DEADLAND'S
HARVEST

The Seven Deadly Sins

with a shambling twist

RACHEL AUKES

DEADLAND'S HARVEST
Book 2 of the DEADLAND SAGA

Copyright © 2014 Rachel Aukes

Surprisingly Adequate Publishing
Edited by Stephanie Riva – RivaReading.com
Cover background © shockfactor – Fotolia.com
Cover art (soldier) © Adrian Hillman – Fotolia.com
Warpaint font © Chepi Devosi – ChepiDev.com

ISBN-10: 0989901815
ISBN-13: 978-0989901819

For my parents.

Thanks for letting me read all the comic books I wanted.

CONTENTS

PURGATORY 1

PRIDE: The First Deadly Sin 151

ENVY: The Second Deadly Sin 181

WRATH: The Third Deadly Sin 207

SLOTH: The Fourth Deadly Sin 231

GREED: The Fifth Deadly Sin 251

GLUTTONY: The Sixth Deadly Sin 287

LUST: The Seventh Deadly Sin 319

NEW EDEN 347

Author's Note 393
Acknowledgments 396
About the Author 397

PURGATORY

CHAPTER I

"Cash!"

I tried to open my eyes, but they were glued shut. I opened my mouth to respond, but my tongue was too parched and swollen. I couldn't even move through the shivers that racked my dew-drenched body.

"Cash! Damn it, where are you, girl? Cash!"

I willed strength into my arms to push myself up, but could barely lift my head.

I wanted to tell whoever was calling to me to be quiet, that the herd had disappeared only a few hours earlier. Instead, I could barely force out a rough, garbled syllable. "*Here.*" Trying to speak choked my sandpaper throat. Blood trickled from my cracked lips.

"Cash!"

The voice was closer and louder now, echoed by other voices, each one calling my name. I pried my eyes open, but the world remained a cloudy blur.

"Up here," I called out louder this time, though the words still came out as only a coarse whisper.

With the last of my strength, I rolled over the backpack that had been propping me up on the angled roof, and let myself roll down. As I picked up speed, I clawed at the shingles to slow my descent, but it did nothing but scrape the skin from my fingers. I fell off the edge and plummeted to the ground ten feet below. Agony shot through my abused body, and I collapsed, my head hitting the ground with a thud.

A pleasant numbness followed, and crystalline stars glittered through my vision. They were the first things in over a day that I could see sharply. As the stars faded, I could make out a man-like shape moving toward me.

A gunshot fired, and the shape collapsed. The acrid stench of plague and rot hit me.

Zed.

Another shape approached, and I tried to kick away, but my limbs weighed a ton, my movements sluggish. Arms wrapped around me, holding me in a relentless grip. I whimpered as I waited for dull, broken teeth to shred my skin.

"Cash, I've got you. You're safe now."

Once the words sunk in, the tension in my muscles gave way, and I inhaled the fresh soapy smell of a man who'd recently bathed. Through my blurry vision, I could barely make out the blond clean-shaven soldier in full gear. "Tyler?"

"Yes, it's me. I've got you. Everything's going to be okay."

I felt myself lifted off the ground and I held onto his shirt. My leg that had a gunshot through it throbbed with each sway of Captain Tyler Masden's steps, but I welcomed the pain. It meant I was alive.

They found me!

It was hard to think, with black clouds drowning my happy thoughts as quickly as they came. I was jostled around and found myself laying on a cold hard surface. The rumble of a big engine starting reverberated through my body. My consciousness ebbed against the soothing engine vibration, but I didn't mind. I was safe now.

"Holy shit, she's alive." I heard Griz's familiar deep voice off to my left, sounding a million miles away.

"Here," Tyler said, lifting my head. "Drink this."

Something pressed against my lips. Cool liquid poured into my mouth and streamed over my tongue. I tried to gulp the water, but it burned, and I choked. I coughed out nearly everything I had drunk. When Tyler held the bottle to my mouth again, he only allowed a trickle of water to pass through. I took a tiny sip. Then another.

"You've been up on that roof for two days?" Tyler asked while I forced down the water my cramping stomach threatened to heave.

I tried to nod, but that sent more water dribbling down my chin and neck.

Tyler pulled the bottle away. "Whoa. That's enough for now. You have to take it slow, or else you'll get sick."

"More," I said, reaching for the water again.

Someone touched my calf, and I hissed. Pain from the gunshot wound burned up my leg, causing me to wince. Blackness tunneled my vision.

A whistle. "That's a nasty infection. You're damn lucky we found you when we did."

"Hurts," I muttered. I didn't feel lucky. I felt like hell.

"Everything's going to be okay," Tyler said, rubbing my shoulder. "You're safe now."

"*We're* safe. Doyle's dead," I said, finally able to get out more than one word just as I felt my body fade into a colorless place between day and night.

"I know. You did well," Tyler said. "We drove through the area yesterday, but the place was still crawling with zeds." A pause. "Damn. I'd just about given up on you, but Clutch was convinced you were still alive."

My jumbled mind tried to process words that made no sense. Clutch couldn't have said those words. It was impossible. That Clutch could've spoken *anything* was impossible. A vision of when I'd last seen Clutch cut through the clouds in my head. "But Clutch…"

Tyler gripped my shoulder. "Clutch is alive. And he's pissed—we're all pissed—you went after the militia on your own."

Thankfully, the next few weeks went by in a blur. When I remembered the flight over Doyle's camp and my attack on his Dogs — the militia — the memories were so fresh that they seemed like yesterday. I could still smell the smoke from the grenade blast, and I could still hear the never ending moans of the zeds surrounding me as I waited on the roof. Had I waited up there to die? To be saved? Hell, to be honest, it was a bit of both.

Fortunately, I didn't have to dwell such things for long. After three days of being confined to bed and on IVs, Doc had cleared me to return to my cabin. It took me another ten days before I'd been able to walk without using crutches, but that didn't stop me from signing up for any tasks to keep busy.

Doc had said I'd gotten lucky that the bullet from the Dog's rifle had been a through-and-through and that it hadn't hit an artery or bone. I was even luckier that the bullet hadn't been dipped in infected blood as the Dogs had become notorious for doing.

Several times a day, I'd rub my leg to remind myself that it hadn't all been a just a bad dream. By some miracle, I'd gone into the pit of hell and came out alive.

Clutch hadn't been so lucky. It had taken another two and a half weeks before Doc had cleared him to leave the infirmary. With the injuries he'd sustained during the Camp Fox attack, he had a long battle ahead of him.

No one said anything when Clutch went through pain-killers and booze a bit too quickly. He was angry most of the time and a muted version of himself the rest of the time. His injuries had pulled him into a dark place that I hadn't yet been able to reach. But he was alive. That was what mattered most to me.

While we recuperated and worked on physical therapy, Fox scouts cleared out Doyle's basement that I'd discovered after killing him. The large underground space chock full of military surplus, weapons, ammo, and food was exactly what Camp Fox's morale needed. With those supplies and the militia no longer a threat, people finally felt like they had a shot at getting through the winter.

"You're wasting daylight, Cash. C'mon, rise and shine!" Jase yelled before jogging out of the cabin the three of us shared, the creaky screen door slamming behind him. Our cabin was the most hidden of all cabins at Fox National Park, which was why Clutch had chosen it when we'd first arrived here. We'd been alone at that time. Now, it was nearly impossible to find a place where we could be alone since the park had become the temporary Camp Fox until the zeds evacuated the real Camp Fox National Guard Base nearly thirty miles southeast of here.

"Off duty," I muttered as I stretched with a groan and rubbed my eyes. I sat up and swung my legs off the bed, and my still-healing calf protested by shooting a burning spike of pain up through my leg. Wincing, I reached for the bottle of water on the floor and took a long swig. God, I loved water. Couldn't get enough of it ever since Tyler rescued me from Doyle's militia camp. I'd been up on that roof for two days, and I wouldn't have made it a third day.

With a sigh, I strapped on my gun belt, and came to my feet. Pink scar tissue tightened over my calf, and it took a moment for the tension to release. The bullet wound always hurt most in the mornings, but I finally felt like I'd climbed out of hell. All the while, Clutch was stuck in hell's deepest tar pits. I glanced at his cot pushed up next to mine. Unmade and empty. The blankets were tangled and draping off the bed after another night of nightmares.

Each night, when I'd move onto his bed to console him, he'd turn the other way. For the past twenty-two days, he'd tell me to leave. The first night I gave him his space, and his nightmares returned worse than ever. The second night I stayed despite his words. He turned away from me, and I draped my arm over him, spooning him. Even though he grumbled, he fell back to sleep and the nightmares stayed away. Every night he tried to push me away, to emotionally isolate himself, but I made sure he knew he wasn't going through this alone. It wasn't easy, and I doubted myself sometimes, but, I kept doing it anyway.

I had convinced myself that what Clutch asked for wasn't what he needed. He'd drawn so far into himself that he pushed others away. Jase and I watched as melancholy dulled his gaze. I loved Clutch's intensity, and it broke my heart every time I saw that strength missing from his spirit.

The third morning he'd left before we woke, Jase and I made a vow to see him through his recovery together, no matter how much of an ass he could be. Clutch had saved both of our lives. It was our turn to bring him back from the hell he was stuck in. We were his family now. Of course, cheering someone up in the middle of the zombie apocalypse was easier said than done.

Just like every morning since he'd returned to our cabin, he'd left before sunrise for physical therapy. He was relentless with his exercises; as if the harder he worked, the faster he would heal.

And, just like every morning, I loosely made all three beds, grabbed my rifle and the long spear that sometimes doubled as a walking stick, and headed out the cabin door.

Several minutes later, I found Clutch at our usual spot by the stream. After every morning PT session, I'd find him sitting there, watching the sun rise and scanning the trees, always ready to kill any zed or bandit who made the mistake of stumbling into our small part of Fox National Park.

I rubbed his shoulder as I walked by him. "Morning, sunshine. How'd PT go?"

He took in a long breath, and his grip on his rifle loosened, but he still stared ahead. "It went."

His short light hair with slivers of gray was still

damp with sweat, and his scruffy face was pale. The veins on his arms stood out like they did every time after weightlifting.

I frowned. "You're pushing yourself too hard. It's only been a couple months. Doc says it's a miracle you're even alive."

Clutch chortled. "Doc was a family doctor before the outbreak. He had no idea how badly I was injured. Hell, he got half of his diagnoses wrong."

"Thank God he did," I said all too quickly and then forced a weak smile. "Doc's doing the best he can. He seemed to do a good job on your broken wrist and fractured leg. Yesterday, you even said yourself that your ribs weren't bothering you as much."

He shook his head. "The only thing Doc did was keep me on my back and drugged up so my body could heal itself with time. Just about any injury will heal in three months."

Just about, I thought to myself. *But not every injury.*

His lips turned upward into a smile that wasn't quite a smile. "The zeds aren't going to wait around for me to get back into shape. We've been too lucky lately, with only groups of two or three coming across the park each day. Our luck is going to run out sometime."

"That's why we have scouts spread out across the park to keep watch. With that and my recon flights over the area, we'll know if any herds are headed this direction."

"I know. It's just, when I'm not out there..." He

rubbed his eyes with his forearm and clenched his fists. "Hell, I hate being useless."

"Whoa," I chuckled. "One thing you've never been is useless. You may be as stubborn as a mule but you're not useless."

He grunted, his tight features unchanged.

I sobered and knelt by him, placing my hands over his. "I'm serious. Do you think Tyler would have asked you to be his second-in-command if you were useless?"

Clutch didn't respond.

I wanted to knock some sense into him, if only a simply smack to the head would work. Exasperation came into every conversation with Clutch lately. It wasn't his fault. He was dealing with things the only way he knew how: by unhealthily shoving his feelings down, making his body a boiling volcano always close to exploding. I forced myself to breathe and not snap at him. "You could be tied down in bed and you'd still be far from useless. Tyler manages the day-to-day stuff around here, but you're the reason Camp Fox still exists. Even though Tyler would never say it, he knows it, too. Everyone knows it. Thanks to you, everyone's trained and prepared." I paused, then frowned. "You know that, right?"

His lips tightened before he finally spoke. "I just hate sitting on my ass all day when there's so much left to be done. Once winter hits, the same tasks are going to take twice as much work."

I sighed. "We'll get by. We always do. But you've got

to give your body time to heal."

He gave an almost imperceptible nod, which I returned with a soft smile before turning in the sand. I pulled off my thermal shirt, leaving on my sports bra. I glanced down at the Piper Cub aviation logo tattooed on my forearm, which reminded me of how far we'd each come. A little over six months ago, I'd sat in a cubicle every workday in a big insurance building. I'd fly for fun every weekend and work on my little bungalow at night. Clutch had been a farmer and a truck driver. His skills had proven far more useful than mine, especially considering he was also a military vet. He'd saved my ass ten times over.

"At the rate you're healing, you'll be back to your old self in no time," I said before I dipped my finger into the cold water and shivered.

Clutch grunted. "Old is right. I've collected plenty of new aches and creaks in this old body."

I smirked at his grumbly response and noticed his eyes focused on my none-too-ample chest. I gave him an appraising look from head to toe and back up again. "Not too old, I hope," I said with a flirty smile.

A hint of lust twinkled in his gaze before his reality dampened his features again.

My heart skipped a beat. Even though it had been a fleeting glimpse, I considered it a success. *Any improvement in Clutch's emotional state, even if for only a second, I took as a sign that there was still hope. In this world, any hope was worth treasuring.*

I turned and splashed cold water onto my face. Goosebumps flitted across my skin as rivulets ran down my cheeks. In my wavy reflection, my cropped dark hair went out in every direction. I used the water to try to tamp it down, with little success. As I washed up in the cold stream, I dreaded what winter would be like. Even the outhouses being built by each cabin were already cold. Sitting in one when it was ten degrees outside would be absolute torture.

On this brisk morning, we shared the stream with three other bathers, but they were all a hundred or so feet away at their personal stations. Only those at a higher risk for infection, like Clutch, could use the park's showers. Until the water froze, the rest of us had to use the trout stream to conserve the half-full rural water tower that fed the cabins and campgrounds. With over fifty survivors—and new arriving each week—at the park, the trout stream was never without someone bathing or collecting water. We'd all quickly learned to shed our modesty, though some still clung to old values and had strung up shower curtains next to the stream for changing and bathing.

Each person had their quirks. Life had gotten hard fast, and every single one of us had found ways to survive without going crazy. Taking a cold bath was nothing compared to learning how to walk again with only a general practitioner for a neurosurgeon. I leaned back on my heels, turned, and saw Clutch watching the horizon. My gaze fell on his wheelchair, and I thought of the battle he still fought. Seeing his trampled body following the Camp Fox attack was the worst image of every image haunting my dreams every night. It was worse than the school full of zombie kids, worse than sitting on a hot roof surrounded by a hundred zeds, even worse than all the different ways I'd imagined how my parents must have died during the outbreak.

I hadn't seen how they died, so I tried to tell myself they went peacefully, that they hadn't suffered. Like anyone else, I hated seeing those I loved hurt. That's what terrified me about Clutch. He had been hurt so badly—and still hurt—that it nearly broke my heart every time I saw him wince from pain. And he winced far too often.

If he'd dislocated his back before the outbreak, modern medicine would have had him walking by now. Except there was no longer such a thing as modern medicine. His bones were healing, and the swelling on his spine was going down since he was regaining more sensation every week. Still, even though he had feeling in his legs and could sometimes move his toes, he might not ever walk again.

Since the attack, we hadn't had sex. While I craved a deeper connection, Clutch couldn't handle intimacy. He was struggling just trying to hold his personal demons at bay. I was afraid a simple kiss could topple his teeter-totter of control. So, I gave him his space, even though I felt so very alone.

The funny thing was that before the outbreak, I

wouldn't have considered dating Clutch. My parents would never have approved of a blue-collar man fifteen years older than me. We were from two different worlds. It would've been a shame, too. Instead, it took a virus to destroy the world for me to find someone whose spirit meshed so perfectly with my spirit.

"What's wrong?" Clutch asked, and I started, looking up.

I shook my head. "Nothing."

After a moment, he gave a small frown and looked back toward the rising sun.

I splashed more water on my face. The rumble of a motorcycle drowned out the sound of the stream and my thoughts. I glanced over my shoulder to see Jase ride down the trail we walked to get to our section of the stream. The sixteen-year-old pulled to a stop, kicking up dirt and leaves, and revved the engine one final time before killing it. His sandy hair was in much need of a haircut, but it fit his personality. He had grown into his body over the past several months, but he was still clearly a teenager.

He gave his famously endearing grin before climbing off the bike, the grin I knew hid nightmares. It was a bad habit he was picking up from Clutch: burying his pain, pretending it didn't exist. Not that those two were alone in that bad habit. I found myself doing it enough, as well as most of Camp Fox. It was a survival mechanism. If we focused too much on the reality, it would swallow us whole. Every now and then, someone would break. Each person was different. Some would cry nonstop, some would eat a bullet, some would take on a blank stare, and some became hell-bent on destroying every zed in the world. I prayed that neither Clutch nor Jase would hit their breaking point.

Just like every morning, Jase pulled out a couple granola bars and tossed one to Clutch and me. For the first week or so after the Camp Fox attack, he'd rarely spoke. He'd lost too much in too short of time to be able to digest it all. Then, one morning, he'd awakened and starting to speak. Acting like Teflon—like he hadn't lost Mutt or his parents—had become his coping mechanism.

He leaned on the handlebars. "Looks like another quiet day."

"Leaves are starting to turn," Clutch replied.

Jase ignored him. "I'm going on a run today. Doc is running low on towels."

"Count me in," I said.

"I'll go," Clutch added on.

Jase's brows rose. "But—"

"I'll be fine," Clutch interrupted. "I'll stay with the vehicle and scan for zeds. It's not like I'm going to jump up and run away."

I clenched my jaw shut to keep from saying anything. Doc would get pissed if Clutch left the park, but I also knew that being caged up was driving him crazy. The idea of him heading out before he was fully recovered bugged me, especially given the lack of any decent modern medicine. If something happened, his temporary paralysis could become permanent—assuming that it was temporary now. Clutch needed action to survive. Every day spent doing nothing but PT at the park, he lost a little bit more of his spirit.

Jase didn't look convinced but he also knew better than to tell Clutch no. "All right. I'll prep the truck. See you guys at—"

We all jerked around to see one of the Jeeps used for guard patrol barreling down the lane. The driver's white hair stood out. Wes came to a stop and stood up in the Jeep. He was one of the newer residents, having moved to the park less than a month ago. "We've got an all-hands call, guys. Captain Masden said I'm to grab every scout I can find and head to the church at Freeley."

I stood up and pulled on my shirt. I was one of the scouts, Camp Fox's protectors. Most were soldiers—National Guardsmen—but there were a few non-military scouts like Jase and me. Tyler had originally called us all soldiers, but then opted for a more neutral, "friendly" term. The label made sense. Scouting for supplies while watching for trouble was ninety percent of our jobs.

"What's up?" Clutch asked while I wiped my face with my sleeve.

"We've just found out about some survivors trapped in Freeley. Sounds like they've gotten themselves surrounded by zeds."

"On my way," Jase said as he revved up the bike and peeled out.

Jase was always energetic like that. Other folks had even started calling him Teflon, since the nastiness of the world around us seemed to roll right off him. But I knew better. Jase had seen a lot of shit and buried his memories, fears, and emotions under a thick coating of that Teflon. Back at the cabin, when he was exhausted after a hard day, I sometimes saw the real Jase. The Jase that was still a kid and was struggling to fake it through each day. He'd toss and turn all night, often waking up in a cold sweat. I'd sit with him until he fell back to sleep. By morning, he was back to being Teflon.

When two survivors showed up at the park with a dog, Jase had avoided them for over a week until the kid—and his dog—cornered Jase one day. I'd noticed Jase's eyes watered as he petted the dog that day, remembering things he tried so hard to forget. He wasn't afraid to pet the dog after that. In fact, he seemed to seek out Diesel. I'd thought about finding a dog for Jase's birthday but had decided it was still too soon. He had too many wounds in his heart that needed time to heal.

"Let's roll." Clutch headed toward the Jeep.

Wes looked confused. "Oh, I don't think you have to come, Clutch. You're—."

"I'm coming," Clutch interrupted. He then turned and pulled himself out of his wheelchair and onto the passenger seat using the Jeep's roll bar and seat.

When I saw the intensity in Clutch's eyes, I said, "It's fine." I came up and grabbed the wheelchair, folded it, and set it in the back before climbing in next to it.

"Uh, okay. You guys need to stop for any gear before we head out?" Wes asked as he sat down and pulled the Jeep back around.

"We're good," I said, knowing that Clutch never left the cabin without being fully prepared for anything, a trait I'd quickly picked up after a run-in at an elementary school.

I checked my rifle. Loaded and ready. I just hoped I wouldn't have to use it.

CHAPTER II

"How many zeds are we talking about?" I asked, my question muffled from trying to talk while chewing on the granola bar Jase had given me.

"A big herd," Wes replied as we drove through the opened front gate, which the two scouts on duty closed as soon as we went through. "Tack's report was twenty, maybe even thirty. Always hard to count when they look the same and keep shuffling around each other. Tack said that the zeds have surrounded a house full of survivors, somewhere in the middle of town."

"Shouldn't be hard to find, not with a town the size of Freeley," I thought aloud.

"These better not be bandits we're risking our lives for," Clutch said as he held onto the Jeep's windshield. "Or else they're going to quickly learn that they'd prefer the zeds' company to ours."

"Amen," I added.

Most survivors had already joined with settlements like Camp Fox. Since the outbreak, civilization had been regrouping, finding strength in numbers against the relentless zeds that kept spreading out from the cities. Camp Fox had become a new home for survivors in central Iowa. Even larger, more powerful city-states were being formed across the country.

Bandits were a different story, and they were becoming more common to see than survivors. While everyone looted empty houses and stores, bandits were greedy outlaws, taking anything they wanted from other survivors and leaving bodies and scarred victims in their wake. I hated bandits more than I hated zeds.

Zeds couldn't control their evil. Bandits could.

We drove past the gas station Clutch and I had cleared out before Camp Fox relocated to the park. We had avoided the station ever since, leaving it to other scouts to loot. No one else had come across the two zed kids that we'd seen there. They'd simply disappeared, even though all the doors to the restaurant were still closed. The pair we'd seen had watched us while holding hands, and it had freaked both of us out.

We'd run across a few non-violent zeds before, but what had really unnerved us was the intelligence in those kids' eyes. Zeds weren't supposed to have any kind of brainpower. If they did have the ability to think, we wouldn't stand a chance. We'd told others about what we'd seen, but no one believed us. Well, no one *wanted* to believe us.

They had racked it up as just seeing a bit too far into something, which was common. After all, when a zed could be hiding around every corner, survival required a bit of paranoia. But, if some zeds could think, it would tip the odds even more against us. Not to mention, I couldn't imagine the horror of zeds knowing who they were and the cannibals they'd become. I prayed those kids' intelligence was just a figment of our imagination.

Wes slowed down once we passed the sign that read *Freeley, pop. 498*. The sun had just crested, sending a warm glow over the trees. Clutch was right—the leaves were showing hints of changing color. Fall had always been my favorite season. But now, rather than enjoying fall, I dreaded the season that would come next. Even with the gold mine we'd found at Doyle's militia camp, we were nowhere near ready in terms of security and supplies. Plus, taking in more survivors meant that we'd have to pull together even more supplies and food before winter hit.

Wes drove the Jeep into the church parking lot near the edge of town. Aside from some corpses, I didn't see any of the zeds Wes was talking about. We pulled up next to the Humvee where two of Tyler's most trusted men stood on the hood. Tack was looking through binoculars while Griz kept watch.

Tack had joined the National Guard a few months before the outbreak. He'd finished basic training, but still looked like he belonged in high school. He was as scrawny as ever, but no one messed with him. He was too damn likable.

Griz, on the other hand, had over a year under his belt in the Army before the outbreak. He had plenty of muscle, and was a Golden Gloves boxing champ. A trader had dared to mess with him once. No one ever messed with Griz again.

Griz eyed Clutch. "You sure you should be out here today?"

"Fuck off" was Clutch's quick response.

Griz lifted his hands in surrender and smirked. "No harm, no foul, man."

Tack lowered his binoculars to look Clutch over. "Good to have you back, man."

I jumped out and walked over to stand at the front of the Humvee. Even from this distance several blocks away, it was easy to guess which house the survivors were in. Hanging from a second story window was a bed sheet with the word *HELP* written across it. And, it was the only house surrounded by zeds.

"Son of a bitch," I said. "There must be forty zeds." We couldn't take that many without burning through precious ammunition. "You sure there are even survivors left inside?" I asked, selfishly hoping we didn't have to go near a herd this size.

"I'm sure," Tack replied, not looking very happy about the fact. "They hung that sign after they saw us. And they've been antsy ever since."

The rumble of a big engine came up from behind. I

turned to find Tyler and several more of Camp Fox's scouts arrive in a Humvee. Tyler jumped out. Sometimes, I thought he seemed too young to be leading Camp Fox, but then I remembered we were the same age. After the outbreak hit, being nearly thirty wasn't seen as young anymore. Especially since there was hardly anyone over the age of fifty remaining. Then again, there was hardly anyone of any age remaining anymore.

When Tyler saw Clutch, he raised a brow, clearly surprised. "Sarge."

"Captain," Clutch said as Tyler approached Tack and Griz's Humvee.

Over the past few months, Tyler and Clutch had *almost* become friends. Well, at least they put up with each other. Tyler respected Clutch's experience, but he'd never gotten over the fact that Clutch had refused to report to duty when the outbreak first hit. Clutch respected Tyler's leadership, but he'd never forgiven Tyler for abandoning me in the middle of a zed-infested wasteland. I knew the only reason Clutch stayed with Camp Fox was because of Jase and me.

Out of over thirty troops at Camp Fox, Clutch was the next-highest ranking officer after Tyler. Always one to follow the rules, Tyler had gritted his teeth as he made Clutch second-in-command of Camp Fox.

"What are we looking at?" Tyler asked, all business.

Tack handed him the binoculars. "A large herd surrounding a house with six or more occupants, including at least one kid."

That a kid was with them was important. It meant that there was a good chance they weren't bandits. Bandits tended to ditch anyone that would slow them down—and they often ditched them by using them as zed bait.

"The front door is broken but barricaded. There are three vans parked outside, but there's no way for them to get through the herd and to their vehicles. I'm guessing they've been in there a while since the zeds aren't attacking, but there are some curious zeds sniffing around the porch. The folks holed up inside look to be in rough shape. I doubt they can hold out much longer."

"Well, they'll have to wait just a little longer," Tyler said, turning to face our group.

"Are we going with the Pied Piper plan?" I asked.

He nodded and then looked over all of us. "It saves our ammo and minimizes risk. The Jeep will lead as many zeds away as possible, and we'll take out the rest. My team will go in for the survivors. Griz's Humvee will take out any zeds that stay behind."

A chorus of *yes sirs* and *hooahs* erupted.

Tyler nodded in Clutch's direction. "Sarge's team is with the Jeep. We need to get the zeds at least three miles out of town before you break and head back to Camp Fox. Call in if you run into any problems."

Tyler had given us the easy job. Lure zeds away while keeping a safe distance. With each passing month, the zeds were moving slower and becoming less of a threat. I wasn't surprised he'd assigned us as the Pied Piper vehicle. It was by far the least risky role to play in this gambit. Wes was old yet often overconfident. Clutch...well, everyone knew Clutch's weakness. Heck, I was surprised Tyler was even letting Clutch participate today. He could've ordered him back to the park.

Then again, we all knew how well orders went over with Clutch aka Sarge.

As for my case, Tyler had always been protective of me, but assigning us as the Pied Piper vehicle was more than for my protection. It was a matter of practicality. For one thing, my injured leg was still slowing me down. Another reason Tyler intentionally kept me on the sidelines of trouble was my unique skill. I was Camp Fox's only pilot. My patrols were critical to helping us stay ahead of zeds in the area. I could easily cover a fifty-mile radius and report back any herds heading our way. We'd finally reached the point of being a step ahead of the zeds. It was our first break since the world had ended.

We were still waiting for a second break.

"Are the streets cleared?" I asked finally.

Tack shook his head. "The north and west has been mostly cleared, I think. But as far as I know, no one's started on the east or south yet."

"Avoid the east and south. Got it. We'll see you back at the park." I grabbed the extra bag of ammo Tack held out to me and headed back to the Jeep with Wes. We waited with Clutch while the attack-force with two Humvees checked their weapons. There were as many homemade machetes and spears as there were rifles. Next to food, ammo was the most valuable resource. We'd collected a couple hundred thousand rounds in Doyle's stash, but we knew that once it was gone, there would be nothing left. So, we were careful with every round.

Tyler turned to us. "You've got a green light. Be careful and keep a safe distance."

Wes started the engine and pulled out. Tyler waved as we headed past.

Two minutes later, we slowly approached the intersection closest to the white two-story house. It sat in the middle of a street surrounded by other houses. At the sound of the engine, the zeds turned in our direction. Some started heading our way. The disease that had taken everyone I'd known in my past life seemed to be slowly eating away at their bodies. Scouting patrols over the past month all reported the same: the zeds were definitely getting slower, smellier, and uglier. Now, if we could finally get a bit of luck, they'd all die out this winter. The poor souls deserved peace. Hell, *we* deserved peace. Until then...

"I'm ready," I said. "Lead the zeds either to the north or west. The south and east might not be safe."

"Let the games begin." Clutch turned on the CD player. Heavy bass blared as Avenged Sevenfold blasted through the speakers. The zeds around the house immediately turned and began to migrate in our direction en masse. A man came to the second-story window and held out his hand, waving wildly. A little girl with golden hair came to his side. She was clenching a stuffed doll against her chest, and she watched us with big eyes.

The zeds became more and more frenzied as they moved in our direction. It had been nearly seven months since the outbreak. The zeds that had managed to avoid the elements and keep well fed were still in relatively good shape. Luckily, most of these had managed neither.

They stumbled, crawled, and shambled toward us.

I let out the breath I'd been holding. "It's working."

Wes revved the engine.

"Not yet," Clutch said.

Wes gripped the steering wheel, his knuckles white.

I got up on a knee, supporting myself against the roll bar in case Wes hit the gas, and I readied my spear. The first zed was less than ten feet away.

"Now," Clutch said.

The Jeep lurched forward, then Wes slowed down somewhat.

Over the next block, I watched as the zeds behind us grew smaller. I yelled to Wes over the music, "Slow down! We're going to lose them. Three miles, remember?"

I kept my spear ready for any coming at us from the

side, but it seemed like every zed in town had been at the house.

The Jeep came to an abrupt stop, and I was thrown against the back of Clutch's seat.

"The road is blocked!" Wes shouted.

I jerked up to see what looked like a nasty car accident blocking the entire street and debris littering the front yards. The wreckage was dusty, and the bodies inside the broken windows were little more than bones. The roads weren't anywhere near cleared enough. *Shit.*

"Then turn around and take the last intersection," Clutch said.

Wes did a hard U-turn, which put the zeds at our twelve o'clock. He stepped on the gas and sped toward the herd.

"Don't turn left," I said, noticing the dead end sign at the upcoming intersection.

Wes cranked the wheel hard left. Wheels squealed.

"I said *don't* turn left!" I yelled.

"You said turn left!" Wes yelled back.

I hollered out a string of profanity.

Clutch killed the music, and winced, grabbing his ribs. "Get us out of here, Wes. In one piece would be nice."

Wes whipped the Jeep around again. The zeds had come around the corner, blocking our escape route.

"Try that yard," I said, pointing to a yard without a fence that looked wide enough for a Jeep.

Wes jumped the curb, and Clutch yelped in pain.

"Careful!" I yelled.

Wes kept driving, maneuvering between a garage and a neighboring house. He knocked off a side mirror on a wood play set in the backyard. He narrowly missed the trampoline in the next yard, drove through two more yards, a chain link fence, and plastic deer. I clung onto the roll bars, unable to do anything except to keep myself from getting thrown out of the Jeep.

"Charlie to Alpha," Clutch said into the radio. "Charlie needs support."

No response.

"Charlie team to Alpha." After no response, he set the radio on his lap. "They must've moved in already. We're on our own."

I pointed to a large shed. "How about in there?"

"Let's try it," Clutch said quickly.

"Okay," Wes said under his breath while he gripped the wheel. He pulled up to the shed with a sign that read *Mac's Auto Shop*.

Panting from the wild ride, I jumped off the back, ran to the first garage door, and rapped on the metal. When no sound emerged, I yanked on the door. By some miracle it wasn't locked, and the door slid easily to the side with an unoiled squawk. Wes pulled the Jeep inside, bumped into a VW Beetle that was sitting in the bay, and pushed it forward. I scanned outside. Seeing no zeds in on the vicinity, I tugged the door shut as quick as I could.

Wes cut the engine. The three of us watched one

another, all with eyes wide open and breathing heavily. I swallowed and forced each breath out slowly.

Zeds were dumb, but they were damn good at sniffing out prey.

CHAPTER III

Wes was already out of the Jeep, searching for zeds around the car and behind toolboxes. With nothing looking or smelling out of place, I'd already figured the place was clean. Zeds were a messy, stinky bunch with no talent for stealth.

I looked at Clutch to find him still gripping the windshield, his head lowered.

I went over and rubbed his shoulder. "Hey, you okay?"

"Yeah." He raised his head. Tension highlighted the wrinkles around his eyes. "Just got a bit bumpy back there."

I'd thrown my back out once, and it had hurt like hell. I couldn't imagine how dislocating it would feel. I gave him the gentlest of hugs. "Hang in there," I said softly.

He leaned back with a wince and closed his eyes.

When Doyle's Dogs attacked Camp Fox last summer, Clutch had been crushed in the stampede of fleeing survivors. Two vertebrae in his back had been dislocated, thankfully not broken as Doc had first guessed. Doc was doing the best he could do. It had to be tough to work in a world without x-rays and emergency rooms. A person couldn't just snap vertebrae back into place like a dislocated shoulder. Doc had been very, very careful to align Clutch's back. The backpack Clutch had been wearing was likely the only reason his back hadn't been broken; it had served as a buffer between his body and the trampling herds. Even then, the swelling on his spine prevented us from knowing yet if it had been permanently damaged or if it was simply the swelling that had paralyzed him from the hips down.

While his back had been his most serious injury, Clutch had also gotten three cracked—or at least badly bruised—ribs, two fractured—or badly bruised—legs, and a broken left wrist. He'd also had a dislocated shoulder and a nasty concussion. Any one of those injuries would have taken him out of action for a bit, but the combination of injuries had left him unconscious for three days.

It was a miracle he hadn't incurred any internal bleeding, deep cuts, or bites in the stampede. At the Camp Fox medical clinic, if someone couldn't heal on his or her own, there was little hope. After the attack,

Doc warned me that if Clutch didn't wake in the first hours, he would likely never wake up due to the severity of his injuries. Doc didn't know Clutch. The Clutch I knew was too hardheaded *not* to wake up.

Aside from some minor memory lapses and random muscle spasms, he was well on the road to recovery. Despite Doc's pessimism, I knew Clutch would walk again because he could feel pain in his legs and wiggle his toes not long after he woke. He'd even been able to lift his legs a bit a couple days ago. It shouldn't be much longer until the pressure was off his nerve endings enough that he'd regain control over his legs and be able to stand on his own. I only hoped he could stand soon because being held prisoner by his own body was taking its toll.

My greatest fear was that if Clutch didn't have use of his legs, it would kill him. Well, he'd kill himself more likely. The idea of the strongest man I knew giving up terrified me. If he couldn't make it, how did Jase or I have a chance?

Wes stopped by the Jeep, his gaze darting to the garage door. "As long as they don't break down the door, I think we'll be safe in here."

I nodded before holding up my hand. "*Sh.* They're coming." It was the faintest sound of shuffling feet and low moans. It sounded almost like a flock of sheep passing through. Except sheep didn't tear apart anything that breathed.

This was the sound that caused me to wake up in a

cold sweat every night. The herd that had followed us from the survivors had caught up. We stood frozen as the sounds outside grew louder. I exhaled as shallowly as I could and leaned on the Jeep, waiting for the zeds to sniff us out. *Please don't find us,* I prayed over and over.

If they found us, it wouldn't take them long to break through the old door. Clutch's eyes remained closed, and I couldn't even tell he was breathing, let alone conscious, though I knew he was listening as intently as I was. Wes kept his rifle aimed at the door. The sounds grew louder. My nerves felt like they were about to detonate. My tense muscles ached.

Something brushed against the shop, and the air in my lungs froze. With no windows on that side of the building, the zeds couldn't see inside. It also meant we couldn't see if they were stopping to sniff around the shop or merely passing through in their quest to find us.

Hours passed as the zeds checked out the shop, brushing against the walls on all four sides. They'd lingered for some reason, but whatever it was, it wasn't enough to work them into a frenzy. None pounded against the building. It seemed like they were more curious than anything.

And so we waited. My back ached from standing in one position. I sat on the ground as quietly as possible, knowing the smallest sound could draw attention. Wes had long since lowered his rifle and sat at a tool bench, but he still faced the door. I could tell by Clutch's pale, pained expression that he needed to be lying down, but he didn't dare move.

The sounds grew fainter until I could hear nothing but silence. Wes looked back and glanced from Clutch to me.

Wait, I mouthed. There'd be stragglers. There were always stragglers. Ones whose guttural wails would call the others back if they found us. And so we waited longer. I didn't take even one step toward the door in case there were any zeds still out there. That they hadn't sniffed us out meant that the various car and old oil smells in the shop had provided better cover than I'd anticipated. Or, the zeds' senses were deteriorating right along with their bodies.

After a forced count to one thousand, I glanced at Wes and then crept toward the sliding shop door. When I reached it, I put my ear to the crack and heard nothing. Taking a deep breath, I pushed the door open an inch. The rollers squeaked, and I cringed. I peeked through the crack.

At first, I saw nothing. Then, movement in the corner of my eye caused me to scan again. Sure enough, a pair of slow moving zeds was focused on the garage.

"Is it clear?" Wes whispered at my side.

I jumped at the unexpected question. "Clear enough. But I don't think we'll want to stick around here all night." I threw him a glance. "Let's go home."

"You don't need to twist my arm," he said before heading back to the Jeep.

Wes started the engine, and the two zeds continued their shamble toward the garage. I shoved open the door, grunting, finding it much harder to open this time. To my right, a zed that must've been pressing against the door spun around and was sent tumbling to the ground. I marched over, twirled my spear around, and skewered its head. The two zeds' moans grew louder.

When it no longer moved, I walked over to meet the pair of zeds. Their groans rose as they reached out for me. I speared the male through its forehead, yanking my weapon back to knock out the ankles of the female zed. It went down on its back, its head making a solid thump against the ground. I stood over it and brought my spear down, putting it out of its misery. I didn't know if zeds suffered, though they'd never wince whenever I cut off a limb or stabbed one. They just looked miserable.

I figured they just were. They existed — without feeling or thought — and with a single urge: to feed. At least that's what I told myself to make it easier to kill what had once been a person. The worst part about zeds wasn't their hunger or viciousness or stench. It was that each one resembled someone I knew before the outbreak. They were reminders of loved ones lost. Then again, maybe I was just trying to anthropomorphize something that was no longer human.

As Wes backed the Jeep alongside me, I turned away from the zeds, grabbed the roll bar, and swung myself onto the open back.

"Let's get the hell out of this town," Clutch muttered, his arm cradling his stomach.

Escaping a town where the herd of zeds potentially waited around any corner wasn't exactly easy. We had no idea if the herd had kept moving or if it had stopped around the next house. Wes drove slowly, creeping up to every intersection so as to not draw attention. We'd gotten lucky today. Once we were back on familiar streets, I think we all breathed easier. The herd was nowhere to be found. At the intersection not far from the roadblock, I finished off a lone zed that approached the Jeep. A block later, another zed lumbered toward us.

Wes sped up.

"Hold up," I said. "I'll get this one."

Wes slowed, and I waited until the zed was close enough that I could stab it from the safety of the Jeep. As we progressed through town, I took out every zed I could because every zed I killed was one fewer zed that would come across the park or join up with a herd later.

By the time we reached the church, the parking lot was empty. We drove by the house where the survivors had been. There were several corpses scattered around on the overgrown lawn outside, but fortunately no bodies wore Camp Fox fatigues.

Once we were safely out of town, Wes stepped on the gas. As we headed back to the park, I shivered in the

October breeze. No one spoke. Without things like movies and sports, small talk had become an exercise of discussing what still needed done before winter hit. A person could only handle talking so much about the lack of skills and supplies.

As we approached the park's entrance, I cringed inwardly at the sight of the newcomers standing outside the gate. It was a larger group than I'd thought. At least ten, but it seemed like a hundred for the amount of food they'd eat. Wearing my actuarial hat, I figured we'd have to add an additional seventeen percent to our calculations of food needed to get us through the winter. The numbers became more and more dismal with more stragglers arriving every week. We'd have to start turning people away or else we'd starve. The question was, would today be that day?

Most of Camp Fox's scouts were on the other side of the gate, standing with their guns lowered but at the ready. Two scouts stood next to Doc while he attended to someone in one of the newcomers' three vans, the same vans that had been parked outside the house in Freeley. The rest of the newcomers were busily drinking from plastic water bottles.

Tyler was sitting in the passenger seat of a Humvee, also drinking water, with his window rolled down, and I had no doubt a rifle sat on his lap. His blond hair was matted from wearing a helmet, yet it did nothing to detract from his good looks. He had a killer smile and when he talked, he made you feel like he was talking directly to you, even if he was standing in front of a group of hundreds. There was something charismatic about him that made men want to be his pal and women swoon. He was a natural leader.

Wes slowed the Jeep down to a crawl as we drove past the newcomers and toward the gate. They were a dirty bunch and looked like they'd been on the road for some time. Some waited at the gate with desperate pleas for help. Four ATVs sat nearby to run down any zeds or chase fleeing bandits.

Tyler would have already informed the newcomers that Camp Fox had protocols. Any newcomer had to be fully vetted by Doc for bites, illness, fleas, and other infectious things before being allowed through the gate. Still, it tugged on the heart strings to stand around when miserable, starving people needed help not even twenty feet away.

Seventeen percent, I reminded myself when sympathy rose in my chest.

Yes, they desperately needed our help. And, if I was on the run and came across a camp, I hoped they'd take me in. Still, I didn't know these people. What if they stole our supplies or hurt Jase? Keeping an image of Jase in my mind helped gird myself against my desire to help them.

Little Benji Hennessey held Styrofoam cups as his grandfather Robert, whom everyone called Frost, filled them with water. Frost's huge Great Dane, Diesel, lay sprawled out at his side. After each cup was filled, Benji handed it to a newcomer. Tyler always called upon the Hennesseys whenever newcomers showed up. It was a smart tactic that worked every time. A kindly grandfather and a young kid with Down Syndrome tended to put folks at ease. Little did any newcomer know that Frost would kill — and had killed without hesitation — anyone who threatened his grandson. Even more impressive, Benji had ridden a bicycle — with training wheels no less — miles and miles through zed-infested country to reach his grandfather. He hadn't killed a zed yet, but he was a survivor, through and through.

Wes pulled onto the shoulder to get around the vans. Clutch let out a pained groan when the Jeep's tires went off the edge of the pavement. I placed a hand on his shoulder. "We need to get you to the cabin and on your back."

"What I wouldn't do to get a woman to say that to me," Wes said.

I rolled my eyes.

That Clutch didn't argue was proof of the pain he was in. I was sure the jarring ride in the Jeep hadn't helped the swelling on his spine.

A small section of the gate opened, and we drove through, coming to a stop at Tyler's vehicle. He stepped out of the Humvee, setting his rifle on the seat. After giving us a once-over, he frowned. "What took you guys so long? You usually beat us back by at least a couple hours."

"Detour," I said. "We really need to clear all the main roads in these towns."

"I'll add it to the list of infinity."

He said it jokingly but it was true. Civilization had collapsed overnight, and it was going to take years to get it back, if it was even still possible.

"Any problems getting the survivors out of that house?" Clutch asked curtly.

"Nothing I couldn't handle," Tyler replied quickly, and then he whistled. "You look like shit, Sarge."

Clutch flipped him the bird.

I rolled my eyes. "In case you guys hadn't noticed, we've got seventeen more mouths to feed standing at our gate."

Tyler's lips tightened before speaking again. "Doc's nearly finished with checking them out. I'm not too worried about these folks. They seem harmless enough. To play it safe, I want every scout on watch once I let them into the park."

"I'm no good to anyone right now," Clutch said, the words sounding forced.

After a moment, Tyler gave a single nod. "Understood. Get yourself to bed."

"I'll take Clutch back to the cabin and get right back," Wes said.

I squeezed Clutch's shoulder just before I climbed out. "I'll see you in a bit."

He touched my hand briefly. The Jeep pulled away.

Tyler watched the Jeep disappear around a curve.

"It's too early. Clutch shouldn't been out there today."

"Our detour today jarred him around too much," I said. "He needs more time in bed, but you know him."

He sighed. "Yeah, I do."

Doc waved toward Tyler and then gave him a thumbs up. The newcomers had been cleared. I walked with Tyler toward the ragtag group of newcomers. When we reached the gate, a middle-aged man with white hair and a scruffy beard stepped forward.

Tyler said, "Thanks for your patience. I apologize for the delay. I know you're tired and hungry, but we have protocols to follow."

"I understand. You've treated us fair," The man said and then held out a hand. "The name's Manny."

Tyler nodded rather than taking Manny's hand. "I'm Captain Tyler Masden, and this is the current base of operations for Camp Fox."

The man smiled. "Oh, I know who you are. We were on our way here to find you when the zeds found us."

Tyler frowned. "You were coming here?"

"I heard Camp Fox was a safe place."

"Word travels. We're the largest camp in the area for a reason. But you nearly didn't make it here. You're damn lucky one of my men saw your sign," Tyler continued. "We only scout Freeley once a month."

Manny smiled. "Luck? No. I'd call it a goddamn miracle you found us. We're mighty obliged you stopped to help. Most folks would have just kept on going. You saved our lives. To tell the truth, we were starting to lose hope."

"We're happy to be of service," Tyler replied. "Nowadays, we have to look out for one another. After all, there aren't enough of us left. So, where are you folks from?"

"Marshall," Manny replied.

"Marshall, Minnesota? You mean the group holed up at SMSU?" Tyler asked. "What are you doing this far south?"

My brows furrowed. Marshall, with all its radio and telecom equipment, had been one of the first to develop an entire network of communities, with Camp Fox being one of its weekly contacts.

Manny cocked his head. "You haven't heard? Marshall was overtaken. When the herds hit the university, we couldn't get back to the student center where everyone else was. We were out on a supply run, and the herds cut us off. Anyone else who couldn't get back to the student center scattered to the four winds. So we radioed the center and took off to scout somewhere safe from the zeds. We'll go back to pick up everyone as soon as we find somewhere safe in case the zeds pass through again. Before we lost contact with them, they'd said several herds were still there. They don't have much food in the student center, enough for a few weeks, maybe."

I gulped in shock. Marshall was a large settlement. With survivors from the Twin Cities, they'd had a couple thousand survivors and had set up walls around the small university. No herd should've gotten close.

"I don't get it," Tyler said. "What kind of herd could get past Marshall's troops?"

"Not just any herd. Many huge herds all moving together." Manny waved his hand. "One was at least a hundred thousand strong."

A hundred thousand zeds. I shivered. A herd of forty nearly got the best of us today. The last thing I could fathom was an endless herd heading straight toward us.

Manny continued. "They're slow, but they make a wide path, and they trample everything. The bastards are relentless. They only stop to feed. As soon as we'd get in front of one herd, we'd run into another. They got my Marcia when we first tried to leave the house we'd spent the night in. I tried to get to her, but...well, she's with them in hell now." He rubbed a hand through his greasy hair. "We'd finally put a couple hundred miles between us and them. We stopped at Freeley when the sun set. We were planning to come here first thing in the morning, but when we'd awoke, a herd had found us. We tried to get out, but we lost several good people. We'd been holed up in that house for damn near a week, losing time that we don't have."

"You think these herds are headed this way?" I asked the instant before I knew Tyler would voice the same question.

Manny nodded with a pained expression. "They're headed this way, that's guaranteed. We figure they're migrating. Near as I can tell, zeds from as far north as

Canada are picking up small herds as they move south, until their numbers become like locusts."

Tyler pursed his lips before letting out a sigh. "Well, shit. I definitely want to learn more about this zed problem, but your folks need food and rest. We can talk more over dinner. Tonight, Vicki is making a rare treat, pumpkin for dessert. You and your people are welcome to stay as long as you need." He pointed down the road to the south. "I have a farmhouse set up about a mile from here for you to stay in tonight. As long as you play fair, you'll see no aggression from Camp Fox. If you want to make your stay more permanent and live within the park, we'll have to talk. There are conditions all residents must agree to." He motioned to Griz and Tack in the Humvee closest to the gate. "My men will take your people into the park for dinner and then to the farmhouse so you can clean up and rest. Sound good?"

The other man nodded. "I owe you my life and my thanks. Your offer is more than fair." Then he held out his hand.

This time, Tyler shook it.

A blond guy approached Manny. I could see the white tip of a thick scar peeking out from the V-neck of his shirt. He reached behind him and I readied my spear. Instead of pulling out a weapon, he held up a picture of a family. I assumed he was the man in the photo, though the beard and a hundred pounds less fat made it tough to tell. In the picture, a middle-aged man posed with a kindly looking woman and a teenaged girl.

All three looked happy. Obviously, it had been taken before anyone had heard of zeds.

He shoved the picture in my face. "Please, you have to help me. My wife and daughter are still in Marshall. If you can give me some supplies, I can go back for them while the others go ahead and find somewhere safe."

"Bill, we've talked about this already," Manny said with a sigh.

"I know, but I can't leave them alone for much longer. I need to get back to them," Bill replied before looking again at me. "Please. It's my family."

My lips tightened. He was clearly trying to get me on his side, likely because I was a woman. He was playing to the wrong person. Of the pair in front of him, Tyler had the softer heart. He was generous, always ready to help someone in need. I was selfish. Everything I did was to protect Jase, Clutch, and me. With every stranger we helped, we put ourselves at risk. Our days were already full from sunrise to sunset with keeping Camp Fox clear of zeds and searching houses and gardens for food. The idea of giving up even one day to help someone I didn't know or trust brought on an instant tension headache.

"We'll consider your case later," Tyler said, pressing Bill's hand down. "You need food and a good night's rest."

The man frowned and fervently shook his head. "No. This can't wait. The herds will hit you here, just like they did in Marshall. Then there will be nothing left. I have to get my family and head south, find an island or somewhere the herds can't get to us. If we stay here, we'll die. Just like you're all going to die."

CHAPTER IV

T yler let Bill ride back to the park square with us so no one else had to listen to his endless pleading. I couldn't imagine how he must've driven the other survivors crazy while they'd been cooped up in that house. Manny rode along, seemingly oblivious to his friend's chatter.

As we headed back to the park square in the Humvee, Bill detailed his plans about getting back to Marshall to find his family. Though, for pointing out all the obvious details, like stopping by farmhouses to look for food, his plan was really simple: drive back to Marshall while watching out for the herds.

Even though his constant talking grated on my nerves, I could relate to how he felt. If I'd been separated from Clutch or Jase, nothing short of death would've stopped me from finding them. However, as much as I understood Bill, I was also disgusted with him. He was too afraid to head after them on his own. It was bad enough he'd abandoned them in the first place.

"We're here," Tyler said a few exhausting minutes later, as he pulled the Humvee into the small parking lot for the park office, where all Camp Fox business took place, including three group meals per day. "Welcome to the Fox Park square. It serves as our command center, chow hall, and the place for just about any other group activity."

"The university's student center was our town square," Manny said, a hint of sadness in his voice.

Bill had quieted when we arrived, likely from the smells of dinner overtaking his senses. Starving, I headed straight for the door, and the three men were right there with me. A couple of the park's residents walked out the door as we approached. Tyler held the door open, and I politely followed the two newcomers inside. Even though Bill was a chatterbox, both he and Manny seemed like decent, albeit smelly, folk. Regardless, it would take longer before I trusted them enough to welcome them into the fold of Camp Fox.

Inside, I found Kurt already hitting on one of the women who'd arrived today. It was par for the course for the Guardsman who treated every day like a frat party rather than the end of the civilized world.

Tyler grabbed a tray, stepped into the cafeteria-style line, and nudged Kurt. "I need you to check on the north gates."

"I'm sure they're fine," he replied all too quickly before smiling again at the young woman basking in his attention.

Tyler's jaw tightened. "I wasn't asking."

Kurt's smile fell, and he stood straighter. "Yes, sir."

On his way out, he winked at the woman, and her flirtatious smile left no doubt as to whose bed she'd be sleeping in tonight. That was Kurt. He hit on every woman. Hell, he hit on me but mostly only when Jase was around, likely because it pissed Jase off. He obviously liked Jase even though he seemed to be constantly picking on him, so I figured it was some kind of friendship hazing ritual. Clutch, on the other hand, was a completely different story. Kurt didn't risk hitting on me when Clutch was around. Maybe because Kurt looked to him as Sarge. More likely it was because that any sense of humor Clutch had was lost in the stampede that crippled him.

The smell of beef stew made my mouth water and drew my attention to the small buffet line. Made with wild greens, berries, and some other local plants that I hadn't yet figured out, it was my favorite meal. As soon as Tyler got a bowl, Nate set a generously sized bowl of stew on my tray. Nate, like everyone else here, performed multiple duties. Like Kurt, he was also a Guardsman and a scout under Tyler, but he was also a damn good cook. Between Vicki and him, they planned all our meals.

It was easy to see that Nate thoroughly sampled each

meal. He was one of the few scouts whose clothes fit tighter since the outbreak. After giving Nate a grin, I moved on and grabbed a handful of nuts and two crumbly chunks of cornbread, our daily staple. One thing the Midwest had plenty of was corn, but there was one big problem. Farmers planted *seed* corn, with only small pockets of sweet corn scattered across the area. Seed corn was made for cattle feed or corn syrup. Hard and bland, it generally wasn't exactly consumable without being ground down into cornmeal. We'd grown accustomed to the simple taste. Hell, I even looked forward to Nate's corn hash every third morning.

That was the way things were around here. Everything had become a routine. Hard-boiled eggs or hash for breakfast, meat as dinner's main course every other day, and only vegetables and grains on the alternate days. Sugar and salt were restricted for medical use only. After a while, a person's palate became accustomed to a blander fare, finding new flavors in things like dandelion tea and root soup. But that wasn't always the case. Some things were just simply flavorless, or worse, tasted like weeds.

Tyler led us back outside to a picnic table. Manny and Bill followed us rather than sitting with their own people.

"Real beef?" Manny asked, swirling a spoon in his stew, while Bill slurped directly from his bowl, completely oblivious to us.

"It's nothing fancy," Tyler replied after taking a bite.

"But it fills the stomach."

Manny chuckled. "No, you don't understand. I can't remember the last time I had meat that didn't come out of a can." He took another bite and frowned. "I can't make out the seasoning."

"It's marjoram," I said. "Deb found a whole bunch of it growing wild around the park. We ran out of spices a month ago and have been trying out what grows naturally. We're still getting used to the new flavors ourselves."

"We've also been collecting all the remaining livestock in the area," Tyler said. "Mostly hogs, but a few cattle and some chickens. There aren't many left, but enough to repopulate into something that can support us."

"Impressive," Manny said. "We've brought some livestock into Marshall, but nowhere near enough to support the numbers we need to support. You've got everything you need right here."

"Not yet, but being smaller helps," I said. "Right now, we're working on harvesting and canning fruit. There are quite a few apple trees, but other than berries, we don't have much variety. Not having enough vitamin C to last the winter is one of our greatest nutritional worries right now. Scurvy is a very real risk we will face unless we can get into town for food or vitamins."

Manny tilted his head. "Well, you're a step ahead of us. For winter, we planted some crops in the greenhouse, but we'd planned on living off anything we could find in houses. The pickings have grown pretty slim the past few weeks. We've gotten desperate enough to start picking around the edges of the Twin Cities. We've been saving seeds. Come spring, we're planting crops anywhere there's grass at the university. That is, if the herds haven't busted things up too bad."

"I'm sure you can rebuild," Tyler said with his famous, kind smile. "Were you in contact with any other survivors from Marshall?"

Manny frowned, and then shrugged. "We kept in touch for the first day before we lost contact. There were pockets heading in every direction. Some headed north, thinking the worst of the zeds were to the south. Some headed east or west, since the herds were moving south. I decided to take my folks south to get as far ahead of the herds while we still could, but as soon as we pulled away from one herd, we ran smack into another. All I know is that once we find a temporary place to hide until the herds migrate, we'll head back to Marshall for the rest of our people and rebuild at the school, if it's still possible."

"It's possible," Bill said, wiping his mouth with his sleeve. "The other zeds will join up with the herds, so they'll all be gone. We can focus on rebuilding, finally, instead of just watching and defending ourselves against the infected every day."

"You really think the herds are migrating for the winter?" I asked, sure that the doubt bled through my words.

"After seeing it with my own eyes, I'm convinced of it," Manny said before taking another bite.

"I think it's a good idea to check out those herds for ourselves. What do you think?" Tyler asked me. "Can you make the flight without a fuel stop?"

I shrugged. "It shouldn't be a problem."

"You're a pilot?" Manny asked.

I gave a quick nod. "If the herds are getting that big, they'd be easy enough to spot from a distance. I wouldn't even have to fly low. Plus, I could make a wide arc back to see if there are any other groups headed our way. It'll give us some idea where the herds are and where they're headed."

Bill's eyes widened. "You have to take me with you."

I held up my hands. "Whoa. I'm scouting the herds. That's all. I'm not touching down anywhere."

"If you could at least fly over Marshall, we can at least see if the herd did much damage," Bill pleaded.

I sighed before turning back to Tyler. "If the flight goes without any hiccups, I suppose I could check out Marshall the same way I did Mason City."

Tyler thought for a moment, and then nodded. "If the weather changes or you get any kind of bad feeling in your gut, turn back. This run should be as straightforward as they come. I also want Clutch with you to check out the herds. We'll wait until he's feeling better if we have to, but I need his experience on this one."

"So, you *aren't* going to check on Marshall?" Bill asked, each word climbing in pitch.

"I didn't say that," I said. "If everything goes as planned, I'll fly over it. If the heavens align, I'll *consider* landing. But if it is in any way unsafe to land, all I can do is drop a bag with any messages you and your friends want to leave."

Using bag drops had been Tyler's idea to improve morale. The first bag I'd dropped had worked like a charm at Mason City. It looked like no survivors had made it in the ravaged area, but that didn't matter. Even if no one came to claim the bag, Tyler was right. The action had brought hope to the families back at the park.

Manny smiled and patted Bill's shoulder. "That's a grand plan. If you have some paper and pens around here, I'll bring notes from my people in the morning. We'd done similar things over the Twin Cities when we still had a pilot with us. Though, I'm guessing Bill would be more than happy to ride along if you have room for an extra passenger."

Tyler looked to me to answer. I didn't like taking people I didn't know on a flight, especially one as desperate as Bill. Too many things could happen in the air that could turn everything to shit. I'd learned that lesson by watching my dad. He'd been a doctor and an avid volunteer in the Doctors Without Borders program. He had learned to fly to get into some of the world's most inhospitable places. He'd taken me with him one summer, where I became hooked on flying but also learned first-hand how easily a single passenger with a panic attack could nearly crash a plane. Now, I never flew anywhere without having someone I trusted on board to handle any passenger.

"Okay," I said and Bill's face lit up. "You can ride in back only if we have an extra seat. Jase is my co-pilot and rides shotgun. We'll try for tomorrow morning. If Clutch isn't up for it or the weather doesn't look perfect, we'll try again for the next day. If any other Fox scout wants to ride along, you lose your seat." I pointed a finger at him. "I'm in charge. You do everything I say. No questions asked. No arguing. I will not risk my plane or my life because you decide to do something stupid. Got it?"

Bill gave a fervent nod, smiling widely. "Yes, yes. I'll do whatever you ask." He cupped my hands. "This means so much. Thank you, I mean it."

I gave a weak smile. "Listen. There are no guarantees on this trip. Chances are, even if we make it to Marshall without having to turn around, there won't be any safe landing strips, so we'll only manage to make a bag drop. You're signing up for what will likely be a dull three- or four-hour flight."

"I understand," Bill replied, his eyebrows high. "We had a road cleared at the university for our pilot to land. You can land there."

"I'm not making any promises," I cautioned.

"Even if you can't land, I can at least get a note to my family," Bill quickly replied. "They'll know I'm safe and on my way back to them. They've got to be so worried right now." Bill reached into his pocket, grabbed a pen and notepad, and started drawing something.

"Much obliged, ma'am," Manny said. "Bill's been riding my back ever since we pulled out of Marshall."

"I'm not surprised," I said with a smirk. "And the name's Cash." I watched Manny for a moment. "What can you tell me about these herds? How are you so sure the zeds are moving south?"

"A scout told us he'd followed the herd for fifty miles before he figured out they were heading straight south. One of our radio contacts in North Dakota noticed zeds all started walking the same direction about the same time the birds started migrating. We put two and two together and figured they're migrating for the winter."

I shook my head. "The zeds around here aren't showing any signs of migrating."

"You're farther south. It's warmer here, so they might not have gotten the itch yet. Or, maybe they're just waiting to join up with other herds."

I thought for a moment. I dreaded seeing if this pair was telling the truth, but I also wasn't going to be an ostrich with my head in the sand. If there was danger headed our way, we needed as much advance warning as possible. Flying was the safest and most efficient way to do that. I sighed, came to my feet, and grabbed my tray. "Well, if I'm going to do this, I better start my flight planning." I turned to Bill. "Be at the park gate by sunrise. Don't bring more than five pounds of gear with you. I like to keep the plane as light as possible when we head out."

"Here." Bill handed me a piece of paper. "Here's a map of the university." He pointed to a long line. "Here's where our pilot used to land."

As I pocketed the paper, Tyler gave me a smile. "Get some rest. I'll try to catch you before you leave in the morning. *If* you leave in the morning, I mean."

"Good night." I gave Tyler a slight smile before stepping back and then paused, thinking of another problem of being cooped up in a small, enclosed space with a newcomer. "Oh, and Bill? Be sure to wash up. You guys really stink."

Tyler's smile widened into a big grin, and I couldn't help but return his smile. I turned and headed toward the food table. After dumping off my tray and grabbing a bag of nuts and an apple for Clutch, I walked back to the cabin. My leg needed the exercise, and I needed the fresh air. Aside from the random raider and zed herd, life had returned to something that vaguely resembled normalcy. I tried not to show fear, but if Manny was right about huge herds headed this way, I was downright terrified. We couldn't take out a single herd. How the hell could we defend the park against something ten thousand times the size of the herd we ran from today?

By the time I reached the cabin, the sun had set. Jase was doing push-ups on the floor while Clutch was sprawled out on the bed sound asleep, with a bottle of pills still in his grip. For a moment, my stress disappeared. These two guys were my family now. Like so many other "families" of survivors in this new world, we were just as close and any real family, and I loved them no less than if we were related.

Jase was a bit like the brother I'd never had, but he was more like a son I'd probably never have. He had a good heart. Even with all the shit he'd seen, there was still an unjaded piece left in his soul. I'd give my life for his in a heartbeat. He was a far better person than I was, and I was thankful that he came to Clutch's farm that day many months ago…the day our family was born.

The idea of a real-life son terrified me. I often thought back to the time Clutch and I had unprotected sex and was thankful that I hadn't ended up pregnant. I shivered at the thought of having a tiny, defenseless, *crying* baby surrounded by zeds.

Shaking the thought from my head, I walked over to the table, grabbed the stack of FAA sectional maps, and opened up the one for Minneapolis. I laid the map next to the hand-drawn map Bill had scrawled during dinner. On it, the buildings of the university were squares and rectangles, with a thick line drawn at the bottom indicating a road he was convinced would work as a landing strip. After lighting a candle, I scrutinized the sectional, circling every airport that had fuel along the route to Marshall and back. Taking off and landing wasn't much of an issue anymore. Any stretch of road without power lines worked, especially since the planes

I flew weren't large by any means. I could feather the prop and land nearly silently. As long as no zeds were too close when I restarted for takeoff, I could be safely in the air before any got close.

"I didn't know you were doing a scouting run tomorrow," Jase said without stopping.

"*We* have a scouting run tomorrow. A long distance one," I replied. "If Clutch is up to it. Tyler wants him on this run."

Jase rolled over. His brows rose. "Really? Where are we heading?"

"The folks from Marshall said there might be some herds headed this way. I want to check that out. They seem to think zeds are migrating south for winter. If that's true, the more time we have to prepare, the better."

Jase's guffawed. "Zeds migrating? Like geese?"

I shrugged. "I suppose so. I thought it sounded pretty farfetched, too."

He simply gave a disbelieving shake of his head. "How big of herds are we talking about?"

I thought about telling him what Manny had said, but decided Jase had enough bad things to dream about already. "I guess we'll find out tomorrow."

Jase's eyes narrowed. "They must be big for Tyler to want you to fly out that far."

I shrugged. "We head out at sunrise. This will be a top-off-the-fuel-tanks kind of mission. If we can, we'll also check out the folks still holed up at the university in

Marshall. Otherwise, we'll at least try to do a bag drop."

"Cool." He then nodded to Clutch. "He was out cold when I got home. I'm surprised he's still asleep."

"Freeley was a bit rougher than we expected," I said. "I think it banged him up a bit."

He frowned for a moment before his features softened. "He'll feel better in no time."

I wished I had his confidence. While I knew Clutch would say he was feeling better, I also knew he would lie about his pain just to ride along. Clutch needed more time to heal, but he also needed to keep his spirit up. Being cooped up at the park was a constant numbing barrage against his spirit. I didn't know how to find the balance, and so I took the easy way out and let Clutch decide.

I circled another airport on the map. "Oh, and one of the newcomers will be riding along. He's got a wife and daughter still at Marshall."

Jase gave a crooked smile. "We could leave early, leave him behind."

"Believe me, I've already considered it, but this guy really needs this. That's another reason I need you along—to make sure he doesn't go stupid while we're up there."

"Won't be the first time."

I snorted. Yeah, the Cessna now had duct tape covering a bullet hole in the fuselage from the last time we gave a newcomer a lift. "Get some sleep. I have a feeling tomorrow is going to be a long day."

Bill was waiting—practically prancing—when Clutch, Jase, and I arrived at the gate the following morning. As we approached in the small red truck, he waved and jogged to the edge of the gate.

I gave him a full once-over. His hair was still damp, and he wore a fresh shirt. That he'd listened to me yesterday and cleaned himself up a bit gave me some confidence that he'd behave on this trip. "Morning," I called out. "Are you ready to go?"

He nodded with a smile, his eyebrows raised high. "You bet. Let's go." He lifted a small duffle. "I also brought some letters and things from the others."

"All right. Go ahead and climb in back." I gestured behind me, where Clutch sat in his wheelchair against the big white portable fuel tank, sipping coffee in a thermos while he eyed the newcomer. Before the outbreak, Clutch had never touched caffeine. Ever since his concussion, he guzzled the stuff whenever he had a chance.

As Jase drove us down the road, I craned my head out the window. Long wisps of white marred an otherwise clear sky. I leaned back in with a sigh of relief. "Fingers crossed, it should hopefully be a smooth flight today."

"Good," Jase drawled. "That last flight was not much

fun. And by 'not much fun,' I mean it was pretty much the worst experience ever. "

I chuckled, remembering Jase's face buried in a sick-sack thirty minutes into a two-hour scouting run. "Poor Jasen can't handle bumpy air," I cooed.

He gave me a droll stare for a moment and then flipped me off, and I grinned even harder.

Jase's stomach couldn't handle turbulence, but it was Clutch's back that couldn't risk any turbulence today. Over the past couple of months, Jase had filled in for Clutch on supply runs, and he'd become my co-pilot. He was no longer the kid who'd come to Clutch's farm — bloody and carrying his dying dog — six months ago. He'd only turned sixteen last week, but, aside from a youthful face, no one would ever mistake Jase for still being a boy.

In his eyes, anyone could see that he'd suffered more than most. Not many had to kill their own father like Jase had. Many would've been broken. Not Jase. He'd become the consummate survivor. He was the best of all of us. He did what it took to survive, yet he somehow managed to retain his humanity, something I felt like I had to fight to hold onto. Whether fighting zeds or on scouting runs, I easily trusted him as much as I trusted Clutch and Tyler.

I also hated bringing him into danger. I wanted to keep him safe behind the park's gates. Every time he left the park, some place deep within my heart panged with dread. A part of me craved to lock him in the cabin, but

I knew that would be a disservice to him. He needed to learn how to survive on his own, and protecting him would only hurt him.

Still, it was hard.

Jase brought the truck around a curve in the road, bringing into sight the Cessna 172 and shot-up Piper Cub sitting in the small parking lot of a rest area, both ready to go at a moment's notice. For most of my scouting trips, I took the slower Cub. For today's long trip, I needed the speed and distance the Cessna offered, even though the 172 could in no way be called a fast airplane.

I kept the planes as close to the park as possible. It made sense given we kept the area around the park clear of zeds, and I felt safer knowing I could be in the air in less than five minutes in case shit hit the park. Jase parked on the edge of the road, and I stepped out. The air was cool and damp, and the early morning sun caused the dew to glisten on the Cessna's wings.

Bill jumped down and stared at the plane. "You take off on this road? Isn't that dangerous with all these trees?"

"Nah," I said. "It's a lot less dangerous than the airport." I headed to the back of the truck and dropped the lift gate. Clutch casually screwed the cap on his steaming thermos and slid it into the bag on his wheelchair. After twelve or so hours of rest, Clutch's pain had receded, and his mood had improved. His face seemed lighter this morning, and I knew he was eager for his first flight with me. I pulled two two-by-sixes out and made a ramp against the truck.

"The airport is close to Chow Town," Jase said, walking past us. "So the risk of zeds getting in our way on takeoff or landing is a lot higher. This road is straight and close to the park. Besides, it's not like we have to worry about traffic."

Clutch wheeled his chair down the primitive ramp, and we headed for the Cessna 172. "The weather looks good today," he said.

I looked out to the sky another time. "Yeah. It's great flying weather." I went down on a knee and began removing the tie-downs.

"Don't you have to land at an airport to get fuel?" Bill asked from behind me.

Once I tugged the first rope from the plane, I moved onto the next. "No. We truck the av-gas in." I pointed to the pickup truck we'd arrived in. "You see that white tank on the back of the truck?"

He looked and then frowned. "That's for the airplanes? I thought it was an extra tank for the truck."

I shook my head. "We have a full-sized gas truck for all of our cars and trucks. We use that tank just for the airplanes." We'd found the fuel tank on the back of some farmer's truck. We'd cleaned out the tank and filled it with aviation fuel at the airport. "It works pretty good," I tacked on before glancing over to see Jase helping Clutch get into the front seat. I looked back at Bill. "We'll be taking off soon. We'll be in the air for a few hours, so if you need to hit the bathroom, this is your last chance."

"It's okay. I'm ready to go." Bill wrung his hands and headed toward Jase.

"Jase can help get you strapped in," I said and walked my preflight checklist. After I made a final circle around the plane, I headed for the cockpit.

"We're all set. Clutch is up front since it would be too much of a hassle to put him in the backseat," Jase said as he held the door open.

"That makes sense," I said. "I guess it's time, then." While Jase stood off to the side of the plane, I climbed into the front left seat of the small four-seater.

In the seat next to mine, Clutch was busy stashing his backpack under his seat.

Bill was strapped in the seat behind Clutch and already had a headset on. I set my spear and rifle alongside Clutch's Blaser rifle between our seats, and buckled into the pilot's seat.

I smiled at Clutch strapped in next to me. "Our first flight together."

He nodded and for the first time in months, a genuine smile emerged. "I've been looking forward to it."

"Jase is my usual co-pilot. But since you're riding shotgun, you want to be my navigator on this run?"

"Sure." A sense of purpose spanned his features. "Do you have a map?"

A smile crept up my cheeks. "It's good to have you

back," I said quietly as I pulled out the sectional maps I'd marked up last night and handed them to him.

He watched me for a moment, and the tiniest hint of a smile curled his lips. He opened his mouth to speak but then closed it, choosing instead to say nothing.

"All right," I said with a sigh. I pointed to black circle that marked the park and moved my finger an inch or so. "We're about here right now and our flight path is that penciled line there. We'll be on a heading of zero-one-zero. The map continues on this side." I flipped the large sheet over.

"I'm a Ranger," he replied with a smirk. "I've read a map once or twice."

"Oh, yeah," I said. "I guess you have." After a moment, I grabbed a pen from my pocket and handed it to him. "We need to mark down every large herd we fly over. Be careful to mark down their current locations. If you can see any kind of path they've trampled, try to note their trajectory, if you can. Hopefully, we'll be able to figure out if any herds will come near the park or if we're in the clear. If any are headed our way, I think Tyler's counting on you to help figure out some kind of response plan."

"I figured as much," he said, his smile fading.

"I'm still hoping Manny was exaggerating, and there aren't any big herds headed this direction."

"We'll find out soon enough," Clutch said quietly.

This morning, while we were at the stream, I'd brought Clutch and Jase up to speed on everything

Manny had said. But, it wasn't until Jase had left to grab the truck that I'd told Clutch just how large the herds were reported to me. I swallowed and gave a tight nod before going through my pre-startup checks. Satisfied, I looked outside to Jase who was busy keeping an eye out for zeds. "Clear," I called out. I turned the prop on the engine and it came to life. The magnetos were starting to run rough. Unfortunately, I knew nothing about the mechanics of an airplane besides the most basic items, and neither did anyone at the park. There were two guys who maintained the Humvees, and they were doing their best to keep the plane in shape as much as their knowledge would allow. If the FAA still existed, they would've grounded this operation months ago. As it stood, it was just a matter of time before I'd have to find a new airplane for transporting cargo and going on longer scouting trips like today's.

Once the engine warmed up, I taxied the plane onto the road and ran through my pre-takeoff checks. It took a few minutes to tame the coughing engine by leaning the mixture and playing with the throttle. Once everything was in the green, I motioned to Jase who, after one final three-sixty, ran over and squeezed inside behind me. Takeoff was the most dangerous part of the flight. There was no way to mask engine noise and full throttle, and even though any zed that neared the park was quickly dispatched, more zeds showed up all the time.

As Jase buckled in, I put on my headset. While there

was no use for headsets to communicate with control towers or traffic, they did make it easier to talk with the passengers and to report in to Tyler when we were returning from scouting trips so he could make sure the runway was cleared for landing. To not draw zeds to the area, I liked to fly straight in and with the throttle pulled back to keep my landing as quiet as possible.

"Everyone ready for takeoff?" I asked.

Clutch nodded. "Ready."

I looked to the backseat.

"I'm ready," Bill said, his voice coming through loud and clear through my headset.

Jase was still adjusting his boom. "Let's rock and roll," he said.

I smirked and then turned my focus onto the road in front of me. I pushed the throttle full forward, and the plane rolled ahead, slowly at first, and then passing each yellow divided highway line faster and faster. I tugged back on the yoke, and the plane lifted off the ground gently, the smoothness of the air instead of tires against rough concrete was the only sense of transition from the ground to the sky. As the plane climbed, I turned toward north on my compass heading.

I set the stopwatch taped on the panel, a backup to help remind me how much fuel I had remaining. I looked at Clutch. "While you look for herds, keep an eye out for landmarks and let me know if we start to veer off our flight path."

"Got it," he replied, all business.

"If I have to ride backseat, I call dibs on the music," Jase said, and I found an iPod dropped onto my lap.

With a chuckle, I plugged his MP3 into the audio input and kicked off the playlist he always listened to on our scouting runs. Flying was one of the few times we could listen to music without fear of zeds, and we always played rock-paper-scissors to see whose music would be played. Though, listening to any music was nice. Pop music filtered through our headsets, and I turned up the volume.

We flew for an hour, everyone given the same task: search for herds. I kept the plane three thousand feet off the ground so that any herds would be easier to spot. Bill nervously chattered, his voice cutting over the music. Once I threated to pull the plug on his headset, he was a better passenger.

The air was smooth and cool, and the sky was clear. It was an absolutely perfect flying day, and I found myself feeling lighter and breathing easier. There was something surreal about being in the sky, removed from the death and destruction below. It was the only time I could still feel completely at peace. After all, the sky was the only place left without man-eating predators.

"There's one! Down there, below!" Bill exclaimed.

"Down where?" I cranked my head around to see him pointing out the window to my right. I looked, searching for zeds. My gaze narrowed on a field of dirt that seemed to go on forever in the distance, and I turned the plane in that direction. As we approached, the dirt morphed into what looked like a giant, flat anthill. Chills covered my body because this was no anthill.

"Holy bejeezus," Jase said. "That's no herd. That's...that's..."

"Fuck," Clutch muttered.

"Yeah," I added, my jaws lax. As we drew closer, the movement began to split into individual humanoid shapes all moving together like fans at a music concert, only far bigger than any concert or sporting event could be. The herd was larger than I could've possibly imagined. Hell had opened up and spurted forth millions of demons from its gorge.

"I told you guys these herds were huge. And it looks like another one in the distance out there," Bill said from the backseat. "Now that you've seen it, can we check on my family?"

"Hold on," I said, as I continued to stare at the mass of zeds below us.

"I wasn't expecting a herd like that," Jase said. "What could we possibly do if it found the park?"

After a tense moment of silence, I pulled off to return to our flight path.

A heavy stone was already growing in my gut. I found it hard to breathe, and my chest pounded like I was about to have a heart attack. I could already guess their trajectory from seeing the relatively straight trodden path over a half-mile wide that went on for as far as I could see. Camp Fox didn't stand a chance.

As I flew north, parallel to the zed path, Clutch continually updated the map while muttering under his breath every few seconds. The herd had crushed all the grass and fields in its path. We lost the path a couple times when we flew over larger towns, but quickly found the path again on the other side.

"God," I sighed. "There's another one."

Clutch looked up and followed my finger. "Jesus."

Another herd, at least half the size of the first, looked like it was only thirty miles or so behind and headed the same direction.

"I'll mark it down," Clutch said as I tried to stay focused on my heading, but my eyes kept darting back to the herd. Worse, not ten miles later, another herd appeared in the distance.

"How can there be so many?" Jase asked from the backseat.

No one answered. In fact, no one spoke for many long minutes. I gripped the yoke and twisted my hands around it. Clutch scribbled on the map. I couldn't tell what Jase and Bill were doing behind me. My mind was too busy dealing with shock. I didn't need to be an actuary to do the math. There was nothing we could do to defend Camp Fox against such numbers.

We were absolutely, completely fucked.

My brows furrowed as I held back a sob. The unfairness of it all pissed me off. We worked so hard to survive. We'd finally gotten to the point where we felt a step ahead of the zeds.

And now this?

Like Manny's group, we could only run, but where could we go? The massive herds seemed to cover an entire line of latitude as they moved south.

Bill lunged forward and pointed straight ahead. "There," he said, wagging his finger. "See that? The university is coming up."

I jumped, startled. "Get buckled in!"

"It's SMSU. We're there," he said, not moving.

I squinted and made out the connected buildings. We were still at least five miles out and I throttled back to slow the plane and descend. "All right, guys. Keep an eye out for zeds."

"They would've all left with the herds," Bill said.

"Do you know that for sure?" I countered, adding in flaps to slow the plane to near stall speed.

He said nothing.

I sighed. "Where's that street I can land on, Bill?"

He leaned forward more. "Birch Street," he said as if I could read street signs from up here. "It's just to the south of the dorms. We kept it clear in case we had to pull out."

"It's east-west, right?" I asked, looking once more at his roughly drawn map.

"What?"

I made a motion with my hand. "Does the road go north and south or east and west?"

"Oh, east and west. You can't miss it. It's the main street for the university."

As we neared the small university, I slowed the plane and dropped in as much flaps as I could without stalling. Once I had the street in sight, I nodded. "I've got it."

I frowned as I took in the university. During a typical scouting run, zeds dotted streets of any town I flew over. Here, other than the random zed crawling across the ground or a rotting corpse, I saw nothing. The entire university seemed devoid of zeds. "You guys see anything?" I asked.

"Nothing yet. Just a few stragglers," Jase said.

"Same here," Clutch said. "From what I can tell, those stragglers look pretty decrepit."

"You're going past the street. Down there! Down there!"

I flipped off the intercom but could still hear Bill's yelling even through my headset. The street was narrow, only two lanes lined with trees and streetlamps. It had a ninety-degree curve on the eastern edge and a forty-five on the west. I could make it work, but there wasn't much room for error, and no room for a late-decision go-around.

Clutch squeezed my knee, and I turned. "You sure you want to try it?" he yelled since I'd turned off the intercom.

I looked back down at the street. I had to make the call. If I continued to circle, the engine noise would draw all remaining zeds into the area. I glanced at Bill. His eyes were wide and pleading. It would've been easy to fly over and drop a bag, letting the survivors make their way to their families and friends on their own. But, if I were in Bill's shoes, this close to my family...

"Damn it," I muttered and dropped in the rest of the flaps. There was no way I couldn't not land. I may have lost my parents, but if it was Clutch or Jase down there, I would have to see for myself. Bill deserved the same.

I lined up for a long final approach. I wanted to land as short as possible because neither the length nor the width of the street was forgiving for a botched landing. My grip was firm on the yoke. I had to get it right. The stall warning sounded, and the ground came up quickly. The wheels hit hard. The plane bounced before settling down. I stepped on the brakes to stop faster than I could with a taildragger.

I pulled off my headset and looked around to find no zeds running out to greet us. I bit my lip. "Well, that wasn't my finest landing."

"We didn't crash, so I consider it a success," Clutch said.

Jase tapped my shoulder. "I'll cover you while you get lined up for takeoff."

I nodded and opened the door. I brought my seat forward. He squeezed out from behind me and hopped outside. Bill leaned between Clutch and me as I started to taxi back the opposite direction I'd landed. Jase walked alongside the Cessna as I taxied, ready to take out any random zed that came at us.

"What are you doing?" Bill asked. "You're going past

the dorms."

"We'll check them out on foot. First, I need the plane ready in case we need to make a quick takeoff."

He muttered something and leaned back. Suddenly, I found myself pressed forward against the yoke as he squeezed passed me. "Hey!"

Bill jumped out of the plane and ran back toward the dorms, carrying the bag of letters.

"Idiot," Clutch muttered.

I shook my head. "He's going to get himself killed." I taxied the plane all the way back to the eastern edge of the street and turned around, setting the plane up for an immediate takeoff. "I'm half tempted to just leave him and head back."

As I cut the engine, Jase walked around the front, still scanning the area.

Clutch grabbed his rifle.

I put my hand on his forearm and fought to say the words I needed to say. "You should stay with the plane, in case we need to make a quick takeoff." I inhaled before he had a chance to speak. "You know us. Jase and I won't do anything stupid. We're just going to check on the dorms, that's it."

"I know. I trust both of you. It's the other guy I don't trust."

"We'll be wheels up in ten minutes. You stay here and sweep for us in case zeds start trickling this way. Okay?"

He sat there, gripping his rifle. After a moment, he

hit his legs, startling me.

"I hate this. I fucking hate this," he said before tilting his head back against the headrest.

My heart ached for him. "I know," I said softly and touched his cheek. "This is a temporary inconvenience, that's all. You'll be walking soon. I know it. We just have to take it one day at a time."

His lips tightened. "I'll see you in ten."

After a moment, I dropped my hand, unbuckled, grabbed my gear, and climbed out.

"Be careful," he said suddenly. "I've got a bad vibe about this place."

I gave a small nod and walked away, glancing back to see Clutch already focused on scanning the area.

Jase came up to my side. Looking around, he gave an exaggerated shiver. "This place gives me the creeps. Everything's been trampled. There's not even a shrub left."

To my right was a parking lot filled with cars. Most were parked askew, as though they'd been forcibly shoved out of their parking space and into the spot next to them. A couple had even been rolled over. I hadn't seen any mobile zeds, but no survivors came out to greet us, either. Both would've heard us fly over.

I slung my spear onto my shoulder and kept my rifle ready. "Let's make this quick."

We walked toward the dorms where Bill had headed. We took slow steps, constantly scanning our full three-sixty, though I knew Clutch had our six covered. While I wanted to get the hell out of there, I didn't rush. Just because Bill had run in half-cocked didn't mean that we had to put ourselves at risk.

A zed without legs reached out like a beggar. I stepped to the side, and it tried to drag itself to us. I didn't waste energy killing it; it was in such bad shape that the only way it could latch onto a victim was if someone fell on it.

The ominous feeling in my gut grew worse as we approached the first dorm. The doors were propped wide open by a mangled corpse. Bones, tufts of hair, and cloth shreds were about all that remained.

Jase and I eyed each other. With a deep inhalation, he stepped inside first. Glass crunched under my boots as I stepped around the corpse. We walked as carefully and quietly as we could, pausing to listen after every few steps.

Something fell on the floor in a nearby room. I swung my rifle around.

We moved as one toward the open door. I listened for any other sounds, but could only hear movement in the one room. When we reached the door, I twisted around and aimed. I lowered my weapon with a sigh. "Jesus, Bill. I nearly blew your head off."

He continued to rifle through papers on the table. "They're not here. I don't understand it. There's no note." He chewed on his bottom lip for a moment before he looked up and over his shoulder. "They must still be in the student center."

"Hold up," I said, reaching for him. That no one had cleaned up the body in the building they lived was a serious red flag. "They probably had to run and didn't get a chance to get back here to leave a note."

"Bill, hold on, man," Jase echoed.

He pushed open the door. "It's lunchtime. Everyone eats at the student center." He headed outside.

"He's a real pain in the ass," I muttered, not caring if Bill heard me or not.

"The idea of ditching him and heading back is getting pretty appealing," Jase added.

I glanced at my watch. Six minutes to go. I sucked in a breath. "Let's get this over with."

We followed Bill as he jogged down a sidewalk and up to a brick building with large glass windows.

"Hold up," I said and grabbed his arm before he opened the door.

He yanked out of my grip. "Everyone will be inside. It's okay."

"Look," Jase said and pointed.

"What?" Bill asked, and then he frowned. He cupped his hands against the glass and squinted. He let out a gasp. "No."

Inside, the student center was a mess. Tables were overturned, chairs were scattered. There was nobody eating lunch. There was nobody, period.

"They must've run," I said hopefully.

Bill grabbed the door handle and yanked it open. As he ran inside, I lowered my head and shook it slowly.

After taking a deep breath, I followed, staying protectively at Jase's side.

There were no zeds, not even any bodies littering the floors. The ominous feeling in my gut had morphed into fear.

Bill was doing a three-sixty, looking around. "Katie!" he called out. "Jan!"

"Sh," I hissed. "Keep it down."

A thump came from somewhere off to my left, confirming my suspicion. There were zeds still around here, all right.

A smile broke out on Bill's face, and the tension fell from his shoulders. "Oh, they're in the theater. Thank God."

"Don't," I warned.

Bill turned back to us. "It's all right. The theater is our emergency shelter. They've probably been staying in there until someone came to give them the all-clear."

"Then why is there a steel pipe through the door?" Jase asked, but Bill either didn't hear or didn't care because he rushed across the open space and to that exact door.

"I don't like this," I said, slowly walking toward Bill.

"I think we should get out of here," Jase said.

"Agreed."

"I'm coming!" Bill called out and glanced over his shoulder. "It's okay. You don't understand. This is part of our emergency procedures. Someone probably locked them in here for safety, so that zeds couldn't get to them. But now they can't get out unless we unlock it for them."

"Then why didn't they lock the door from the other side," Jase asked dubiously.

Bill slid the pipe out from the handles and pulled open the door. He stood there, staring into the darkness. "Katie? Jan?"

Moans echoed. Jase and I both lunged for the door the same time a zed tumbled from the darkness. Bill cried out and shoved it down. Jase slammed the door shut, and I slid the bar back into place. I spun on my heel to see Bill holding the zed back with his hands pressing against its shoulders.

Hundreds, if not thousands, of fists pounded against the metal door. It sounded like the entire theater was filled with zeds.

Jase swung his machete, taking off the top of the zed's skull, and it collapsed.

"Holy shit," Jase said, sucking in a breath.

"Yeah," I said breathlessly before turning around to find Bill frozen behind us. After wiping sweat from my face, I grabbed his arm. "We need to get out of here. Now."

Both Jase and I pulled at him, but he dug in his heels. "The theater was safe. No windows. How'd the zeds find them?"

"Someone was probably infected before going in there," I answered.

"That door isn't going to hold them for long," Jase

tacked on. "We need to get out of here. Because those are going to be some fresh and fast zeds in there."

Bill collapsed onto the floor with his head between his knees, hugging himself. "I never should've left. I should've come earlier."

Jase and I looked at each other, hopeless. Neither of us spoke. I didn't voice the truth, that his family had probably never stood a chance.

The sounds of fists pounding against the doors echoed through the center. The bar through the door handles clanged as the door moved against it in a rhythmic wave. It would take minutes, at most, for them to break free.

I nudged Bill. "We have to go."

He shook his head. "What's the use in going on?" He looked up, tears running down his cheeks. "It's my fault. I should've come for them." His voice grew louder with every word, and I tried to shush him. Bill shook his fist at the theater. "You bastards! You're all bastards!"

I eyed Jase and he nodded. "We need to go now," he said, enunciating every word.

I nodded. We each grabbed one of Bill's arms and pulled him to his feet.

He tore away. "No!" He fell back onto his butt and sobbed.

I pursed my lips. "Bill, it's not your fault what happened."

"There's nothing you can do, Bill. Your family would want you to save yourself."

Bill didn't respond, instead he continued to sob.

We tried to pull him up again, but he shoved away and fell back down. The zeds' moaning and pounding were growing louder, echoing throughout the student center.

This time when I eyed Jase, his features hardened, and he shook his head slowly. I swallowed and glanced down at Bill one more time. The man had reached his breaking point. He'd chosen to give up rather than to keep on living. I wanted to yank him along with us, but I knew it would be pointless. If we took the time to drag him, we'd never get out of there alive.

My throat tightened and I stepped back. Then Jase and I ran back to the plane, leaving Bill behind with a theater full of zeds.

CHAPTER V

"Where's Bill?" Clutch asked as Jase and I piled into the Cessna. I dumped my gear onto Jase's lap and pulled the door closed.

A distant scream broke through the silence.

"He's not coming," Jase said as I started up the plane without taking the time to go through any checklist, let alone buckle my seat belt.

Clutch didn't say anything else, but I could feel his eyes on me as I tried to smooth out the engine as quickly as I could. As soon as its rough grumble of fouling spark plugs cleared somewhat, I throttled full power and started my takeoff roll.

"A shitload of zeds coming in fast at our two o'clock," Clutch said loudly at my side.

"*C'mon, c'mon, c'mon,*" I muttered, pulling back on the yoke, trying to force the plane into the air. With the tanks only half full and one less passenger, the Cessna lifted off at the edge of the dorms. Zeds came running around the buildings and onto the street below. I leveled off my climb to build up speed just out of reach of the zeds below, because I didn't want to risk stalling and losing what little lift I had.

Once I could manage a decent rate of climb, I looked down at the crowded street below. If we'd been five seconds later, zeds would've collided with the Cessna, and we never would've gotten off the ground. I let out the breath I'd held on takeoff. "That was close."

Clutch craned his head to watch the scene below, and then turned to me.

I put my headset on, and he did the same.

"What the hell happened back there?" he asked.

"No one made it out of Marshall when the herds passed through," I said.

"They were still at the student center," Jase added.

His lips tightened and he looked over both of us. "You two okay?"

I nodded. "Yeah."

"That was too close," Jase said before sighing heavily into the headset.

After getting the plane set up on its heading back to Camp Fox, I turned on Jase's music. No one spoke the entire flight back to the park. We passed over the herds again, as they chewed their slow but relentless path toward our home. One herd had stopped at a farm and had all of its buildings surrounded. I hated to think what they were after.

Poor Marshall had never stood a chance, and it'd had a hundred times the population of Camp Fox. The herds could eat right through us and barely slow down. Seeing what had happened at the student center made me realize one thing. We couldn't defend the park against the herds like we'd done before. We had to run, and we had to do it soon. Because if we waited until the first herd was in sight, it'd be too late.

Clutch, Jase, and I could fly somewhere far enough north that we'd be safe easily enough, but I'd never be able to get the others out in time. Tyler, Tack, Griz...they'd all be doomed to certain death. *No.* I couldn't live with myself knowing I'd stranded fifty or sixty people for execution.

I spent the rest of the flight trying to think of viable escape plans that included everyone and our livestock at the park and the only solution that came to mind was a tall building. But I quickly dismissed it as too risky. No skyscrapers existed anymore after all major cities had been bombed. If any had survived, they wouldn't be structurally sound. As for tall buildings in smaller towns, most buildings wouldn't be more than five floors high. Sure, a herd could likely not reach us on the top floor, but if they knew we were inside, they could have us surrounded until we all starved to death. Or, worse, eventually they'd climb over one another to get to us.

We needed a better option.

When the park came into sight, Clutch radioed Tyler.

Clutch simply said, "Come out and meet us."

I had no doubt it got the point across.

Sure enough, by the time we landed, Tyler was waiting for us. He watched from where he sat on the Humvee's hood as I taxied to my usual parking space.

Tyler jumped down and started tying down the plane as soon as I cut the engine.

I opened my door, and Jase squeezed out from behind me. "I'll get your chair, Clutch," he said from outside before opening the baggage compartment and pulling out the folded wheelchair.

After checking everything, I grabbed Clutch's and my gear and climbed out.

With Jase's support, Clutch lifted himself out of the plane by holding onto the spar and lowered himself onto the chair. I handed him his rifle and backpack.

Tyler came over and scrutinized each of our faces. "Well?"

I opened my mouth to speak but couldn't find the words. I searched for something to say, but nothing coherent formed. How could anyone describe what was headed our way? No one else spoke either, likely unable to find the words as well.

After a long pause, he clenched his fists and kicked at the ground. "Shit!" He took a deep breath and looked back up. "How bad is it?"

"Imagine your worst fucking nightmare times a million," Clutch said bluntly.

"I've never seen anything like it," Jase said. "Huge

herds. Each one has thousands and thousands of those things."

Tyler was silent for a moment. "Do any pose a risk to the park?"

I swallowed. "We have a week, maybe two, until the first herd gets here. If we were a hundred miles east, we'd have longer. But the park is right in their path."

"God," Tyler muttered.

"Camp Fox is not equipped to hold off that many zeds," Clutch said. "The park's hills and waterways will slow them down, but they'll still plow right through the park. We'd burn through all of our ammo, and there'd still be more."

"We have to run," I added.

"Where will we run to?" Tyler asked quietly.

I shrugged. "I don't know. We can keep ahead of the herds for a while. Maybe Montana or Wyoming where they're building those super-cities we keep hearing about."

Tyler shook his head. "The herds could already be hitting through those areas now."

"Okay, then. We could go gypsy. Keep on the move until they pass through," I said, frustrated that I had no better answer. "As long as I have a plane I can scout out areas and make sure that we're not heading straight for another herd. Or, we can try the Pied Piper plan and lead them away from the park. That plan has never failed. If we're lucky, the herds will stick to the roads and steer clear of the park completely. After all, it's pretty secluded."

Even I didn't believe my words. Hungry zeds had a knack at sniffing out prey. A few dozen people in a small area would be a tasty snack for a herd.

"But if the plan failed, we'd be doomed," Clutch said.

"We can't sit on our asses and hope they bypass the park. I've already reached out to all my radio contacts. We have one potential option," Tyler said finally. "How'd Marshall fare? Did Bill find his family?"

I shook my head. "It's been completely wiped out."

Tyler sighed. "I was afraid of that. It's going to devastate Manny's people." He scratched his head. "And Bill?"

I gave him a slow shake of my head. He didn't need to know the ugly details.

"Damn it." He kicked a pebble on the concrete. "I need time to think. We'll talk more after dinner. I'll meet you all at the square," he said and took off.

As though we hadn't just seen the Grim Reaper headed our way, a grin grew across Jase's face and he hustled toward the truck. "Good. I'm starving."

Food, the best temporary medicine for a shitty day. It was the only time I knew Jase wasn't faking his happiness. Everyone loved food now, likely because we all knew how precious it was. Without the convenience of drive-throughs and grocery stores, food took on a whole new meaning. That, plus all the hard physical work we did each day, made mealtime an almost religious experience.

I glanced back at the plane. "I'll refuel in the morning. I didn't see any zeds worth worrying about in the area," I said when I saw Jase already loading Clutch onto the back of the truck. I hopped in, and Jase started the engine and stepped on the gas.

As we drove back into the park, many of the residents were outside working on their assigned tasks, such as gathering food, tending to gardens, and doing laundry. All were completely oblivious to the horde of death headed straight for them.

Jase headed straight for the park square and parked next to Tyler's Humvee. In front of the log building, three of the park's older residents were busy cracking walnuts, hazelnuts, and acorns that the kids had found. Everyone had a chore. No one got a free ride. Even the kids' games had a purpose. Flag football was a popular one, where we taught them how to escape zeds. There was no football involved. One kid started without flags, and they played the role of zed. Every kid whose flags the zed took had to join its herd and go after the others. It sounded a bit morbid, but we had to train them to protect themselves. For little kids, running and hiding were their only real options.

I forced a smile and waved at the trio cracking nuts on my way into the park square.

Tyler held the door open for us. "I should warn you. They've been waiting here since morning,"

Clutch rolled himself in first, and Jase and I followed.

The chow area was empty except for Manny and his

people. The moment we stepped inside, all eyes turned to us. Manny stood with a wide smile and headed our way. "You're back!" He slowed down as he looked past my shoulder, then at me. "Where's Bill?"

I'd been expecting the question and didn't hesitate. "He decided to stay behind."

Faces lit up. Except for Manny, whose smile had been replaced by a dubious squint of his eyes. I tried not to make contact as I followed Clutch to the food line. Jase had somehow found his way to the front of the line. A woman hustled to me and held a picture in front of my face. "Did you see my husband?"

I shook my head. "I didn't see him." I picked up a tray and grabbed some leftover potatoes, nuts, and berries.

Manny's people quickly surrounded us.

"Are they okay?"

"Did you talk to Lyle?"

"What did you see?"

"Did you give them our letters?"

"Please tell us more!"

The woman who'd showed me the picture of her husband grabbed my arm. "Please take me north like you did Bill. We don't have to land, just look for Mike. I know he's out there. Please help me."

"I'm sorry, but I can't help you," I said, not wanting to be the one responsible for crushing their precious hope. "The chance of seeing anyone from the air is so miniscule that—"

"You took Bill there. I need to get back to my husband!"

Clutch wheeled between us, forcing the woman to loosen her grip. "Cash can't help you. None of us can," he said.

Even though he had to look up at her, he still radiated strength. The woman's lips pursed in anger. She spun on her heel and left us, mumbling, "Assholes."

"Will you go back tomorrow?" someone else asked.

"No," Clutch and I said at the same time.

"There's no place to go back to," Tyler said from behind us.

His words smothered the room. Even the sounds of silverware on plates silenced. In a rush, Clutch and I grabbed the rest of our food and headed to a picnic table in the corner.

The man who'd asked the last question followed. "What do you mean, 'there's no place to go back to'?"

I glanced down at Clutch, and then took a deep breath. "It's not safe there."

"What do you mean? Why won't you tell us? What happened? If it's not safe, why did you leave our people behind? Those are our families back there!"

I ignored him, eating with one hand while holding my Glock on my lap with the other.

"Because there was no one left to get out!" Tyler bellowed out as he sat down.

Manny clenched his eyes shut for a moment before opening them again and speaking. "We were too late."

I pursed my lips before I finally spoke. "Some had to make it out. If they made it to cars and stayed ahead of the herds, they could've made it." I wasn't lying; I believed my words. After all, someone had to have locked the infected in the theater from the outside. Whether they got away in time...chances were no one would ever know.

"I thought they'd be safe," one of the newcomers muttered without any inflection. "I thought the herds were following us."

"God," someone else said. "So many kids...lost."

"We should've gone back for them."

"My Ginny," a man said, pulling at his hair.

"Maybe they got out in time."

"We have to try to find any survivors," the woman who'd first showed me a picture said, though the picture was now crumpled in her grip. "Manny, we need to go back."

"We have to go back and find anyone we can."

The man who'd been pulling at his hair screamed, "Stop it! Stop it! You all know they didn't get out. They're dead! We left them there to die! They're all dead or they're zeds!"

Manny held up his hands. "Whoa. Enough. We don't know that for sure. Some might have gotten out. Even if they did, there are all the herds between us and them. We can't search for them if we're dead. We have to look out for ourselves first. Once the herds pass through, then we can go back."

"How will we survive the herds? If Marshall couldn't survive, we have no chance here!" a woman cried out.

Tyler stood up. "I have an idea, but it's a long shot."

CHAPTER VI

The following morning's flight was a bumpy one, and I had to keep both hands on the yoke. The weather was unseasonably warm, and the heat caused thermals to pop up in the air. Tyler was strapped in next to me in the Cessna 172. Sitting behind us, Jase scanned the countryside for anything useful while Griz slept soundly, his snores coming over the intercom every once in a while.

Clutch, as Tyler's second-in-command, was in charge of the park whenever Tyler was offsite for longer than a few hours. When Camp Fox had relocated to the park, the pair had reached an agreement to never ride in the same vehicle because the park couldn't risk losing both of our seasoned military officers. Even though their knowledge and leadership had saved our collective ass many times over, I suspected the other reason they didn't ride together was because they pissed each other off as much as they needed each other.

Clutch couldn't come along today for three reasons. First, the air was too turbulent for his back. Second, Tyler was the only person who'd spoken with the guy we were meeting today. Third and most important, Clutch was shit as a diplomat. He was great at getting people in line—and was likely running all the residents through the training wringer right now—but when it came to begging for help, Tyler's smooth personality was needed.

Tyler currently had his head propped against the glass, looking outside, his hand tapping to the beat of the music piping through our headsets. He had his iPhone plugged into the plane's audio system, and the connector charged the device while it played. Right now, music from the Nadas filled my headset.

"The zeds around here aren't showing any signs of migrating yet. I wonder if they do leave, how far south they'll go," he said without looking up, the music volume auto-muting while he spoke.

"Who cares as long as it's a long ways from us," Jase replied from the backseat.

"I don't get it," Tyler said. "The zeds are rotting away. Why would they migrate when they're probably going to be dead within a year, anyway?"

The zeds still owned the area, but their bodies had slowed down as the plague ate away at their flesh and muscle. With how decayed many were, that they hadn't died off already made no sense. Then again, that anyone could have their throat ripped out and yet return as a zed made no sense either. The virus, in its cruel effectiveness, was terrifying.

Still, on this trip, our greater risk was survivors, not zeds. Most zeds remained near towns, with only herds roaming the countryside. If only I'd flown over these roads before and mapped out any roadblocks or signs of raiders, we could've driven today. This was the first time Tyler was meeting with this radio contact. I would've preferred to drive so that we could have taken more reinforcements.

Tyler's contact, a riverboat captain named Sorenson, had a community roughly the size of Camp Fox on a riverboat casino. He'd told Tyler he was confident his people would make it through the migration unscathed, and Tyler had believed him. The question was, would Sorenson take Camp Fox under his protection as well? That he had offered to meet with Tyler gave us all hope.

Right now, everyone at Camp Fox was busy packing up their belongings and pulling together all the food, livestock, supplies, and weapons for winter under the assumptions that Tyler's diplomacy would succeed and we could temporarily relocate to Sorenson's riverboat. If Tyler failed in gaining Sorenson's help today, our only option was to run. I hoped to God Tyler wouldn't fail.

On the ground, a few zeds dotted the landscape. Nothing like the herds Clutch, Jase, and I had seen north of us. Every hour I hoped the herds would stop their migration or at least pass through without coming near Camp Fox, but I knew better. I'd seen the herds and the paths they'd trampled. They moved like locusts intent on a mission. "Maybe the zeds in Chow Town will head out with them," I said, thinking of the only possible benefit of the migration.

"We can only hope," Tyler said. "It would be great to be able to get into town and clear out the stores before bandits get to them."

Right now, around three thousand zeds lurked in the streets of Fox Hills, now called Chow Town. I'd made the unfortunate mistake of getting myself stranded in town not once but twice, and I'd barely gotten out alive each time. No one was crazy enough to venture near Chow Town. Zeds had laid claim, and no one dared challenge them for it.

Every day, a few more would trickle out of Chow Town, and our scouts would put a quick end to them. Still, at that rate, it would take years to clear out the town that had once been Fox Hills.

We couldn't wait a decade for the zeds to clear out of Chow Town. We needed food and resources *now*. After Clutch's farm and Camp Fox were destroyed, it was too late to replant, leaving everyone to harvest wild crops and the few gardens that had been planted. It scared the beejeezus out of me knowing there were even more zeds on the way, eating everything in their path.

Swallowing, I glanced over my shoulder. "Hey, Jase. Did you bring the map that's marked up with the herds?"

"Got it right here."

"Good. If we get the chance to make a fuel stop, I'll fly us north. What do you think, Tyler?"

He nodded. "It's a good idea to see if they're still on track for what we calculated. I think we'll need to start scouting to the north every day."

"I'll use the Cub. It burns less fuel, and I don't want to use this plane except when we have to because it's in desperate need of an overhaul." I paused. "And we have another problem."

"Oh?" Tyler asked.

"The fuel tank at the Fox Hills airport is nearly empty," I replied. "I can get two, maybe three, more refills for the portable tank from it. Jase has marked every airport in the area that might have av-gas, but if I have to travel farther for refills, I need a bigger portable tank. A gas truck would be perfect."

Tyler chuckled. "Easier said than done. Every gas truck we've found is needed for ground support in case Camp Fox needs to become mobile. We can't sacrifice a single truck right now."

"I guess I'll start searching for a plane that runs off auto fuel."

His eyebrows rose. "There are planes that run off regular gas?"

I nodded. "Quite a few, actually. There weren't any at the Fox Hills airport, but I'm sure there's one at a nearby airport."

"Hey, it looks like a grass strip down there," Jase said.

I scanned from side to side and found a yellow crop duster sitting in tall grass. A single building and white tank sat near it.

"That's a good one. Be sure to mark it on the map."

"Already got it," he said. "There's no town for miles. The land is wide open. Might make a good fuel stop on the way back."

"The grass is awfully tall, but yeah, it could be perfect."

We flew in silence for the next several miles. I kept an eye on my flight path while Jase and Tyler scanned the countryside.

"That looks like a camp down there," Tyler said, his finger pressed against the glass.

"It could be a bandit camp," Jase said. "I don't see any kids down there."

"I'd rather warn bandits than not warn good people," Tyler countered.

I slowed the Cessna and descended a hundred feet. Finding survivors was rare, but they were easy to spot. All we had to look for was signs of fortifications, and nearly every camp we'd found was at a farm.

"Can you get any closer?" Tyler asked, ruffling through a duffle.

I smirked. "Afraid gravity won't catch the bag?"

"No, but it'd be nice to actually drop it within their fence."

I bit the inside of my cheek to keep from gritting my teeth. I'd grown an aversion to flying over camps. Every time I did, it brought back memories of Doyle's camp and getting shot at, even though I suspected most folks were out of ammo by now. With one hand wrapped too tightly around the yoke, I dropped in some flaps, slowed the 172 to near stall speed and brought it in to circle the settlement. A half-dozen or so people came to stand outside, looking up, and shading their eyes against the sun.

The engine began to rumble roughly, and my heart lurched. I added in power. "Damn engine is getting worse. We've really got to get it fixed," I muttered.

Tyler opened the window. Cool air blew into the cockpit, and he dropped out the hazard-orange painted bag filled with dirt and a single written warning about the herds heading south. He pulled the window shut and I turned back on course.

"Thanks," Tyler said. "Any time we can warn others about the herds is potentially another life saved."

Tyler had brought three more drop-bags, but we didn't use them. We'd flown over what had definitely been a camp, but it looked like it had been abandoned or overrun some time ago. I often saw signs of abandoned camps, but I hadn't seen a new camp pop up in over a month. Maybe people were moving west where the government was supposedly pooling all resources into building new "city-states" defensible against zeds.

The rumored city-states gave us all hope, but they were too far away to be considered a possibility yet. The largest rumored city was in Montana, with three states of zeds between us and them. Until we had better vehicles, the trip was too risky. We had to survive on our own in zed country.

Mid-sized groups did the best out here. Too small of a group, resources were spread too thin between fending off zeds and finding food. Too large of a group and it became a magnet for every zed in the vicinity. Camp Fox, just crossing sixty residents if the newcomers stayed, was going to become quite tempting to zeds.

The wide blue landmark in the distance caused me to refocus. "We're coming up on the Mississippi. Start looking for our bridge," I said to no one in particular as I strained my eyes, searching the Mississippi River for its bridges.

If the GPS had still worked, it would've brought me straight to our destination since Sorenson had provided the bridge's coordinates. Now, I had to fly by sight, and I was often a mile or more off my destination. It was my fault. Like most, I'd become way too reliant on technology before the outbreak.

"Wait, I've got it. I'll check in," I said to no one in particular as I lined up to the giant yellow X that had been painted on a bridge. I pressed the radio's transmit button. "Cessna to Camp Fox. If you can still hear us, we're descending to land at the RP. Over."

Dead static came as the only response.

"Clutch might have heard us, but there's no way I could pick up his handheld from this distance. I'm not even sure he can pick us up," I said. "We both figured that'd be the case."

On the right day, the radio signal could cover the entire state, especially with the lack of other signals to hinder it. Today didn't seem to be one of those days.

As the river grew larger, I descended and slowed. No signs of zeds and—unfortunately—no sign of the riverboat yet. I flew over the bridge with two steel arches. "Everything looks clear, but I'm not seeing our guys. You guys see any zeds?"

"No. Nothing," came the response from my crew.

I lined up for the bridge again, this time running through my landing checklist. Touching down this close to the river set my nerves on edge, even though the highway was open for a quarter-mile before the bridge, and I had plenty of runway ahead of me. Still, it was discomfiting having all that iron and open water surrounding me. It wouldn't take too much to veer off and hit a wingtip, and then we'd be stranded over two hundred miles away from Camp Fox. And, once down, I'd have to taxi onto the bridge so we didn't have to walk to our destination.

The engine sputtered a couple times on final approach, and I throttled forward just enough to keep it from cutting out completely while still making the landing.

"That engine doesn't sound good," Tyler said.

"It's been acting up more and more lately. Joel says it needs some new sparkplugs," I said as I pulled the plane to a stop in the middle of the bridge so that I could take off in either direction at a moment's notice.

"He's been busy with Humvee Three, and that's his first priority right now. But I'll ask him to take a look," Tyler said.

"Yeah, I figured that." After double-checking to make sure everything was powered off, I set my headset on the dash and unbuckled.

"Rise and shine, Grizzly Bear," Jase said, and I heard Griz grumble something unintelligible.

Tyler smirked, grabbed his bag, and climbed out of the plane. I grabbed my backpack and rifle. Before I opened my door, I glanced back at the red five-gallon jugs filled with emergency av-gas to make sure they were still bungeed together in the baggage compartment, and then headed outside. Jase and Griz followed.

Griz stretched under the sun while I locked the Cessna's doors and turned to Tyler. "We're all set. Barring any big change in weather, we should easily make it back to the park without having to refuel." I thought for a moment. "I miss getting the weather forecasts. They sure did come in handy with flight planning."

"I kind of prefer the lack of news," he said as he pulled out his sword. "It was always sensationalizing the bad things."

"I'll check out the area to the east," Griz said. "I need to stretch my legs."

"I'll go with you," Jase offered, and the two sauntered off with their weapons drawn.

I started to head in the opposite direction.

"Weather reports were inaccurate as much as they were accurate," Tyler said. "I miss pizza delivery more."

I chuckled. "I miss pizza, too."

We both quickly sobered. It was no fun dwelling on things that we could never have again. We all had a trigger that brought everything we'd lost to mind. Shaking off memories of loved ones I'd never see again, I scanned the distance in silence, looking for any zeds that might have heard the airplane and come to investigate. The bridge and rural highway had no cars for as far my eyes could see. This area was rural enough that it didn't have the telltale scars of wreckage and bodies that populated areas had.

The sun glistened off the blade a trader had given Tyler in exchange for penicillin. It was a nice weapon but it'd be far too heavy for me. I preferred my lighter weapons: the spear I'd made from an old broom handle, a machete from our first looting run in Chow Town, and a large tanto knife Clutch had given me right after the outbreak.

I checked my M24 rifle. We'd been through plenty together, and it bore as many scars as I did. Tiny scratches marred the black metal from a grenade blast that I'd never expected to survive.

"You look sad," Tyler said. "What's wrong?"

"My poor rifle has seen its share of abuse," I answered.

"We all have," he said softly.

I pointed to a gouge on the barrel that had shown up sometime between the time I was imprisoned at Camp Fox and when I got the rifle back. "This one wouldn't have happened if you hadn't thrown me behind bars."

He raised his brows. "Seriously? You're still beating me up over that?"

"Always," I replied. "After all, no one forced you to arrest me."

"I did it to save you from the Dogs," he said, referring to the Iowa militia. "Besides, you did break the law. No matter how you look at it, killing someone is still breaking the law."

"*Hmph.* You and I both know that scumbag Dog had it coming for what he'd done to that poor girl."

He nodded. "Maybe. But that wasn't for you to decide. You took away his right to a fair trial. I'm not saying he wasn't guilty and didn't deserve what he got. I'm just saying it wasn't the right way to go about it."

I could've brought up the young girl the accused had raped and beaten, but Tyler had heard it all before, and he still refused to budge from his stance on traditional justice. After the outbreak, I'd reverted to an "eye for an eye" brand of justice because mistakes and crimes committed now nearly always caused someone's death. We didn't have the time or resources for a full court system anymore.

"At least it was one fewer Dog to attack Camp Fox," I said instead. "But that's all water under the bridge now," I said, watching a sizable tree limb float down the river.

"I agree. I'm glad things worked out and that you decided to stay with Camp Fox." Tyler shaded his eyes as he looked down the river. "No sign of the riverboat yet."

Tyler had reached this guy Sorenson on the radio a month or so ago by sheer luck. He spent twenty minutes every day scanning all the AM, marine, and aeronautical frequencies. One day, they had both been scanning and reporting across the same marine frequencies at the same time. It was through Tyler's diligence that we'd connected with the folks in Marshall as well as several tiny groups scattered across the area. Sadly, for every settlement he reached, he seemed to lose contact with another.

Of all Tyler's contacts, Sorenson was best equipped to survive the herd migration. He was a riverboat captain and, since zeds couldn't swim, anyone who could navigate the rivers had done pretty well since the outbreak.

Tyler believed Camp Fox had found an ally in Sorenson.

I was doubtful. There was a big difference between talking on the radio and asking Sorenson if he'd take another sixty mouths to feed onto his boat. That's why we'd flown all the way here today — to beg Sorenson to add Camp Fox to his crew. Temporarily, of course.

After turning around and heading back toward the plane and across the painted X on the bridge, my stomach growled. I pulled out a plastic bag filled with jerky. Without freezers, all lean meat was made into jerky. Jerky and nuts comprised our protein staples on scouting runs. I chewed on a piece and held the bag out to Tyler, who grabbed one.

"Any thoughts on a backup plan to our backup plan?" I asked. "Just in case Sorenson doesn't come through."

"Besides running?" Tyler sighed and then shook his head. "No. We really need Sorenson to come through."

"Even if he does let everyone from Camp Fox hop a ride until the herds pass through, it's still a three-hour-plus drive over here, best-case scenario. Longer with the roadblocks we've marked on the maps." With the Cessna, I could only bring a couple people with supplies at a time. I'd never be able to transport everyone before the herds reached our latitude.

If today fell through, my assignment was to fly over potential routes and mark any roadblocks and herds on the maps. Even then, driving a convoy full of people and livestock in any direction was a dangerous plan. We'd surely draw out any zeds in the area.

Griz and Jase met up with us at the plane. "All clear to the east," Griz said, snatching a piece of jerky from my bag.

Jase grabbed the entire bag and dug in.

"Same to the west," Tyler said. "If the engine noise didn't draw any in, we shouldn't have anything beyond the random grazer to worry about today. Sorenson picked a good area. I can see for miles in every direction."

An engine noise in the distance snapped all of our attention to the river. Shading my eyes, I searched for the source of the sound.

"Over there." Jase pointed to the southeast.

I followed his finger and saw a white deck boat coming out from behind an island of trees and toward us.

As the boat approached, I could make out four men. They pulled to a stop where an aluminum extension ladder had been securely chained to the bridge.

A muscled man grabbed a hold of the ladder while a man with weathered skin motioned toward us. "Come on down. We're here to take you to meet Captain Sorenson."

Tyler didn't move. "I was under the impression that Sorenson was coming here to meet me."

The man shook his head. "You're meeting Captain Sorenson on the *Lady Amore* today. We've all seen the herds. He can't risk leaving the boat anymore. Now, we're burning gas. Are you coming or not?"

Tyler shot each of us a look before turning back to the men on the boat. "Yes, we're coming, though I don't appreciate the change in plans."

Griz took the lead down the insanely long ladder, and I followed, noticing that the ladder was actually three extension ladders fastened together with chains. It would be no fun for anyone scared of heights, like me. My muscles were tight, and I gripped too hard with each rung I descended.

One of the men helped me off the ladder at the bottom, and I looked up to see Tyler sliding his sword into its sheath. I stood off to the side, ready to pull out my machete in an instant if anyone tried to injure Tyler. After all, Captain Tyler Masden wasn't just the commanding officer of Camp Fox, he was its face. Clutch was a better strategist and a stronger leader, but he lacked Tyler's finesse in working with people. If something happened to Tyler, morale—which was thread-thin already—would snap.

Tyler climbed down, with Jase right behind him. One man motioned Griz and me to sit up front. As I walked past the boat pilot, I noticed the rifle propped next to him, and I swallowed. We'd have run out of ammunition months ago if I hadn't found Doyle's stash of old military surplus.

Once we all sat down, the driver throttled the boat forward gently, and we pulled away from the bridge and headed toward the small island. With every minute, I felt farther and farther away from Camp Fox.

Over a half hour later, the boat curved around the northern edge of a small island, and riverboat casino came into view. It was still a good ways off, a mile or so at least, and our boat pilot seemed to be in no hurry, burning precious daylight.

As we neared the *Lady Amore*, my eyes widened. The riverboat casino was massive, yet perfectly hidden from anyone—or anything—on land and from air. Our boat rocked gently as it pulled up alongside the riverboat which was filled with people watching us from the deck above. At least six of those people had rifles pointed right at us.

CHAPTER VII

"The password?" a white-haired man—who looked like the fellow on frozen-fish boxes—called out from the deck above.

"Mae West had nice tits," the man who'd spoken to us at the bridge yelled out.

"That password is correct, Otto. You all may come on board." Sorenson motioned to the armed people with him. "Lower your weapons. Everything's clear."

"His own guys have to use a password?" I muttered.

"Every time we have newcomers," the man named Otto replied. "It's a safety precaution in case we're being coerced into bringing bandits on board."

"It's smart," Tyler said as he came to his feet.

A ladder extended down the side of the tall riverboat. We climbed up in the same procession as we had at the bridge. At the top of the ladder, two men lifted me up and onto the deck.

Griz was already chatting with the white-haired man I assumed to be Sorenson. A small terrier sat by his feet. The man said something that brought out Griz's deep chuckle, and then the man narrowed his eyes at me. "You must be the pilot."

I nodded.

"It'd be handy having one of you around, especially nowadays. I'm Captain Sorenson, and welcome to the Lady Amore." He held out his hand, and I accepted it.

"I'm Cash."

Tyler stepped onto deck, quickly followed by Jase. Sorenson smiled. "And I take it you're Captain Masden."

Tyler gave his irresistible Homecoming King smile. "It's great to finally meet you, Captain Sorenson. Under normal circumstances, I would've delayed our meeting until the spring, but some factors arose that forced the issue."

Sorenson nodded. "I've seen the herds with my own eyes, Captain Masden, so I'm not the least bit surprised at your visit." He gestured to his men. "You've already met four of my men. Otto, Hank, Chuck, and Pedro."

Tyler dipped his head at the men who'd just come up the ladder.

"You didn't come all this way to swap nicknames and exchange pleasantries," Sorenson said. "You've got a zed problem headed your way, and you need my help. Let's go somewhere where it's more comfortable to talk." He paused. "I'm a fair man, but I won't allow aggression on the Lady. All weapons must be holstered or sheathed at all times, or else they will be confiscated. Aggressors will be dealt with harshly. I'm assuming you find no issues with that?"

Tyler looked at all three of us first, then back at Sorenson. "I can assure you, no weapons will be drawn as long as there's no reason for them to be."

"Fair enough. I'd never ask for more than that," Sorenson—with his dog as his heels—led us to a side door and entered. We all followed into a well-lit hallway. I glanced back to see Otto and Pedro stepping in behind us, and Otto closing the door. Inside, the hallway was straight with doors every ten feet or so. It reminded me of an old-fashioned hotel, and I realized that was exactly what the Lady Amore was.

The end of the hallway opened into a winding double-staircase that led down to an enormous open area. Twenty or so poker tables dotted the colorful open space. Couches, bean bag chairs, and camp chairs looked out of place in the ornate room that reminded me of a scene from Titanic. The new furniture was likely replacements for the missing slot machines, and the area was now filled with people chatting and eating. At the far end of the casino was the restaurant area where a large buffet was set up against a wall. Twenty or so people stood in line.

Sorenson had a good setup here, a safe little paradise that no zed could get to...though I suspected it was a different story each time they had to go to land to refuel and restock.

He led us down the stairs and through the area, nodding, chatting, and smiling at folks as he walked. Beyond the buffet line, there was another winding stairwell. After climbing a flight of stairs and taking several hallways, we entered a bland corridor with beige walls and no artwork.

"This used to be the staff quarters. My quarters are right on the end up here," Sorenson said. "We're a bit cramped around here, so this is the best place to chat openly."

"I would've taken the biggest room if I was the boss," Jase said softly behind us.

"A family of eight lives in the Presidential Suite," Sorenson replied as he stopped at a door. "They need the space far more than I do. Besides, these quarters have been my home for nigh on thirty years. They're plenty enough for my needs and suit me just fine." He opened the door, and his dog bounded inside. Sorenson walked in and held the door open for the rest of us to enter.

Inside, the area seemed to be as large as any suite, which I supposed was probably common for captain's quarters. The room we stood in was a medium-sized living room area with a large wood conference table in the middle. A couch and TV sat in the far corner opposite a small kitchenette. Next to the refrigerator was an open door to a bedroom.

Sorenson gestured to the table. "Have a seat," he said before he opened the refrigerator and pulled out a bowl.

I took a seat next to Tyler, and Otto sat on my other side.

Sorenson set down the bowl. "Pickled bass. Help yourselves."

His dog yipped, and Sorenson picked out a large piece of fish and tossed it in the air. The dog jumped, caught the chunk, and swallowed it in a single bite.

Tyler reached in and grabbed a small piece of fish. "Bass? Haven't heard of that being pickled before."

"You can pickle just about anything that can be eaten. It keeps food from going bad and doesn't ruin the taste," Sorenson replied. "But we steer clear of the bottom feeders. In fact, I lost one of my people from bad catfish. Too many fish have ingested zed-infected bits to be safely eaten anymore. It makes fishing more challenging."

"I can imagine," Tyler said, after taking a bite. "We no longer hunt wolves since they've started going after zeds. We can't trust that they don't carry the virus."

"Speaking of zeds," Sorenson said. "Looks like a heap of trouble about to pass through."

Tyler gave a tight nod. "We have a theory that they're migrating south for the winter."

Sorenson cocked a brow. "Interesting idea, and what I've seen would support that. But I wouldn't put much weight on that theory. I've yet to see the herds do anything logical."

Tyler shrugged. "I doubt it's a planned event. I think it's nature. As they get cold, they just start heading to where it's not so cold."

Sorenson chuckled. "You're assuming they can feel anything. I've speared a zed right through a kidney and it didn't even wince."

"Call it a sense of preservation, then. Who knows what's driving them, but we've mapped their paths, and all signs point to the herds moving south and picking up numbers along the way."

"Which is exactly why the Lady is going to head further north to find safe ports and food," Sorenson said. "Once they pass through, the pickings should be easy."

What's left of them, anyway, I thought to myself.

"What's your plan when you come face to face with one of the herds?"

"Same plan as we have when we come across a herd of twenty. We're safe as long as we are careful under bridges and keep plenty of water between them and us."

"What will you do if one of these herds comes across the Lady Amore? What then? You think they'll ignore you just because they can't get to you?"

"No, they're persistent bastards. We'll head down river. If they're migrating, then they'll get the urge to keep moving. There are enough islands and turns in the river for us to break visual contact. You know zeds. 'Out of sight, out of mind' and all that."

Tyler looked dubious. "You're assuming the urge to migrate is stronger than their urge to eat. I'm guessing these zeds are hungrier than ever since they're moving."

Sorenson leaned back and cracked his knuckles. "I'd worry more about what you're going to do. You don't have a boat. What's to stop the zeds from walking right through the park? There ain't nobody out there with enough firepower to cut down one of those herds." A sly smile crossed his lips. "Then again, that's why you're here."

After a moment, Tyler nodded. "We need your help. If we can come aboard this riverboat, just until the herds pass through—"

Sorenson lifted a hand. "I'll stop you right now. The Lady Amore is at full capacity already. She can't handle any more people. We can barely purify water fast enough the way it is. As for food...well, that's all dependent on our next restock."

My heart plummeted. I wanted to jump in to talk about how they wouldn't have to feed us, but I didn't dare speak. Tyler was our leader, and we had to show we were one hundred percent behind him. We needed Sorenson to believe that Camp Fox would make good passengers on the Lady Amore, but after seeing the riverboat, I'd already suspected Sorenson wouldn't risk the good thing they had going by doubling his crew with strangers. We were desperate, and it pissed me off, but I couldn't blame him. I had the exact same mindset when survivors passed through the park. Still, knowing that we'd be on our own devastated me.

I looked across the table at Jase and Griz. Both looked the same way I felt. Filled with utter despair.

"It would only be for a week or two. Once the herds pass through, we'd head back to the park," Tyler said. "We'd bring enough food to cover all Fox personnel while on board. With more hands for boiling water —"

"You don't understand. It's not the manpower, it's the facilities," Sorenson interrupted. "We're boiling water twenty-four hours a day as it stands. We'd have to turn on another bank of stoves, which would burn more fuel, and that's our biggest concern. Fuel is our most precious commodity. It's not easy finding safe ports to refuel. Hell, siphoning from crippled boats is nearly as dangerous."

Tyler held up a hand. "I understand. I'm asking you for a favor I might never be able to repay. Believe me, if we had any other option I wouldn't be here. But the only way we'll all survive in this new world is by working together. If I put my people on the road, any direction we head except south, we'll run into more herds. If we run south, we'll just be staying one step ahead of the herds. Eventually, something would happen, and the herds would get us. We need your help, Captain."

"Please," I said softly, pulling my girl-card. But I wasn't acting. I desperately hoped he would help us, and I wasn't above begging.

He came to his feet. "I never said I wouldn't help

you. Unfortunately, the Lady is full. I'm sorry, but I simply can't take on any more souls. Not without risking the lives of the ones on board now."

Tyler came to his feet as well. "Your riverboat is doing okay now, but just wait. What about the trade agreement we'd discussed? Your fish for my livestock. If Camp Fox has to go on the road, we won't be able to tend crops or share our livestock. Hell is coming our way, Sorenson. Don't be so naïve to think that it's going to bypass your boat."

Sorenson headed to the kitchen. He opened a cabinet and pulled out a bottle of whiskey.

The room sat in silence before Tyler finally sighed. "I get it. I know the strain taking on my people would add to an already full boat. I wouldn't ask if I knew of another way."

After taking a drink, Sorenson screwed the cap back on, turned around, and leaned against the counter. A moment later, he looked up at Tyler, then at his two men in the room. "As I told you before, I'll help you, but I can't take any more onto the Lady."

Tyler frowned. "Then what can you do?"

Sorenson paced the room. "Awhile back, I came across a decent-sized towboat that's run aground not too far from here. It'll work better than any building would for keeping zeds out. I'd been planning to use her for overflow survivors we find. I can mark it down on a map for you."

Hope sprang from deep within. There was a chance!

Tyler shook his head. "None of my people have any experience running a towboat, especially one big enough to support sixty-plus souls, our livestock, and food."

"There's no need for that. That towboat isn't going anywhere. It's dead in the water. It ran aground on a small island that goes underwater every spring. A few of her barges have broken off, but there's enough still connected that should hold you through until the island floods come spring. Even then, she should still hold together for a year or two."

I watched as Tyler thought for a long moment.

He finally nodded slowly. "It could work. We should only need it for a couple weeks. Until spring, that is, when the zeds might return."

Sorenson pulled out a stack of papers in the top drawer and headed back to the table. He dropped a paper on the table. A map.

Sorenson opened the map and pointed at an X marked on the water. "Here's the island you're looking for. It isn't far from the mainland, so you'll have a higher risk of zeds floating ashore, especially with how tiny the island is. But it's the best I can offer. We've already had to start turning away survivors. If we bring on any more, we risk the lives of the ones already on board. I can't allow that. These people are my responsibility."

Tyler sat down and examined the map before sliding it to me.

I looked at the small island toward the east side of the river, and not far south of a four-lane bridge. I much preferred the idea of being on the riverboat casino. From what I'd seen of the Lady Amore, they had plenty of space to take on more survivors. Hell, the boat was so large it was like a mountain on the water. The idea of being stranded on an island made me feel like a sitting duck. If any herd spotted us, there'd be no running. "So, zeds can still get to the island?" I asked after sliding the map across the table to Jase and Griz.

"Unfortunately, yes," Sorenson said. "They can't swim, but any that fall in the water could wash ashore easily enough. The towboat also likely had a crew of ten or twenty on her when the outbreak hit. That she ran aground isn't a good sign. She might have been evacuated because I didn't see any zeds on her deck. Even if she's not empty, with enough firepower, it shouldn't take you long to clear her out.

Tyler sighed deeply and leaned back, closing his eyes. I placed my hand over his and he gripped it.

"It could work," I said quietly, as much to support Tyler as to convince myself.

"Oh, it can work all right. Trust me," Sorenson said. "Once you get the towboat cleared out, you'll only have to deal with zeds that get to the island from the water. I'm sure the barges are all clear. I don't see any reason why you couldn't start moving your people and supplies over right away. From what I've seen of the herds, you have about two weeks before they make it this far down the river. You've got a lot of work to do between now and then."

"Except there's a herd already coming straight through the center of the state," Tyler said. "We have to be over here within a couple days or else we risk getting cut off." He paused. "It can work. We'll make it work."

"You'll need to get moving then," Sorenson said.

Tyler nodded and motioned to us. "Agreed. Thank you for your help, Captain. I don't have any marine experience, but I'll take you at your word that this towboat and barges will make for a defensible position and that I'm not condemning sixty souls."

"Aye, she'll be safe as long as you're discreet and don't do anything to draw attention," Sorenson said. "I've kept an eye on her for just this sort of need. I'll make sure there's a pontoon or two for you to get to her by tomorrow. Be sure to bring enough folks to clear out the boat and possibly do some patching. The towboat is named the Aurora II. She's built for a small crew, so she won't hold sixty people. Maybe thirty if you push it. You'll have to use the barges to house the rest of your people and supplies."

"Fair enough." Tyler looked at his watch. "Sunlight is half gone. We'd better head back. We've got a lot of work to do."

"You're more than welcome to stay the night on board the Lady Amore," Sorenson said.

Tyler smiled and held out his hand. "Thank you, but we have to get started on preparations. We've got a lot of work to do."

Sorenson shook Tyler's hand before he headed over to the door and opened it. "Otto will see you back to the bridge. I'll see if a couple of my people will volunteer to help you patch up the barge once you clear it."

Suddenly feeling a hundred pounds lighter, I came to my feet and followed Tyler into the hallway. For the first time since seeing the massive herds, I felt like we stood a fighting chance to make it through the fall.

After Pedro, Otto, Griz, and Jase joined us, Sorenson shut the door, staying in his room. I wondered how much time he spent in his quarters to avoid having to deal with all the problems of having people living in a floating hotel.

Our trip back to the plane was uneventful. The sun had warmed the air, and I enjoyed the afternoon breeze blowing through my cropped hair as the boat cut through the water. When we reached the bridge, we said our good-byes and cautiously climbed the ladder, and Otto and Pedro pulled away.

Fortunately, no zeds had come across the plane or blocked our takeoff path. In fact, the countryside was still wide open. We piled into the Cessna, and I started the engine. It coughed and sputtered and growled. On the third attempt, it kept running but was rough. "Keep your eyes peeled for zeds. This could take a while," I yelled over the engine as I throttled up and checked the mags. The right mag had been running rough but now both sounded like metallic beasts about to explode. I leaned the mixture, trying to clean the spark plugs, to no avail. For several more minutes I tried to smooth the engine, all the while cursing and begging the plane.

After I knew it was hopeless, I pulled the mixture all the way out and the engine quit. I leaned forward, resting my head against the panel for moment, knowing I was about to let everyone down. I hated times like this. My first urge was to cry, but I refused to be the weak one, the one the guys felt sorry for.

"What's the problem?" Tyler asked quietly at my side.

I leaned back and opened my eyes. "You heard the engine. This plane's not going anywhere. With both mags running rough, it's not going to be running for much longer. If the engine goes out while we're in the air, we have to land, and it doesn't matter if there's a town of zeds below us or not."

"Will it help if you let it sit for a while?" Jase asked.

"I don't think so." I scratched my head. "Fuck, I don't know. I'm a pilot, not a mechanic. I have no idea how to fix it. I just know it's not safe to fly it like this."

"Then we won't risk it," Tyler said. "We'll find another way back home."

We climbed out of the plane and stood on the bridge.

"Can I see the map?" I asked Jase.

He dug into his cargo pocket and pulled out the folded sectional.

"Thanks." I knelt and spread it out on the pavement.

Tyler came down on a knee next to me while I could

feel Jase and Griz at my back.

I pointed to a spot on the map. "The closest small airport is here. It's not far, but it's on the edge of town. If we can't get to the airport, we should at least be able to find a car. Jase has been marking the routes on the map."

"Too bad Otto didn't stick around," Griz said, looking out over the river. "A lift could've saved us hours."

"That would make things easier," Tyler said. "But I'm not seeing any boats around here that we can use, so it looks like we'll be hoofing it. There should be a few farms between us and the next town. One of those farms is bound to have a vehicle we can use." He came to his feet. "Take five, and then we head out."

I was already dreading how much my leg would ache tonight. I headed back to the plane. I tried to reach Clutch on the radio but had no luck. Giving up, I rummaged through the baggage compartment. I pulled out a plastic bag and handed it to Griz to add to his rucksack. "There are a few protein bars, a couple bottles of water, and a first aid kit in there."

"It's time," Tyler said. "Let's get a move on. We've got less than four hours of sunlight left to get back to Camp Fox."

CHAPTER VIII

After an hour of jogging, we switched to walking once we realized there was no way in hell we'd make it back to the park before dark. My calf had ached for the first forty minutes until pleasant numbness finally settled in.

The rural road was rough but wide open, with trees to our right, where the river was, and fields to our left. A group of four zeds emerged from the trees and blocked our path. Luckily, only one of them was fresh enough to be halfway fast. Tyler took it down with a heavy swing of his sword. I pulled out my machete, and the rest of us each took down one without firing a shot. The zed I killed had been a man, wearing stained khakis and a golf shirt. My first swing knocked it to the ground. My second swing put it out of its misery.

Sounds came from the trees, but thankfully no more

zeds emerged. Still, we made haste to continue on. The first farmhouse we came to we didn't dare approach. Jase had counted at least three zeds inside, and we had no intention on riling them up. The truck in the driveway sat with the driver's side door open and no keys in the ignition. When Jase tried to hotwire it, nothing happened. The battery was dead.

We fared no better at the second farmhouse. A zed was enclosed in the SUV in the open garage. When it saw us, it pounded on the glass. Jase checked it out, but the SUV had been left running and had long since run out of gas. So, we moved on.

It took us another thirty minutes before we found a vehicle we could use. The white sedan we found sat in the attached garage of a newer looking farmhouse that showed no signs of zeds lurking within its walls. The four of us stood in front of the split-foyer house. Griz and Jase had already run around it, looking through each window. Luckily, the garage door was one of those with windows in it, making it easy to see the car as well as tell-tale signs of notoriously clumsy zeds.

"It looks clean inside," Jase said.

"Should we try the house or the garage first?" I asked.

Tyler stood quietly for a moment, his sword in one hand. "I'd say we waltz right up and try the front door." And he did exactly that. He cut through the lawn and onto the pebbled path leading to the doorsteps. Large bay windows were to the left, making it easy to see if any zeds came from that direction. To the right of the door was a wall, so we were going in half-blind.

Griz, Jase, and I followed. Tyler stood at the front door and knocked. A short pause later, he grabbed the door handle and turned but didn't open the door. He glanced back at us. "It's unlocked."

As I gripped my machete, I noticed both Griz and Jase tense as well. They stood a couple steps behind Tyler and me, in case we needed to jump out of the way. I stood off to the side, careful to avoid making myself a target through the windows. I peeked through the edge of the bay window. *All clear,* I signaled with my hand.

Tyler nodded. He threw the door open and then jumped back.

No zeds came at us. After taking a deep breath, I met Tyler at the door, and we stepped into a large living room. Griz and Jase came in behind us. I sniffed the stale air and picked up the telltale putrid sweetness of decay.

"It's not clear," I said softly.

Tyler motioned for him and me to take the left half of the ground floor, and for Griz and Jase to take the right. A couple minutes later, we met back up in the kitchen.

"All clear," Griz said.

"Same here," I said. "Other than the smell, there aren't any signs of zeds up here."

Tyler frowned as he looked at the basement door. "That means the smell is coming from down there."

We pulled out our headlamps and put them on. One

by one, we headed down the stairs. As soon as I was off the last step, I saw the source of the odor curled up against a door. It was the corpse of a woman dressed in jeans and a sweater, and she still held a picture against her chest. A glass and empty bottle of pills lay next to her. With the rate of decay and her clothing, she'd likely killed herself not long after the outbreak.

Griz emerged from the single bedroom and covered the corpse with a sheet. "May God grant you peace," he said.

A thump against the door behind the body answered.

I jumped.

Tyler and Griz moved first. Griz grabbed the corpse's jeans and pulled the body to the side. Tyler stood at the door and knocked. The thumping became fevered. He gripped his sword in one hand and held the doorknob in the other. "Ready?" he asked Griz, who nodded in return, his machete held out in front of him.

Jase and I stood to each side, each holding our machetes ready. Tyler turned the knob and kicked the door open, sending the zed tumbling back. Stench wafted from the room. A zed, who'd been a teenaged boy, tried to pull itself up by grabbing on a black comforter. It looked to be about Jase's age. Its hair was even the same color, and a lump formed in my throat.

Griz rushed forward and slammed his machete through the zed's skull and it collapsed face-first on the floor, and I refused to look at it again. Tyler entered the room and looked in the closet and under the bed.

"Clear," he called out.

Griz and Tyler hustled from the room, and I slammed the door shut behind them, as much to block the smell as to close us off from the zed that reminded me a bit too much of Jase. I breathed through my mouth, but the stench of putrid death always seemed to burn through my pores.

"All right. The house is clear. We'll camp here for the night," Tyler said. "Let's secure the perimeter. Griz and Jase, you guys check the doors and close all the curtains. Cash and I will check the garage. Once everything is secure, we can scout the house for supplies."

No one lingered in the foul-smelling basement. My leg was beginning to ache, but I forced myself not to limp as we walked through the small kitchen and toward the garage. On the wall near the door, a key rack hung on the wall, and I smiled. I shuffled through the sets of keys and pulled off a key chain that had a Chevy logo on it. I held it up and gave it a happy little shake.

Tyler returned my grin. "Let's hope the battery's not dead."

Undeterred, I followed him. Dead batteries had become a common occurrence, and I'd grown adept at jumping cars, but I'd always had a running car with me. We didn't have that tonight, and I suspected there weren't any new car batteries lying around.

Tyler opened the door slowly and carefully, just in case we'd missed a zed while checking the house earlier. Fortunately, silence and fresh air greeted us. A white four-door car sat in the shadowed garage.

I opened the car door and slid the key into the ignition and turned. The engine started without a hitch, and the gas gauge climbed halfway. I let out a whoop. "Looks like we've got ourselves a ride."

I turned off the car and stepped out. Tyler gave me a high-five. "It's about time we got a break."

He checked the garage door to see that it would open easily, and we headed back in the house. In the kitchen, Griz had several cabinets open and small stacks of canned food sitting on the counter.

Jase emerged from the bathroom with a bottle of rubbing alcohol. "I'll have a camp stove built and going in no time."

"The car runs," Tyler said. "We'll head out at dawn. If the airport isn't viable, we'll drive back to the park."

"Fingers crossed the airport is clear and has something I can fly. It will save us time."

Tyler wrapped an arm around my shoulder and gave me a hug, and I found myself leaning into his warm comfort. "It will," he assured. A moment later, he squeezed before letting go, and then led the way down the hall.

As Jase worked on making dinner, we searched every room for anything that could be of use. Over the next thirty minutes, we loaded the trunk with all the food, pills, and supplies we could find.

After we dragged two mattresses from the upstairs bedrooms into the living room, I plopped into a chair at the table and sighed as I rubbed my calf.

Tyler took the chair next to me, grabbed my leg, and massaged it. "How bad is it hurting?"

I shook my head. "Not bad. It just feels good to sit."

Even though Tyler touched me often, I knew he had no romantic feelings for me. Physical human connections helped ground him, and his touches didn't bother me once I realized that he was just seeking comfort and wasn't flirting. I was surprised that he hadn't taken any women to bed yet. It wasn't for lack of admirers. Tyler had plenty of those.

Tyler rarely touched me when Clutch was around, which was wise. Clutch wasn't in any way the jealous type, but it didn't take much for the two to get on each other's nerves. With their tense relationship, even something as simple as a harmless touch could set them off.

We watched the sun disappear beyond the horizon. With the smell of food cooking overpowering the ever-present scent of decay, the tension in my muscles slowly bled away.

"We'll rotate two-hour single shifts tonight," Tyler announced. "That will give everyone at least six hours of sleep."

"Dibs on first watch," I said.

Griz grumbled. "Just because you're a woman, I'll let you have it. I've got second shift, then." He put down a plate in front of me.

I leaned forward. "Spaghetti?"

"Yeah," he said, taking a seat across from me. "The pantry had a pretty good selection. Jase cooked the noodles in sauce and water, so it might be a bit gummy."

Jase guffawed. "You're lucky to have a hot meal." he handed Tyler a plate and then sat down with his own. "I'll take third watch, I guess."

Griz clasped his hands. "Lord, thanks for this food that we're about to eat. And thanks for another day where we get to eat food and not get eaten."

"Amen," we all murmured.

Silverware clinked against plates as we all dug in. Sitting around a table, eating spaghetti, felt like home. It almost felt like the apocalypse hadn't taken place around us.

Almost.

CHAPTER IX

I could barely keep my eyes open after my watch, but unfamiliar surroundings and dreams of massive herds made sleep fitful, and I woke up every hour or so. I finally passed out sometime during Jase's shift.

"Cash."

I lunged awake, grappling for my machete.

"Whoa there," Tyler said and pressed me back. "There's no emergency. I just thought I'd wake you."

It took a moment for the night's fog to clear from my mind. I rubbed my eyes. "Time to head out?"

"Soon." His features softened. "You were having a nightmare."

"Yeah," I said breathlessly, my heart racing, remembering flying a shiny airplane with gold stripes. I sat up and wrapped my arms around my knees.

He kept a hand on my shoulder. "Want to talk about

it?"

I thought back to the dream. Clutch, Jase, and I were flying somewhere. The engine stalled over endless fields filled with zeds. Tyler had woken me just before we crashed. "Just the usual stuff," I said after a bit.

He rubbed my shoulder and gave me a gentle look. "It was just a dream. We're all haunted by them. Don't let it get to you." He cupped my cheek before coming to his feet. He strolled over to Griz who was sprawled out on the mattress we'd dragged into the living room and nudged him with his foot.

Griz grumbled, and Tyler nudged him again.

I made out the words "go away" this time.

"Wake up," Tyler said. "There's some oatmeal on the table. We're heading out in ten."

I rolled off the king-sized mattress we'd taken turns sleeping on, stood, and stretched with a groan. With its cracks and pops, my body sounded—and felt—like it belonged to a fifty-year-old rather than one who wasn't even thirty yet. "I could've used another hour of sleep."

"I could've used another five hours," Griz said as he geared up.

I pulled all my things together, and we ate standing up at the table. A few minutes later, Jase lifted the garage door, and the four of us climbed into the car. Tyler backed the Chevy out of the garage and into the quiet darkness of early morning. We drove down the long winding road parallel to the river until the sun was halfway above the horizon.

Tyler turned at an intersection that had a green airport sign pointing to the left. "If you see anything that seems off, we'll abort and drive the two hundred miles. We'll find a fuel stop on the way."

"Let's not," Griz said, with his eyes still closed. "We need to get back to the park today if we're going to make a mass exodus to a shipwrecked boat before the herds arrive. We're on borrowed time already."

"We can't help our people if we're dead," Tyler replied a bit too quickly. He inhaled before continuing. "But, yes, I also agree with you. We don't have time for delays."

"There's the airport." Jase pointed. "Looks okay from here. No cars around. That's a good sign."

Tyler slowed as we approached the small municipal airport. Up ahead, the road became a roundabout, with turns in three directions. To the right were two large corporate hangars. To the left stood a row of T-hangars, each one large enough for a single airplane. Straight ahead was a single building surrounded by a wide tarmac that was unfortunately empty of aircraft. The pickings would not be so easy here.

Tyler stopped at the roundabout. "Which way do we go, Cash?"

I sighed. "Straight ahead. We need to hit the terminal building first. Lucky for us, it's a small enough airport that there probably weren't many people around when the outbreak hit, so there wouldn't be much reason for zeds to stick around here."

"Except for the ones still stuck in buildings," Jase tacked on.

I nodded. "I wouldn't be surprised if we find at least one in the FBO building."

"FBO?" Jase asked.

"Fixed Base Operator. Whoever ran the airport."

"Can we skip the FBO and go straight for the hangars?" Tyler asked.

"The keys to get into the hangars will be in there." I pointed at the building standing ominously alone just beyond the open airport gate. "We have to check it out."

"You sure?" Griz asked.

I shrugged. "I've never seen hangars left unlocked before."

"All right. We'll take it slow." Tyler stepped on the gas ever so slightly. The car crept through the open gate and he parked about forty feet from the FBO. It was an escape trick we all knew well. Zeds kept getting slower as they rotted away. If we had to leave in a hurry, putting a little distance between us and them made it easier.

I climbed out and breathed in the fresh morning air. No one moved far from the car. We took our time to scan for zeds. Jase was the first to head toward the building after taking several steps in a wide three-sixty. I followed him across the tarmac, crossing the white T-line marked for airplane parking and stepping over cracks in the old pavement. He stopped at the red door and looked through the glass pane.

"How's it look?" I whispered as Griz and Tyler joined us.

"Not sure yet. Give me a minute," Jase replied, taking a step back. "I'm going to check the other windows."

With that, he took off at a run around the building. Jase was Camp Fox's fastest runner. He was his high school football team's first-string tight end and a state track hurdler for a reason. Nothing could catch him.

I looked through the window and saw some papers scattered on the floor by the front desk. No blood or stains marred the walls or floor.

I heard a rustle and turned to find Jase returning from the opposite direction he'd left. He slowed down and then stopped. "I couldn't see any zeds through the other windows."

"We're burning daylight," Tyler said.

I grabbed the door handle. "You guys ready?"

"You open, I'll go in first," Tyler said from right behind me.

I twisted the handle and pulled. Fortunately, the door was unlocked, and Tyler went in, holding his sword before him. Griz went in next, followed by Jase. I stepped inside and closed the door with only the quietest *click* to signal someone had entered.

The air didn't stink of death, which was a good sign. Still, we moved through the building to make sure no zeds or bandits were lurking in shadows.

"This wouldn't be a bad place for a small group to hole up," I said after we cleared the building. "I mean, there's the fence on the side facing the road, which would deter looters, and on the other side gives a full view of the airport to see zeds coming from a mile away."

Glass shattered, and I jumped around to see Griz rummaging through a vending machine broken wide open.

"Not a bad place as long as you always had scouts on guard," Tyler said before joining Griz at the machine.

I walked around the front desk where papers had been scattered. Behind the desk, a small window was opened a few inches. "The wind must've blown the papers." On top of the desk was a clipboard with flight schedules. N-numbers and airplane makes and models were listed on each row, and I smiled. These were planes I could fly. Hanging below the counter of the desk hung several sets of keys. I set down my machete and leaned on the desk to rifle through the keys.

One keychain held a couple dozen nickel keys. It had a plastic fob with "hangars" written in black marker. The other key chains each held only a couple bronze keys, with Cessna or Beechcraft logos on the fobs. "We got lucky," I said. "All the keys are here. We have our pick."

I started plucking key chains off their hooks until a movement caught the corner of my eye. I looked down at the desk in time to see a rat—not a mouse but a huge fucking rat—run across my hand. "Ack!" I tumbled back, launching myself into the file cabinet. My head connected with the corner. Sharp pain blinded me, and I took a nosedive to the ground. Once the starred blackness in my vision began to recede, I let out the longest string of profanity I'd ever accomplished in my life.

Someone grabbed my arm. "You okay, Cash?"

I blinked until the two kneeling Jases became one. Warm liquid tickled my cheek. I touched it and then saw the blood on my finger. "Yeah. Damn rat. Surprised me, that's all."

Tyler stood behind Jase, frowning. "That's one hell of a cut." He turned away. "Griz, see if you can't find us a kit."

Tyler grabbed a box of tissue sitting on the desk and yanked out several. He handed them to Jase, who dabbed at my forehead and winced. "Dang, Cash. It was just a rat."

A moment later, Griz brought over a first aid kit from somewhere. Jase made room for him, and Griz came down on a knee. He grabbed the tissue from Jase and dabbed at my forehead and cheek. As the seconds passed, the numbness became a throbbing ache. Griz tore open a towlette and just before touching me, he paused. "This is going to sting."

"Just do it," I muttered, and he wiped my cut. I hissed and clenched my eyes shut. Burning needles shot through my skin everywhere he touched. Jase grabbed my hand, and I held on tightly. "Jesus. It feels like half my face is on fire."

"I can imagine," Griz said and he continued his torture.

I opened my eyes after a couple seconds of no new pain and found Griz sifting through small items in the first aid kit. He pulled out a suture kit and my eyes widened and my jaw dropped.

"I don't need stitches."

Griz chortled.

"Yeah, you do," Jase said at my side.

"Trust us," Tyler added. "Griz will do a good job. He's done this plenty of times."

I swallowed and positioned myself against the cabinet. "All right, but if that rat shows up again, you sure as hell better squash it."

The antiseptic wipe was nothing compared to getting stitches. The next ten minutes were raw agony. I begged for whiskey and morphine, but all Tyler gave me was a couple aspirin and a warm Coke. My hands were sweaty but I never let go of Jase.

Griz leaned back with a look of admiration. "That might be my finest work yet."

I chugged down more of the Coke before Jase helped me climb to my feet.

"Be careful to keep the wound clean. That cut could get infected easily enough," Tyler said, coming back over. He distributed the remaining candy bars from the vending machine, which we all dug into like kids opening Christmas presents. "Take as long as you need. If you're not up to flying, we'll drive."

I shook my head, and I instantly regretted the movement. My face throbbed, but I said in between chews, "It's just a cut. I'll be fine. We've already wasted enough time on me."

"All right. Let's head out, then," Tyler said.

I grabbed my machete off the desk and noticed a small mirror propped next to the PC. I looked at my reflection and nearly dropped the mirror. No wonder getting stitched up hurt like a bitch. A jagged enflamed line cut across my forehead and down my cheek, which looked almost like the number seven. I touched the skin around it. "Wow, that's *really* going to leave a mark."

No one said anything. I don't know if they were afraid I was going to cry or what, but the urge didn't even cross my mind. Times had changed. Before the outbreak, even though I'd always been a tomboy, I would have dreaded a big scar across my face. Now, the creek by our cabin was the closest thing to a mirror I had. Chances were this cut would leave a hell of a scar once it healed. Yet I'd probably not even notice it as long as it didn't hurt.

I swiped all the keys, all the while keeping a careful watch for the mutant-sized rat. We headed out of the building and back to the car. "Let's go for that row of hangars closest to the FBO first," I said, pointing. "The doors will be easier to open, and that's where the smaller planes will be."

"You need to learn how to fly a bigger plane," Griz said as Tyler drove us toward the row of hangars. "I hate small planes."

"How would you know?" Jase asked. "You sleep through every trip."

"Sleep is underrated," Griz said. "And I still think Cash needs to find a bigger plane."

"No, I don't," I said. "Bigger planes are more complicated to maintain. They require a longer runway. Besides, since I have no experience in them, the risks of me making a mistake go up exponentially. None of those constraints fits our current lifestyle," I said.

Griz cocked his head. "Good point. Small planes are good."

Tyler parked the car, and we went about checking the hangars, first for zeds, then for a plane that met our needs. When I unlocked the fourth hangar, I smiled. "This is the one."

While Jase walked around the hangar, I checked the plane over. Griz and Tyler pushed the large metal door open. Metal creaked against metal, making a horrendous screech. "Make it quick," Tyler said after dusting his hands off on his pants. "It looks like we've attracted the attention of a couple zeds in the field off the runway."

Unveiled by sunlight, a nearly new Cessna 172 sat in the hangar, the N-number on its tail matching a number on one of the key chains I carried. I stepped on the spar and looked at the sticker by one of the fuel tanks. "Hey, this one takes auto fuel! Let's get this outside." I grabbed the prop. Tyler and Jase each grabbed a strut.

We pulled the plane straight outside. I unlocked the baggage compartment and Griz dumped an armful of food and supplies from the trunk of the car.

"I'm going to get this ready while you guys finish loading up whatever fits."

All three went to work at unloading the car into the plane. It didn't take long. The baggage compartment in the 172 was small, and with four of us, we were grossly overloaded. I started the engine, and it ran smoothly. "Thank God," I murmured as I ran through the checklist.

The guys climbed inside, and Tyler took the front seat next to me. "Better hurry because we're going to have a party in another couple minutes."

I taxied out without checking all the instruments. "Oh shit." My heart beat faster, and my eyes widened. "Zeds are on the runway already."

A few shapes peppered the middle of the runaway, but many more were headed straight for the pavement from the trees.

"There are too many for us," Tyler said, his brows furrowed. "Can you take off or do we need to drive?"

I looked at the airport for a long second, knowing this was one of those life-or-death decisions. "I'll take off on the taxiway." I did a quick pre-takeoff check and then throttled full forward on the taxiway. It was narrow, less than half the width of the runway, but I'd gotten used to landing on highways. At the halfway mark, the 172 was still grounded. At the two-thirds mark, I could almost get her wheels up.

"Uh, Cash?" Tyler asked, gripping the dash.

My heart raced, and my head pounded. Visions of last night's dream flashed through my mind. Maybe the plane was too overloaded. *Come on, come on.* After the three-quarter mark, I was able to force the wheels off the ground in time to miss the lights at the end of the taxiway as the plane struggled to climb. If there'd been trees, we would've flown straight into them. Slowly, the plane climbed out above the field and into the sky.

"Well, that was exciting," Jase called out from the backseat since we had no headsets.

Once we reached a safe altitude, I let my muscles relax and I leaned back in the seat. I handed Tyler the map. I didn't look back at the airport. I already knew a couple dozen zeds hungrily waited down there if we'd had a botched takeoff.

"Looks like you'll want a heading of one-nine-five, give or take," Tyler said, holding the map open.

I nodded and set us on course. I glanced back to find Jase looking out the window, jotting notes down for any roadblocks or zeds. Griz was already sound asleep, his head leaning against the window and his mouth open.

During the flight, Tyler, Jase, and I talked about how in the world we'd safely relocate Camp Fox across two hundred miles of zed-infested country. We'd need a crew to prep the shipwreck before the rest of Camp Fox arrived. All this before the herds passed through within a couple days. For the plan to work, everything had to go absolutely perfectly. Nothing could go wrong.

I didn't think we'd have a chance in hell to make it work until after I landed and taxied over to where I used to park the old 172. Standing there, with no wheelchair in sight, was Clutch.

Hope blossomed. We just might have a chance after all.

PRIDE

THE FIRST DEADLY SIN

CHAPTER X

Thirty-one hours later

Wes and I pulled to a stop behind the first Humvee at the bridge crossing over the Mississippi. Even with having all the roadblocks mapped and only two small herds to detour around, it had taken over eight hours to make the journey. I would've preferred to have flown over, but our scouting party and supplies would have required a plane three times the size of the 172. So, we'd loaded up two Humvees and driven the route mapped for convoy to make sure it would work.

Tyler, Griz, Jase, and Nate climbed out of the Humvee in front of us while Tack stayed on the back of their Humvee to man the .30 cal machine gun. He scanned the area while Tyler and Griz talked between themselves by the river.

When Wes reached for the door, I stopped him. "We're not supposed to leave the truck unless Tyler gives us the all-clear."

Tyler's Humvee was the lead vehicle, while ours was jam-packed with tools, food, and weapons. It was our job to secure the boat, and we wanted to make sure we had all the gear we needed to get the job done.

Tyler had to lead this mission since he needed to be here to meet with Sorenson's people. Clutch had wanted to lead this mission, but his legs weren't strong enough to handle the stairs on the boat. He could stand now — thanks to the swelling finally going down enough and with the help of crutches. I loved seeing signs of the old Clutch return in his face. The glint had come back to his eyes, and his expressions were more alert now. It was like he'd been half asleep and was coming back to wakefulness. Walking was still beyond his reach, but it wouldn't be much longer with how hard he was working at it. He had a renewed energy in everything now.

I think even Tyler wished we had Clutch's experience on this trip. Clutch had been in plenty of situations in the Army before the outbreak, while Tyler, Griz, Nate, and Tack were much younger. Aside from Griz, who had also been in the Army, none of the other soldiers at Camp Fox had seen action before the outbreak.

Even from a wheelchair, Clutch was Camp Fox's strongest leader. Tyler was trusted and loved, but Clutch was obeyed. No one argued with him, which made it all the more important he stayed behind to lead the convoy. If anyone could relocate sixty people and all our livestock across a zed-infested state smoothly, it was Clutch.

He wasn't thrilled that Tyler had asked Jase and me to come on the mission. Tyler had said he needed Jase's limber speed for scouting the barges, and my small size for squeezing through tight spaces, but I knew it was really Tyler's way of showing Clutch who was in charge...and to piss him off even more.

That Clutch had freaked out when we'd arrived home a day late with my face cut up was an understatement. He was downright livid at Tyler, even though it wasn't Tyler's fault. He'd blamed Tyler since he was in charge when my clumsy accident happened. Clutch had jumped from his wheelchair faster than anyone expected and tackled Tyler. Jase, Griz, and Tack had to tear them apart to prevent a fight.

Yeah, this mission had come at the right time. The pair needed space, and a couple hundred miles was just about perfect. Except that Clutch wanted Jase and me with him and not with Tyler right now. But even he knew that the safety of Camp Fox came first, and if Tyler said he needed us, then we had to trust his judgment. If something happened to either of us on this trip, I would dread being in Tyler's shoes.

This morning, even though he was still pissed about having to be separated again so soon, Clutch had acknowledged that he trusted Tack and Griz second only to himself when it came to looking out for Jase and me. It was the first time he openly admitted that someone besides the three of us had earned his faith.

Wes nudged me. "Tyler's heading this way."

I turned to see Tyler, Griz, Nate, and Jase walking toward our Humvee. I rolled down my window. The breeze hurt my stitches, and I tried not to wince. As Tyler approached, Tack came jogging over.

"I see only one pontoon tied to the ramp right now," Tyler said. "It's enough for us, but we'll need to round up more transports to handle all the back-and-forths to the *Aurora* when the convoy arrives. I wish the towboat and barges were better camouflaged, but the towboat was clearly shipwrecked. No one should suspect anyone's there if we're careful, and since no zeds can walk there, it should be a great spot to hide out."

"We'll make it work," Jase said.

I looked out over the Mississippi at the small cropping of trees and a white towboat and eight long rectangular steel barges over twice the tiny island's size still attached to the boat, with two more barges that looked like they would break off at any moment. Four of the barges were plowed up on its bank, nearly out of the water. A couple more barges floated at an odd angle in the river, as though they were about to break away from the rest. "That's a lot of boat."

Griz frowned. "Yeah, we could really use more troops to clean it out. You think we should still go for it, Maz?" Griz watched Tyler for a moment, then Tack and

Nate. He didn't look at Jase, Wes, or me. Something about the military guys. They always looked to each other for decisions, never to civvies. It didn't matter that I'd seen every bit as much action as most of those guys had. On the flip side, I could see where they were coming from. None of them meant any harm; they truly thought they were doing the right thing by protecting us.

Still, it pissed me off, but I was done grumbling about it because it did no good. They saw Jase as a kid — I was glad they saw it, too — and they saw me as a woman. Since men outnumbered women over four to one at the park, every woman was treated like delicate china. I was lucky that I had both Clutch and Jase on my side, or else I would've been relegated to only fly scouting runs a long time ago.

"Well, Sorenson seemed to think the barges *should* be clear since there was no reason for anyone to be on those. We should only have to clear out the towboat. We've got Camp Fox counting on us," Tyler said, then shrugged. "I don't see an option. We go in."

I squinted at the boat a couple thousand meters away. "Sorensen seemed to think there wouldn't be much of a crew on that small of boat. It should be an easy in-and-out."

"Except it's going to be dark in just a couple hours," Jase said.

"We'll park over there. On the slope under the bridge on the east bank looks like a good spot," Tyler said, pointing to an outcropping not far from the pontoon.

"That's got to be a thirty-degree incline," I said.

Griz chuckled. "It won't be a problem. Humvees can handle over forty degrees."

"Let's get them down there," Tyler said. "Time's a wasting."

The guys spent the next half hour hiding the Humvees and loading all the ammo, food and tools they could onto the pontoon. It sat low in the water, and there was still more in the Humvees. While they all worked as quickly as they could, I stood behind the .30 cal and scanned for danger, even though the area was rural and no zeds showed up. The only benefit of having less upper body strength was that I always got the easier job of keeping them covered while they hauled supplies. They could carry more and faster than I could.

Tyler wiped his hands on his cargos. "That's all that we can get on this trip." He waved to me, and I jumped down and met up with the men by the pontoon.

"I'll get the ropes," Jase said as he started to untie the yellow ropes that held the boat to the ramp.

Tyler looked back at the motor and climbed into the captain's seat. "It's been awhile since I've driven one of these things."

Having no experience with boats, I grabbed a seat across from Wes and near Griz, who held his rifle ready at the helm. Tack did the same at the back of the boat.

Tyler started the engine and looked up. "Okay, Jase."

Jase loosened the first rope and then the second. He jumped on board and climbed on top a crate full of tools.

Tyler revved the engine, and the pontoon slowly pulled away from the ramp. The boat swayed in the rough water. As we moved into deeper water, waves lapped at the sides, and I was forced to hold on so I wouldn't get knocked around.

"It's bumpy out here today," Wes said, stating the obvious.

I sat there and focused on the distance closing between us and the white towboat with *Aurora II* painted on the side. I wondered how many zeds were in the river, either buried in the murky bottom or floating just under the surface.

"Does anyone see a good place to tie up?" Tyler asked as he brought the boat around the backside of the *Aurora* so that no one could see our pontoon from the bridge, making us safer from bandits.

Jase stood on the crate, which was an impressive feat in the rough water. He pointed to the hull. "I might be able to get a hold right up here."

"It won't take long to get a basic dock built," Wes said. He'd been a handyman before the outbreak, so Tyler had considered him critical to have on this mission. The rest of us were Wes's manual labor. At least the guys were. My job was to squeeze into small spaces, to do tasks like looking for broken cables, if needed. I didn't enjoy my job, but someone had to do it, and I was the smallest of all the scouts.

Tyler throttled all the way back just before we bumped up alongside the hull of the *Aurora*. The deck of the towboat was nearly ten feet high in the water. Sorenson was right. As long as we were careful, it'd be a good place to hide during the zed migration.

We were all pitched forward as the front of the pontoon slid up against the sand. I looked over the side and saw something bloated with scraps of clothes floating just below the surface. "Possible eater here," I said. I poked at it with my machete. A chewed up hand rose to the surface, but the zed's most dangerous feature—its mouth—remained underwater. I swapped my machete for my knife and slammed the blade through the zed's skull. I rinsed the blade in the water and reclaimed my seat. "Nothing to worry about."

We all scrambled to grab ahold of the towboat's hull to steady the pontoon. Jase hopped up and lassoed the towboat's railing. Tack, Nate, and Griz climbed off the pontoon and onto the beach. While Tack helped Jase secure the pontoon to a fallen tree, I jumped off and watched the woods. Wes joined me a few seconds later while Tyler stayed on board at the wheel.

"This island looks pretty empty," Wes said. "There's nothing here but trees and a shipwreck."

Of course, at that moment I saw movement in the trees. "Way to jinx us." I slung my rifle over my shoulder and pulled out my machete. I walked toward the tree, careful to make sure nothing else waited in the shadows. The zed that emerged was ugly — horrendously ugly — bloated with river water and weathered. Its balding head was the only thing that hinted at its gender when it'd been infected. It came toward me, arms outreached, as though it wanted to embrace me. It moved slowly and stiffly. I swung and took the top of its head off. It collapsed, and I immediately looked for more.

When no more zeds emerged, I headed back to the small beach to put space between the trees and me. By then, Jase had the pontoon securely tied to the towboat, and Tyler was checking his rifle. A pile of grain had poured out of one of the barges that had crashed onto the island. "I wonder if all the barges are full of grain," I thought aloud.

Tyler glanced up, and his brow lifted. "We can only hope."

"Yeah, hope that it's not rotten already. My uncle had a farm, and I helped him clean out a bin once. Man, rotten corn is nasty," Griz said as he walked around the towboat, with Tack at his side. He was searching the *Aurora*, though I wasn't sure what he was looking for. Nate stood, watching the water.

Tyler looked around. "I know it sucks, but we're down to an hour of sunlight left. Once we're aboard, we'll need to secure the towboat for tonight. In the morning, we'll clear out the barges so we can unload the supplies and get set up for Fox's arrival."

We'd left before sunrise this morning, while it was

still dark, because we knew well the roads in the Fox River valley. We needed all the sunlight we could get for the long, slow drive over here. We'd known it would take several hours, but none of us had figured it would burn through nearly all of our sunlight hours coming here.

Griz went back to the pontoon and rummaged through a crate. He pulled out an armful of nylon cables and rappelling hardware. Tack helped while we watched him throw a hook over the first railing. He tugged on it and then turned to us. "See you on top." He climbed the short distance in under five seconds flat.

"I'll go next," Jase said, rubbing his hands together.

"Be careful," Tyler said. "No unnecessary injuries."

"I got it." He slung his rifle over his shoulder and grabbed the rope and made his way up to the deck.

I swallowed and glanced at Wes who looked like he was thinking the same thing. "Friggin' spider man," I muttered.

Tyler motioned to us. "Who's next?"

"I guess I'll go," I said, and I heard Wes let out a sigh. I dragged my feet over to the rope and snapped my sheath shut. I grabbed the rope.

Tyler pressed a warm hand against my back. "Use your legs and walk up. You'll find your rhythm soon enough."

If I hadn't had over twenty pounds of gear on me, it would've been easier. I definitely never found the "rhythm" Tyler had spoken of. Even though I was diligent with my workouts, I never had much upper body strength. Every vertical foot was a clumsy struggle, especially as I approached the railing and there was less slack in the rope. Two pair of hands reached down. I grabbed ahold of Jase and then Griz, and let them pull me the rest of the way. Below me, Wes was just getting started, and he was faring only slightly better than I had.

"Geez, Cash. I thought you were going to take a nap on the way up," Jase joked.

I flipped him the bird.

Griz helped me to my feet. "Don't listen to the kid. You did good, girl. It takes a while to get the hang of rope climbing."

I knew he was just being nice, but it still made me feel better. I unsheathed my machete. "Help the others. I'll stand watch."

A couple minutes later, we all stood on the deck of the *Aurora II*. It had three windowed levels above the deck, the second level half the size of the first, and a small high-sitting bridge on top. Anyone could see there were no zeds on the deck.

"The bridge will give us a three-sixty view of the area. It should be the most secure place to hole up for the night," Tyler said as he set down a huge duffle bag with a thud.

"The crew quarters should at least be comfortable when it gets colder," Griz said.

"Where's that?" Tyler asked.

Griz pointed. "I'm guessing either the first level or below decks. I've been on bigger boats. Towboats are new to me."

"This boat wasn't empty when the outbreak hit," I pointed to the round, first-level window as a shadow lumbered by.

"We'll start on the top and work our way down," Tyler said. "I'm thinking we'll set up common housing in the barges. They'll be drafty, but open enough to have fires running for heat should we have to stay into the winter. Our first imperative is to get this boat cleared so we can get some power turned on."

"Then, let's do it," Griz said.

"Yeah, I'm getting hungry," Nate added.

"What are you making us tonight?" I asked.

Nate scowled. "MREs are all we have for tonight. The real food is still boxed up."

"C'mon, then," Griz said. The seven of us walked across the deck and climbed the first stairs.

"This room looks to be a good area for Doc's clinic hospital," Tyler said as he peered inside.

"It was probably the captain's quarters," Griz said.

The sun was beginning its descent, casting a softer glow on the wide river. Except for the road and bridge to the north, all I could see was water and trees for miles. "The view is really beautiful from here," I said, climbing the second stairs.

"Yeah, a regular vacation getaway," Jase said drily.

I grinned at his sarcasm but my smile faded as I kept

focus on the task at hand. We slowed as we approached the bridge. It was a good sign that I saw no zeds in the windows. Since zeds rarely sat down, it meant that if there were any in there, they were either under three feet tall or in bad shape.

Tyler was the first to walk up to the window. He stood for a moment, and then turned to face us. "We don't want to stay in the bridge tonight."

"Why not?" Wes asked, and we all moved closer to look through the window.

Inside, three bodies lay sprawled on the floor, each one with a gunshot wound in the skull. A single revolver lay in the hand of one. They'd been dead for some time, with how their discolored skin clung to their emaciated forms.

Zeds were easier to deal with than corpses. I could convince myself that their humanity was gone, but corpses...they reminded me of what I was doomed to become someday.

"All right. Let's check the next level," Tyler said.

At the bottom of the stairs, we all went up to the glass to peer inside.

"Looks fine to me," Wes said, his nose pressed against the glass. "I wonder if the captain is one of the fellows we came across in the bridge."

Inside, the table and couch seemed undisturbed with no signs of violence and no place for zeds to hide.

"Good. At least one room that shouldn't stink like a shit storm," Griz said.

I glanced at the stairwell. "Ready for the galley?"

"We don't have much time until we lose our sunlight," Tyler said. "Let's go. Tack, you take point. Griz and I will cover. Everyone else, stand back until we clear this level."

Tack was Tyler's go-to guy for taking point, so he was used to it. He moved smoothly and rarely talked, but more important, he never freaked out. The slender man walked up to the door, held up his hand, and then motioned forward. Griz opened the door and Tack swung. A zed that had been on the other side of the door went down. Tack headed inside, followed closely by Tyler. Jase held the door when Griz followed.

I watched through the window as Tack and Tyler finished off the lone zed in the room.

"All clear," Griz called out, and we entered the large room. "Ready to check below decks."

"It'd be nice if there were only four in the crew," I said.

Tack was already at another door. Tyler and Griz joined up with him. He opened the door, and after a quick second, he touched his nose. A signal we'd come up with at Camp Fox for scouting runs.

The smell that caused Tack to signal us wafted through the air from below decks. The all-too-familiar rotten stench of zeds.

Damn it.

There were more than four in the crew.

CHAPTER XI

Tack held up four fingers. He turned to face us. "They're all at the bottom of the stairs."

Four zeds. Relief blanketed my nerves. Four more zeds we could handle.

Tyler looked across our faces. "Griz, since they can't get up the stairs, you want to clear out these one at a time?"

Griz nodded. "No problem, Maz."

"Okay then. Splitting up will save us time. Wes, you stay up above deck and start figuring out what needs done to get this boat ready for Camp Fox," Tyler said. "Tack and Nate are with me. Jase and Cash, you're with Griz. Griz, your team will clear this room. Move slow. It's going to be dark down there, so we have to be extra careful. We have sixty-plus souls counting on us, so there's no room for mistake. Tack, Nate, and I will start at the back and work our way toward you from below decks. Come to the deck if you hit 1900 and we haven't come across each other yet. Everyone clear?"

We all voiced agreement. Tyler, Tack, and Nate headed toward the back of the towboat.

I paused as I walked toward the door. Lying on the table was an open journal. On its cream pages was a beautiful drawing of a cloudy sky. I turned the page to find an ink sketch of a landscape. I flipped through pages of stunning art, and seeing it panged my heart. The outbreak had taken so much talent. It had murdered gifted people and criminals equally, children and the old. All that was left behind was remnants. I didn't have any special gifts. Before the outbreak, I was just one out of billions. Now, I was *necessary*.

The loss of a single life could bring us one step closer to the brink of extinction.

Ha. Who was I kidding?

We were already there.

I snapped the journal shut and looked up to find Jase watching me. His gaze questioned me, and I noticed that both he and Griz had their headlamps on; I clicked on mine. "I'm ready," I said quickly. The band rubbed uncomfortably against my stitches, but it was better than going in blind. Griz stopped outside the door, and I refocused on the mission.

As we stood behind Griz, I thought on Tyler's words. He didn't tell us anything we didn't already know. We all knew that this boat was Camp Fox's best hope.

That's why I'd come along, even knowing it was a political play on Tyler's part. I sure as shit wasn't here because I enjoyed walking into the dank interior of a towboat with who-knew-how-many hungry zeds waiting around every corner and in every shadowy nook.

Griz glanced back at us. "We stick with the usual plan. I'll be on point. Jase, you're at my six. Cash, you'll be sweeper in case we need to break out the artillery."

"Yeah, got it," Jase said.

I nodded. "Just give me a minute to set up before you make contact."

Griz opened the door, his homemade machete ready. The stench wafted out. He stepped onto the top of the metal steps that led into the dark bowels of the towboat. Jase followed, and I brought up the rear. It didn't matter if it was Griz or Tyler. They both always put me in back. They kept Jase in back, too, if any of the other soldiers were involved. I figured it was because we didn't have military training, and they had some kind of idea that the military was the first line, that they were there to protect us civilians. I didn't waste the breath explaining that Clutch had been training Jase and me since the outbreak.

Griz paused at the top step, and I could hear a rustling below. Jase gave him plenty of space to retreat, but he didn't move back. Then, he descended a couple steps and waited. I stepped onto the first step in the darkness and looked down. My headlamp shone on the four zeds waiting at the bottom of the stairs, clawing out at us. Unable to climb the steps, they were almost comedic. Almost.

I lined up the sights on my M24. "Ready," I said.

Jase moved around me, and the two men descended down the steps. Griz swung first, taking down the closest zed. Jase stayed behind. The second zed tripped over the first zed and tumbled toward Griz. Jase swung, and then kicked the lifeless thing away. Griz brought his sharp blade onto the head of the other zed.

He held up a hand. "Stay here." He jumped over the bodies and paced around what looked to be the crew quarters. After he checked every shadowed corner and around every bed, he called up, "Clear."

I lifted my rifle and moved down the metal steps. With only our headlamps for light, shadows danced around the lockers and beds. We gathered around the next steel door.

"We can wait here, or do you guys want to keep going?" Griz asked.

"Keep going," Jase said quickly.

"I want to get this boat cleared," I added.

Griz smiled and then opened the door. A zed lunged at him. "Agh!"

Jase lunged forward and slashed the badly decayed zed across its face. Griz shoved the body off him and rolled to his feet, slamming his machete into the zed's head.

Moans erupted from the darkness. Jase jumped back

and Griz slammed the door shut.

Ah, hell. We weren't even close to being done yet.

CHAPTER XII

Once we had a chance to regroup, Jase opened the steel door, and Griz tossed a snap light into the room several steps below. A green glow lit up the open space. Several dark shapes clumsily and erratically ran into one another to pounce at the light.

Jase whistled. "There's got to be a dozen of them down there."

Griz let out a sigh. "It's too dangerous to take them out hand-to-hand. We could wait for Maz's team, but either way, sweeping the area is our safest option." He turned to me. Shadows danced across his face. "Cash, you're on. Jase, stand by the door. I'll yank Cash back if they get too close, and you shut the door."

"Yes, sir," Jase said, and he squeezed past me to the door.

I couldn't tell if he was being sarcastic or obedient,

but I also didn't care. I had a job to do. Griz would never put me face to face with a zed where I could get hurt, but he had no problem with me taking them down from a distance. I didn't mind as long as I didn't feel useless. I was actually looking forward to some target practice. I still remember the first zed I killed. Hell, I remembered all of them, but when I killed them, I'd learned to compartmentalize. What I killed wasn't human or even *feeling*. It was a target, nothing else.

I ran a thumb over my M24. It showed some wear, but it shot true. After checking the stability of the handrail, I leaned onto the metal bar and aimed. "Don't worry. This won't take too long."

The zeds had begun to disperse from the snap light, having discovered that it brought no flesh that they craved. As soon as the first one sniffed us out, they all headed toward us. Still, I fired only when I was sure I had a kill shot.

My personal motto, *get 'em where I want 'em*, repeated over and over in my mind.

One. A zed fell. The shot resounded off the metal walls.

Two. Another fell. *Three. Four.* My ears rang.

I fired eleven shots in total and killed ten zeds. No one spoke while I fired. It was kind of like talking in someone's back swing. It just wasn't cool.

When I lifted my rifle, Jase smiled and gave me a thumbs up.

"Like fish in a barrel," Griz said with a pat on my

back. "Good job, Cash."

He motioned forward, and then headed down the four steps and into the room holding what I assumed to be the mechanicals of the boat. I swapped my rifle for my machete; even though noise no longer mattered, ammo was a precious commodity. We checked the bodies to make sure they were good and fully dead. Not that I was worried. Each one was a solid head shot.

"God, it stinks down here," Jase said.

I nodded. "We need to find an air freshener warehouse."

"Boats need to be well-sealed or else they'd sink," Griz said, holding his forearm over his nose. "It's a good thing if we have to stay here through the winter. But damn, it's going to take a while to air it out. Jesus." He gagged and bent over. I thought he was going to throw up, but after a moment, he stood, pulled a scarf over his nose and stepped over a zed carcass.

Metal creaked.

"We're coming in!" Tyler yelled from the opposite side of the room.

"All clear!" Griz shouted back.

Beams from three headlamps emerged from the darkness.

"Everything covered from the back?" Griz asked.

"That's affirmative," Tyler replied.

He walked in and looked at the bodies.

"There were eighteen beds in the crew quarters," Griz said. "Add on one for the captain, we shouldn't come across more than nineteen zeds, and that's assuming they were running a full crew and not carrying passengers." He counted on his fingers. "Three on the bridge, one in the galley, and the pair in the crew quarters. We came across another ten in the equipment room, and they all looked like crew. No passengers. So, that makes sixteen."

"Make that nineteen," Tyler said. "We took out two hanging around the engines, and we found the final crew member dead on top of an engine, likely from dehydration. So there shouldn't be any more left."

"Sonofa—" Nate's cussing was cut off by a ruckus of metal crashing and shouts.

We all sprinted to Nate's position. My headlamp shone onto Jase's back as he slashed something on the ground. When he moved, I saw that it had been a zed. More noticeably, it had been female, wearing a skirt and sporting a badly broken leg. The likely scenario? The crew had brought her on board during the outbreak, not realizing she'd been infected. Their compassion led to their deaths.

"She bit me. She fucking bit me!"

I stepped around Jase to see Nate's wild eyes. Blood poured from his cheek and head. The zed had taken a couple good-sized chunks. He had less than an hour.

Jase knelt by the collapsed locker. "Aw, hell."

"Nate," Tyler said, falling to his knees. He shoved against the locker, trying to push it off the guardsman.

Jase breathed deeply and then joined in, and they

pushed the locker off Nate.

Nate must've been in shock because he didn't seem to notice the locker. He only lay there and held his cheek. He stared at Tyler. "She bit me."

Tack leaned on his machete.

"Damn it," Griz said.

With a straight arm, Tyler pushed Jase back. He pulled out his sidearm and pressed a hand on Nate's heart. "You're a hero, Private Hawking. You've saved lives, and you've earned the peace that's coming to you."

Nate squeezed his eyes shut as Tyler lifted the sidearm. His hand shook, but he didn't waste any time. I jumped at the single gunshot. It still echoed through the room as Tyler stood and walked several feet away from us.

Griz came down on a knee, clasped the cross he wore around his neck, and prayed.

By the time he'd finished, I came to accept the fact that Nate was gone. It seemed like the more death I'd seen, the faster I moved on. I wasn't so sure I liked that change in me.

"The zed must've reached out and startled him," Jase said. "He must've banged into the locker and it fell over on him."

It'd been my job to clear this room. My fault. "I can't believe I missed one," I said breathlessly. My brows furrowed as I stared at Nate's body.

"It was hidden behind the cabinet," Jase said,

grabbing my shoulder. "You couldn't have seen it."

I still couldn't help but think I *should* have seen it.

After a long minute, Tyler returned. "Let's wrap things up and get the engines running and lights on. We have less than forty-eight hours to get this towboat and barges ready for Camp Fox. We have to assume there could be more zeds wandering around here. Tack and Griz, you take the private above deck. Cash and Jase, you stay behind me."

We silently fell in line as he headed back toward the engine room.

"I hate these enclosed spaces," Jase said in a low voice, walking beside me. "If zeds got in here, there'd be no way out."

"We're safe now," I forced myself to say even though I didn't believe the words. Jase needed my support, not my doubts. "Zeds would have to climb the side of the boat to get in here, and that's not going to happen. This place will be a vault for Camp Fox, trust me. Once we get it cleared it, you'll be safe here. I know it."

"Easy for you to say," he replied. "You've been through more shit than just about anyone else out there. I still don't know how you made it through that elementary school."

"It wasn't fun, but it was nothing compared to Doyle's camp."

"The Dogs, then all the zeds...man, I can't imagine how much that must've sucked," Jase said after a moment.

"Yeah," I replied in a quiet voice. "But you know what? The Dogs and the zeds weren't the worst part."

He paused. "Then what was?"

I chuckled drily. "Everyone thinks I went after Doyle to save Camp Fox."

"You did."

I didn't answer.

"Didn't you?"

"Yeah, but I didn't need to go it alone. I also went after him because I was cocky enough to think I could pull it off all by myself without anyone else getting hurt."

Jase grabbed my arm, stopping me. "You *did* pull it off. You killed Doyle and took down the militia still loyal to him. You survived and no one got hurt."

"It was by sheer luck." I shook my head. "No. It was a miracle. I realized that when I was lying on the roof, waiting to die. Hell, if I had half a brain, I would've stayed in the cellar with all the weapons and food until help arrived. That just goes to show you how unprepared I was."

"You're being too hard on yourself."

"No, I'm not. I've made so many stupid mistakes that not only could've gotten myself killed, but also you or Clutch. It was at Doyle's camp when I finally came to realize that I needed to get my act together and quit thinking I had everything under control. I found out I didn't and I don't. Hell, if I were a cat, I'd be on my ninth life by now."

He smirked. "Well, then at least you still have one left."

I sucker punched him in the arm. "Funny, ha ha."

"Seriously, though," he said. "No one's perfect. We all make mistakes, and as long as you can walk away from them, it'll work out in time. Look, even your cut on your face is healing."

I lifted my hand to touch my stitches, but then dropped it. "Come on. Let's clean out our new home."

ENVY

THE SECOND DEADLY SIN

CHAPTER XIII

The following morning

"**A**men." Griz said after a lovely *hooah*-style prayer for Nate. Tyler and Griz rolled Nate's body off the edge of the deck, and he splashed into the river below. After him, we tossed over every member of the crew and the zed girl. Luckily, we hadn't come across any others during our search last night.

We still had no power. The towboat's fuel tanks were empty, and Wes couldn't get the engines started last night with only the five gallons he'd brought with him on the pontoon. Without heat, last night had been cold. The smell of death had managed to leak into the second level captain's quarters—in some part due to our clothes—so we'd left the door open to air out the room. The sweet, sickly stench had a way of seeping into everything and becoming a permanent part of a place. Zed stench didn't exactly smell like potpourri. In a way, it was like smoke. Once it got into a person's clothes, the smell lingered and nothing short of a heavy head-to-toe scrubbing could get rid of it. Our best defense for this night was the minty medicated ointment to help clear the lungs. We put a dollop of the stuff under each of our noses and took turns sleeping and standing watch.

Earlier, Tack and Griz had fastened a ladder onto the side of the boat to make it easier getting to and from the dock Tyler and the guys were building. Jase had lost at rock-paper-scissors, and he had to scrub away the old blood and bits of brain on the bridge floor. Thankfully, it wasn't carpeted, but it still stunk something awful.

I turned and went back to the pile of supplies we'd been carrying up one load at a time. While the ladder made climbing much easier, it was still a tiresome, slow progress carrying one load at a time up the side of the *Aurora*. Wes was busy building a pulley system so we could pull up larger loads, but there were some things that couldn't wait for Wes to finish.

I rummaged through the pile and found the cardboard box I was looking for. I untied the rope around it and pulled out two brand new cans of disinfectant. There was a gold star on each can that read, *Kills 99.9% of germs*, and I chuckled. If only killing zeds was that easy.

I headed to the bridge, took a deep breath, and entered. I didn't leave until I'd emptied half a can. In the galley, I finished the can. In the crew quarters, where there were fewer windows, I used an entire can. The other rooms would have to wait. With all the windows and doors propped wide open, I hoped for a good breeze today to freshen up the towboat. I was hoping we'd be able to sleep in the crew quarters tonight where we'd have real beds and it'd be warmer. Somehow I suspected the crew quarters would take a couple more days to air out.

"All done in there?" Tyler asked as I stepped onto the deck, savoring the fresh air. He was wiping his sweaty brow. Tack and Griz were each drinking water.

"For now," I said.

"Good. Everyone, check your gear."

I headed for my weapons, and Jase took the empty Lysol cans from me.

He lobbed them over the water with an impressive throw.

"You've got a quarterback's arm," Griz said, walking over.

"Nah," Jase said. "I could never throw long straight."

"All right. Quit playing around and grab your gear," Tyler announced. "We have Camp Fox arriving tomorrow and barges to prep, so let's get to it," Tyler said.

One day later

Jase and I stood on the wood deck of the *Aurora*, watching the convoy approach down the highway from the west. We had hung the U.S. flag from the bridge, and it waved proudly in the fall breeze. The flag was our all-clear sign to the convoy. If the flag had been upside down or missing, our mission had failed and the *Aurora* wasn't safe. I could only imagine how nervous everyone in the convoy must've felt until they saw the flag.

I looked through the scope of my rifle. I counted fourteen vehicles in all. With the exception of a sports car for our scout vehicle, the other vehicles were all heavy duty: HEMTTs, Humvees, SUVs, trucks—one stacked with crates full of chickens—and a large semi pulling a trailer full of cattle, hogs, and goats. That the vehicles looked unscathed, coupled with the fact that they were slightly ahead of schedule, meant their journey was—hopefully—casualty-free. I continued to watch the vehicles, searching for signs of damage or injuries to their occupants.

Clutch sat in the passenger seat of the first Humvee. He was wearing sunglasses, and his arm rested on doorframe, his window open. I slung my rifle onto my shoulder and gave Jase a wide grin. "Everything looks good. I see Clutch in front."

He returned my smile and let out a deep breath. "Good. I was hoping we hadn't stirred up any herds on our way over. I'll go tell the others." He jogged to the galley and toward the engine room where Wes and two of Sorenson's people were finishing repairs. The *Lady Amore* had stopped by yesterday, and Sorenson had left three of his people, including his daughter, to help us get up and running. Their help and expertise were invaluable. His daughter, Nikki, had been born with sea legs, and she had a salty demeanor that came from spending most of her life on the river. She had been the one to get the engines running. Over the last twenty-four hours, we'd completed far more than we could've done with everyone from Camp Fox combined.

Not that Sorenson had done all that out of the goodness of his heart. The new world was built on bartering, and he was one of the best at it. For three of his people to stay two days, Tyler gave him two pallets of MREs, which cut our MRE supply in half. Sorenson had delivered two more pontoons in exchange for the .30 cal on the back of Tyler's Humvee. I told Tyler he was being too generous, but he believed it was more important to get the towboat and barges set up to sustain Camp Fox.

If we had to stay the full winter on the *Aurora II* or took on any more survivors, we didn't have a single ration to spare. Tyler counted on any remaining zeds in the area to clear out and migrate with the herds, leaving the Midwest free for us to get what we needed from the bigger stores in towns. I didn't have as much confidence. I knew for a fact that some buildings had quite a few zeds penned inside. I wasn't looking forward to finding out which buildings those were.

"Shit. Is the entire group soldiers?" Nikki Sorenson asked at my side.

I started, not realizing she'd come up behind me. I looked at the now-stopped convoy on the east bank, where people were getting out and stretching, including Manny. Until Manny and his people had arrived, Camp Fox only had about ten civilians, the rest being soldiers—mostly Guardsmen. It hadn't always been that way. After the outbreak, there had been well over a hundred non-military residents at Camp Fox. Doyle's attack on Camp Fox had changed all that. The head of the militia had attacked when nearly all the soldiers were fixing the camp's perimeter. No one had ever expected the attack to come from inside the base. The camp's population had been decimated, and I'd almost lost Clutch.

Only forty-two survivors had made it to the Fox National Park to rebuild Camp Fox. Even with stragglers coming in every week, soldiers outnumbered civvies three to one. I think that was part of the reason why Tyler and Griz were overly protective of Jase and me. They still saw us as civvies rather than soldiers.

"Most are, I guess," I said finally.

From this distance, even most civvies could pass as soldiers. Many of the Fox survivors, including myself, wore desert tan or olive drab from Camp Fox's supply rooms as it was our most abundant source of durable clothing.

"Must be nice to have that kind of protection," she said, her tone caustic.

I shrugged. "Yeah, I guess so, but it's not like we're not pulling our own weight. We all look after each other in some way."

Jase emerged from the galley and headed our way. "Wes says they're nearly done down there. We'll have power tonight, but there's not much diesel fuel left for the engines. We're going to have to go on a fuel run soon."

"Ha. Good luck with that," Nikki said. "There's no diesel fuel along this river for fifty miles in either direction. You'll have to go onto dry land to find any."

"We'll find some," I said.

"As long as you're not taking what the *Lady Amore* needs," she quickly added.

My brows rose. "We're not competing. We're all in this together."

With her droll look, I could tell Nikki wasn't convinced. "The *Lady Amore* needs fuel or else we're dead in the water. The *Aurora* isn't going anywhere, so it's not like you need it."

I chuckled. "We don't need it for the boat. We need it for the generators. We're just shooting for a couple luxuries to keep morale up: lights in the barges, some hot water, some portable heaters, and a couple working toilets."

"Hmph." She pursed her lips. "I don't even

understand why you couldn't just hop in a jet and fly all your people to safety."

My hands slid to my hips. I'd heard this all before, and it pissed me off every time. "Just because I have a pilot's license doesn't mean I can fly anything out there. You have a driver's license. Does that mean you can drive a big semi-truck or bulldozer?"

Jase cut between us. "It's all going to work out," he said. "Don't be so sensitive. Sheesh."

After a moment, I sighed. "We're all trying to just get by."

"Say that to the river towns," a man from the *Lady Amore* chimed in as he approached. I tried to remember his name.

"Hey, Bill," Jase said as he fidgeted with his binoculars.

Ah, Bill.

Bill nodded to Jase before continuing. "Those towns that aren't completely infested by zeds are having walls built around them. It's getting harder and harder to find an open dock that's big enough for the *Lady*."

"The towns are closing off their docks?" I asked.

"No, they charge docking fees. Not to mention the outrageous fees for fuel and food," he replied.

"It's a cutthroat world," I said, not knowing what else to say. Yeah, times were tough, but I'd seen the *Lady Amore* in action. They were managing just fine.

"Looks like they're getting ready to load the pontoons," Jase said at my side, looking through a pair of binoculars.

I lifted my rifle and looked through the scope. Everyone in the convoy, with scouts on the outliers standing guard, was busy unloading supplies around Tyler by the three pontoons. Two dead zeds floated face-down nearby.

"I wish we had a better place to secure all the vehicles," Jase said. "It sucks leaving them out in the open like that."

The vehicles, still laden with anything worth taking from the park, had been backed into a semi-circle around the dock to both protect the small boat ramp as well as enable efficient unloading. Soon, everything on the vehicles would be moved onto the *Aurora*, though I suspected loading the livestock on the pontoons would make for an entertaining afternoon show.

I pointed to the tree line near the dock. "Tyler thought we'd park them just off the road by the woods."

"We could try to camouflage them," Jase said. "Even so, I don't see how we can possibly hide an entire convoy. Is Tyler planning on keeping at least one scout on land to keep an eye on them?"

"I think so." I thought of long, cold nights outside ahead of us and shivered.

"Until the herds come," Nikki added. "Then you'd better hope there's no one still there."

Being reminded of the reason for this journey quickly sobered me. "Yeah. Until the herds come."

"Let me see, Jase," Nikki said.

I glanced away from my scope to see Nikki holding out her hand. Jase handed her his binoculars. After several long moments, her mouth slowly dropped open. "My God, it looks like the Army is moving in. How much stuff are you guys moving?"

"Stuff?" I shrugged. "Just the usual. Anything we can eat or use, we're bringing onto the barge to keep it safe."

Nikki watched me for a moment before looking through the binoculars again. "You should be careful. The more you have, the more you have to lose."

CHAPTER XIV

Nikki Sorenson's words pierced any hope I had at sleeping. It wasn't so much what she'd said. It was *how* she'd said it, like she was taunting us at how much we had to lose, like she knew something we didn't. Or it could've been just another one of her catty remarks. Unlikely the former, probably the latter.

I tossed and turned in my bunk, trying not to wake anyone else in the crew quarters below decks, which had become the new residence of Camp Fox's scouts. We filled up all eighteen beds, and eleven of the bunks were shared by scouts working alternating shifts. Using the crew quarters made it easier to rotate shifts than bunking with the civvies in the large, steel Number One barge, which would add at least five minutes onto any scout's response time.

The four barges closest to the towboat were in good

shape, and two of Sorenson's people had been busy moving enough grain from the barges closest to the towboat to the barges further away so that we could use some of the areas for the general residence and livestock. Finding eight barges of grain, with most of it not rotten, was a goldmine. Of course, Sorenson's guy immediately claimed one hundred percent rights to the grain, but fortunately, Tyler talked him down to fifty percent more quickly than I'd expected.

Giving up on the idea of sleep, I shoved the blanket off me, sat up, and climbed out from the bottom bunk that had belonged to one of the towboat's previous crew. Probably one I'd shot.

From the top bunk, Jase rolled over. "What's up?" he asked, sounding wide awake.

"I'm going to check on the Number Three barge," I said softly so I wouldn't wake anyone in the crew quarters. "Something Nikki said earlier. I just need to make sure everything's secure. Then I'll be right back."

Jase sat up. "So it wasn't just me. Yeah, I got a bad vibe, too. How about I join you."

"Thanks." I reached up and grabbed my belt that hung off the corner of my bunk and latched it around my waist. By the time I'd finished fastening my holster and sheath, Jase was armed and ready to go. We headed up the stairs and into the galley, which made up the entire first level of the towboat. A lantern was lit on a table in the center, and Frost was reading a paperback that had seen better days. Diesel was missing and likely serving as a bed for Benji like the dog did every night.

"Where are you two going?"

I turned to see Clutch watching us from the couch that he'd turned into his bed. It was too much hassle for him to sleep downstairs in the crew quarters. He had regained minimal coordinating movement in his legs and still struggled with stairs. Every day, he made it a few more steps with crutches than the day before, but it was clearly exhausting for him.

I rolled my eyes. "Is everyone awake on this boat?"

"We're going to check out barge Three," Jase said.

He sat up. "Barge Three? Why?"

"We both had a feeling," I said simply.

"I'm coming, too," he said, tugging his legs over the edge of the bed.

"You don't have to," I said. "It's probably nothing. Just a suspicion that's been nagging me."

Clutch slid onto his wheelchair and grabbed his crutches. "And if it's not?" He took the lead, and wheeled out of the galley. Frost never even looked up from his book, though I'm sure he'd listened to every word.

As we crossed the deck of the towboat, I looked up at the bridge to see Tyler drinking coffee as he went through papers. He should've been sound asleep by now, but he was one of those folks that felt the need to always be in control. He bore all the weight of Camp Fox on his shoulders. Sometimes, I thought he was afraid the community would collapse without his leadership. Maybe he was our white knight. But maybe he just needed to have faith in the community we all had a hand in building.

I tripped over Clutch's chair and barely caught myself from tumbling over him. "Oomph. Sorry," I muttered.

"Graceful," Jase teased with a grin, his white teeth easily seen in the starlit night.

With a sigh, I saw the large, rectangular-shaped barges in the night sky. The general residence had been set up in Number One, the barge closest to the island and in the row of the four closest to the towboat, making it the safest barge from any bandits who might come across the highway bridge and notice us. Make-shift wood plank bridges had been built from to the towboat to each barge. None of the barges were cozy by any stretch, but they would work.

Next to One, Number Two was our commons area. Numbers Two and Three were the easiest to get to from the towboat for a reason. As we crossed the manmade bridge of two-by-sixes to Number Three, Clutch's wheelchair made a nearly-silent rolling sound over the wood, while Jase's and my boot steps made thumps in the night.

Number Three held all our stockpile of canned and dried food, weapons, and other supplies. It was our own Fort Knox, making it critical that we could get to it easily from the towboat. To its right, the livestock was set up in Number Four, the barge facing the highway bridge. Cattle mooed softly in the night air. If the livestock were any closer, people would constantly complain about the smell.

The second row of barges wasn't used except for storing grain. Number Five, on just the other side of Number One, had hit the island at the wrong angle, and its hull had been compromised. Grain had dumped out onto the ground. The remaining three viable barges were full of precious grain. When we'd discovered it yesterday, we danced like maniacs and whooped like fools. For the first time, we knew with confidence that we'd get through the winter, let alone spring and summer, without starving. We'd get sick of grain and likely have some serious nutritional deficiencies, but we'd survive.

As we approached the wide opening to Three, our steps became softer and slower. I could hear nothing out of the ordinary. In the distance, Kurt waved before turning back to his guard duty. Wes had opened the bays to the first row of barges to air them out of the dangerous grain dust.

Jase looked down the narrow, metal stairway, pulled out his rifle, and clicked on his flashlight. "I'll take lead."

Clutch pulled up to the edge of the open bay. He set his crutches on the deck next to him and laid his rifle on his lap. "If either of you see anything suspicious, flash your lights in my direction."

I pulled out my sidearm and snapped the small

flashlight onto it. The Glock and all its accessories had been a surprise from Tyler for my birthday. I think it was his way to finally show that he wasn't angry with me anymore for leaving him behind when I went after Doyle on my own. I peered into the darkness, my nerves making my senses hyper-sensitive. "It looks quiet down there. Knock on wood, everything will be just fine and we'll be back in bed in no time."

Clutch narrowed his eyes at me. After a moment, I shrugged and couldn't help but smirk at his superstitious nature. He was a firm believer that if any of us said something would be easy, it was sure to have problems. Just because he was right *most* of the time only made the superstition a coincidence, not a fact.

Oh, and Clutch also didn't believe in coincidences.

Jase gave me a slow shake of his head before taking the first step into the barge. I followed him down the steps, slowly scanning the floor and pallets with my mounted flashlight. Nothing seemed out of place. No tarps had been torn off. No supplies were scattered. The tension in my muscles eased. My imagination had been working overtime. Everything was fine. I'd been overreacting.

As I reached the last step, I could make out an almost imperceptible, powered hum, and I frowned. "Do you hear that?" I whispered.

Jase paused and looked at me and then did a three-sixty. "Yeah," He replied just as quietly. "Sounds like it's coming from that way." He pointed with his flashlight and led us toward the long side of the barge.

Wes had gotten the engines running, but they weren't running right now, and there were no generators running on this barge. Tyler had mandated we needed to save power until we found more fuel and the temperatures dipped below freezing. There were several small gas-powered generators spread across the barges to help with lighting, cooking, and plumbing, but there should be none in a barge being used only for storage. Yet, the noise grew as we drew closer.

"What the hell is a generator doing on down here?" Jase asked.

My eyes narrowed on a tarp against the wall. Unlike the other tarps that sat squarely over pallets, this one seemed misshapen and tight against the side of the hull. There, on the edges of the tarp, warm light bled through the edges of the tarp.

"I don't like this." I raised my Glock and turned the light on and off three times. A light from the deck above did the same back at us.

Jase turned off his light to have both hands on his rifle. Seconds later, I heard the sounds of boots pounding down the steps.

The tarp moved, and a masculine shape crawled out from under it. "Lay off. I said I'll check it out."

As he stood, I leveled the light in his eyes. "Don't move!"

Philip from the *Lady Amore* held a hand over his eyes, and then spun around. "Run!"

The tarp was thrown open and two more shapes bolted out.

Jase stepped up to Philip and coldcocked him with the butt of his rifle. The man fell to the ground with a solid thud. The other two ran behind pallets, and we both took off after them.

Jase quickly took the lead and cut between the pallets while I ran straight ahead and took the next chance to get behind the pallets just in time to see Jase tackle a smaller shape.

As he yanked her to her feet, I noticed it was Nikki.

My mouth dropped. *Son of a bitch.*

"I've got her," Jase said. "Quit wiggling, dammit."

"Do you need help?" I asked, glaring at the woman.

"No, I've got it covered," he quickly replied.

"Right!" I took off running in the direction the two had been headed. When I reached the end of the barge, I made a hard right and climbed over a pallet of boxes. Pain shot through my scarred leg, reminding me that it wasn't fully healed. I needn't have hurried. Several feet away, Kurt had Bill from Sorenson's crew restrained, while another scout was dragging an unconscious Philip across the shadowed floor.

I headed back to Jase to make sure he had Nikki under control. She must not have behaved, because he now carried her lax form over his shoulder. "The other two guys are secure," I said. "I'll check the generator."

I jogged toward the tarp now hanging limply off to one side. Under it sat two work lights and the small, still-running generator they'd snagged from somewhere. Hooked up to it was the acetylene torch I'd seen Wes use many times. Confused, I went down on a knee and examined the wall of the barge. Chalk lines were drawn to make a large square on the wall, large enough to slide a crate through. "Son of a bitch," I muttered and jumped to my feet.

I zigged and zagged around pallets and up the steps to the deck, where a small crowd had gathered near the open bay to barge Three. Tyler stood next to Clutch in his wheelchair.

Bill and Philip stood before them, while Nikki — held tight by Jase and Tack — was just coming to.

" — too busy doing whatever it was they were doing, they didn't even see us coming," I heard Jase tell Tyler and Clutch as I approached.

"They were going to cut a hole through the hull!" I said breathlessly. In spring, when the water levels would rise, the barge would likely flood. Until then, where the barge was currently located, it made a perfect exit point for dropping supplies onto a small boat hidden between the barges below. "These bastards were going to rob us."

Frost shook his head slowly. "With all the grain dust around here, they would've set the whole barge on fire."

Tyler cocked his head at the three prisoners. "I made a generous deal with Sorenson for your time and assistance. Tonight, you've broken a trust between our communities. We have zero tolerance for theft."

"It's not like you don't have enough to share," Nikki spat out.

Clutch guffawed. "Does it look like we're any better off than you? We've had to completely uproot our home and are camping on a shipwreck."

"That barge is full of food and ammunition. I've never seen so much in my life," she retorted.

"Aside from sharing the location of this shelter, the *Lady Amore* crew hasn't offered my people a single thing without demanding heavy payment in return," Tyler said, his voice steady and calm but laced with anger.

"You don't understand. We are struggling to get by," Bill said. "Every day, we don't know if we're going to find more diesel or more food."

"Grow a pair," Clutch scolded. "We're all fighting to survive here. The world's a shithole. Deal with it."

Nikki grunted and twisted out of her captors' grasp and sprinted forward. Tack reached for her, but she jumped to the side. She must've twisted her ankle because she tumbled down and fell partway over the edge. Jase lunged after her, sliding on his belly to grab her, but she swung him away, loosening her hold, and she plummeted into the darkness below.

"Nikki!" Bill shouted.

Her scream was cut off by the sound of her body hitting the hard steel floor nearly twenty feet below. No one ran down to check on her. A drop from this height wasn't just deadly, it would've been *messy* deadly.

Everyone stood in stunned silence.

"What the hell just happened?" Tyler asked.

Jase climbed to his feet. "I don't know. She'd been standing so still. Then she just freaked out and tore away."

"You killed her!" Bill yelled, trying to lunge forward, but his scouts yanked him back.

"No," Tyler said harshly. "It was an accident. You saw for yourself."

"The captain's not going to see it that way," Philip said quietly. "That's his daughter down there."

Clutch grabbed his crutches and pulled himself to his feet. "He's going to see it that way because you're going to tell him the truth. You're going to tell him what you were doing here and exactly what happened. I'm going with you to make sure you do."

Tack stepped forward. "No, Clutch." He sighed. "I need to go. She was mine to watch."

"Bullshit," Jase said. "She was as much my responsibility. I'm going."

Tyler watched Tack and Jase for a moment before speaking. "Okay, by morning, the *Lady Amore* shouldn't be more than thirty miles or so south of here. You are both going, but under no conditions are you to board the *Lady Amore*. You drop Sorenson's daughter and his men in a raft and double-time it out of there. I'll write a note to make sure he knows the truth. It's our only shot at keeping our trade agreement. Whatever you do, don't let them get a bead on you. That's Sorenson's daughter lying on the bottom of Number Three. I don't trust him to be rational when he sees her. You drop the package and run. Got it?"

"Yes, sir," they both replied.

"You-you can't just dump us in the water," Philip said. "There are zeds in the water. If it's shallow at all —"

"You should've thought of that before you tried to steal from us," Tyler interrupted. "The only reason I'm allowing you to return to the *Lady Amore*—instead of staying on the *Aurora* for trial—is because of our trade agreement."

"Just let us go," Bill cried out. "We'll tell the Captain the truth. I mean it. You don't have to worry about anything. Please. Just let us go. Nothing will happen. I swear!"

Tyler ignored Bill's pleas and instead looked at the scouts holding the thieves. "Get these two out of my sight. Put them in the galley for tonight and keep at least four armed scouts on them at all times." He then looked to all of us. "I need volunteers to prep Sorenson's daughter for the trip in the morning."

Deb, one of the Fox survivors who volunteered for everything, unsurprisingly stepped forward. "I'll take care of it."

"I'll help," Tack said in a rush.

Deb gave him a sweet smile. "Okay. Thank you."

As the two headed into the barge, I couldn't help but grin. Deb may have been ten years his senior, but Tack didn't seem to care. The two had hit it off the moment she'd arrived at the park, and even though they thought they were hiding their relationship, everyone knew about it.

The crowd dissipated.

"I'm going to hit the sack," Jase said, sounding utterly exhausted. "I'm guessing Tyler is going to want us to get those guys off the *Aurora* at the crack of dawn."

"Listen, Jase," Clutch said. "If you want me to go, if you want an extra gun—"

"Relax. No worries. Tack and I've got it." Jase patted Clutch's shoulder. "Like Tyler said, we just toss them into a raft and bust out of there. Trust me, I don't plan on getting anywhere near Sorenson." With that, he turned and started walking away.

Jase spoke the words so nonchalantly, yet I had a hard time believing that an accidental death wasn't tearing him up inside. He'd seen so much death that he'd built quite the mask. So good that I couldn't even tell anymore if something was bothering him.

"Good night," I said, watching him. "I'll be in soon."

Clutch sat down in his chair and set his crutches across his lap.

The edge around the barge and deck had mostly cleared. Lanterns and flashlights blinked off one by one. I looked out over the river, the water peacefully reflecting the moonlight. In the far distance, wolves bayed. While people and domesticated animals had been devastated by the outbreak, some wild animals had flourished. Packs of wolves had become a new risk to scouting runs. I took in a deep breath of cool air. "Well, isn't this is a mess."

"I don't have Tyler's optimism," he said. "Any hope for a trade agreement is lying dead at the bottom of the barge."

"With the grain, we have enough food. We don't need a trade agreement," I said, pushing his chair. "So we're on our own. Then again, we've always been on our own."

"Yeah, but you're assuming Sorenson is going to let us be."

WRATH

THE THIRD DEADLY SIN

CHAPTER XV

Mid-afternoon, the following day

"You're getting a sunburn. It could slow your healing," Clutch said.

I touched my cheek where Doc had taken out the stitches a couple hours earlier. The bright sun warmed my skin. I looked down at Clutch. "What's taking them so long? They should've been back hours ago."

"Maybe the *Lady Amore* was farther out then Tyler thought."

"The herds could be showing up as early as today."

He shook his head. "The latest recon to the north shows them at least two days out, longer if they stop along the way. Jase will make it back okay."

Clutch didn't leave my side, so I knew he was as concerned about Jase as I was.

Just before the sun had crested this morning, we'd

watched Jase and Tack disappear around the bend of the island. They'd been in the fastest deck boat we had, tugging behind it a large yellow tube containing the trio from the riverboat. Before the outbreak, the tube would have carried squealing kids as they bounced over the waves. Today's passengers were far more somber, especially considering one was dead.

Since Jase and Tack had left, Clutch and I had circled the deck countless times, taking breaks only for food and when Doc came for me. My anxious nerves were making it impossible to focus on anything. At noon, Griz begged Tyler to let him take a small crew out to find Tack and Jase. We all hoped that the reason they weren't back yet was because they'd had trouble finding Sorenson's boat. Any other alternative meant something had gone seriously wrong. I tried to focus on the positive, but as the day went on, horrible imaginings began to cycle through my mind.

I shaded my eyes against the sun and looked out over the river for any sign of either boat. Even with sunglasses, the glare off the water gave me a headache. An engine noise to my right pulled my gaze to find Kurt returning on a Jet Ski from his scouting run in the north. The Jet Ski, which we'd found at a dock a few miles upriver, had extra plastic fuel tanks strapped on both sides, and Kurt wore a large backpack. He'd had enough fuel and food for a three-day trip, but he'd been gone only two days. "I wonder how close the herds are now," I said.

Clutch wrapped his gloved hand around my mine. "Come on. Let's head back to the galley and grab a snack. There's nothing we can do out here except wear holes in the deck."

I looked to the south another time, still seeing nothing. "I guess you're right."

I moped as we headed back toward the galley. Clutch rolled slowly over the deck boards. After several feet, he came to an abrupt stop, peeled off his worn gloves, and picked at a blister on his hand, grumbling under his breath.

I picked his gloves off his lap and rubbed at the soft leather with holes and slashes. "Wow. These are worthless. You really need a new pair."

"That's not going to happen. I can't find any more. What I need is to get rid of this chair and back on my feet."

I wanted to snap back at his infuriating refusal to give his body time to heal. Instead, I dropped his gloves with a smack on his lap and gripped his shoulder. "A week ago you couldn't even stand. Just be patient."

"It's hard to be patient when we've got a shit storm of zeds heading this way."

Good point. I left my hand on his shoulder while I looked to the north. I forced a smile. "The zeds aren't here yet. So you can be patient a little longer."

"Hmph," he replied.

As I turned to look back down at Clutch, something in the distance caught my eye. I stepped back and lifted my rifle to look through the scope. Off the edge of the island, a deck boat with several people in it came jetting around the corner. I quickly made out Jase's sandy, shaggy hair.

I lowered my rifle and let out a whoop. "They're back! They must've had boat trouble since they're all loaded up in one."

Clutch narrowed his eyes and scrutinized the incoming boat for a long minute.

"Come on," I said. "Let's go meet them at the top of the ladder."

He didn't move. "I only count four on the boat."

"What?" I asked. "Are you sure?"

"Yes."

When I'd seen Jase, I hadn't bothered counting the crew. I squinted in the sunlight as I counted. Clutch was right. Griz had gone out with two other scouts today. There should have been five on that boat. "Maybe the fifth man is still bringing in the other boat," I offered hopefully.

"Maybe," Clutch said. "Let's get over there."

We hustled over to where the rope ladder and pulley-driven elevator platform hung. Deb was already there, watching each man climb up the ladder. Consternation filled her face.

Jase was the second man up the ladder. I grabbed onto his shivering, wet form and helped him climb over the railing. He collapsed on the deck, and I wrapped my arms around him to share my body heat. "What happened? Are you hurt?" I asked.

Clutch put a hand on Jase's back.

Deb kneeled by Jase. "Where's Tack?"

"Don't-know," Jase replied between chattering teeth and started to pull himself up.

I helped Jase to his feet. "Let's get you a hot shower."

By then, the others had reached the top. Griz's sleeves were wet, but everyone else was dry. He gave Clutch a hard look. "I think it's safe to say Sorenson is headed this way."

Clutch nodded. "I'll meet you on the bridge in five."

Griz and the other two scouts jogged across the deck, followed closely by Deb, who kept asking them about Tack.

Clutch looked up at Jase. "I need you to tell me exactly what happened."

Jase nodded, his whole body shaking against mine, as we took slow steps toward the galley. "We-we drove until we s-saw the riverboat." He sucked in a breath. "We c-cut the tube loose and took off. They must've seen Nikki or something 'c-cause they sent a speedboat with—swear to God—our own .30 c-cal after us."

"Shit," I muttered under my breath. "Thank God you didn't get shot."

"Tack?" Clutch asked.

Jase sniffled. "When they got close, they shot out our engine. W-we were dead in the water. They kept their distance until we ran out of ammo. They came up alongside, and Tack and I got ready to take them on, but then he shoved me into the water and took on all three guys by himself."

"Oh, God." That sounded exactly like something Tack would do. Even though he was only a few years older than Jase, Tack had taken him under his wing. I figured it had something to do with the fact that Tack had a younger brother about Jase's age. After the outbreak had hit, he searched but never found him.

Jase winced and then rubbed his hair. "I saw it all from the water. They tackled him. Then they tied him up and came after me. I had to ditch my life jacket and swim. I got lucky and hid under a tree trunk floating down the river. They got really close but I heard Sorenson on their radio and he called off the search. I think he assumed I was a goner."

He looked at each of us, his eyes pleading. "We've got to go back and get Tack."

"We will," Clutch said without hesitation. "We don't leave any of our own behind."

I hugged him. "We'll get him back. We have a hundred times the firepower that Sorenson has."

"What if they've already killed him?" Jase asked.

"If they wanted him dead, they would've gunned you both down in the water. I'm sure he's safe. Sorenson needs Tack as a bargaining chip," Clutch replied.

I tried not to frown, but whenever Clutch threw in extra words like "I'm sure" or "maybe", he didn't really mean it. A chill ran down my spine. Did he really think

Sorenson would kill an innocent man? I swallowed and made a mental note to ask him as soon as we were alone.

When we reached the galley, Clutch stopped, lifted himself on his crutches, and turned to me. "You got this?"

I nodded. "Yeah, we'll be fine."

He started to climb the stairs to the bridge while Jase and I headed inside and down to the crew quarters. I propped my rifle against the wall, and helped Jase strip out of his gear and boots. His fingers were shaking too much to unbutton his shirt, so I took over, gently brushing his fingers away. Once he was down to just his pants and a t-shirt, I opened the utility closet near the shower and kicked on a generator hooked up to a small, tankless water heater Wes had brought on board. Within seconds, warm water came out of the shower. Jase stepped under the spray without bothering to take his pants off and stood, leaning against the stall.

I went to his bunk and sifted through his trunk for a change of clothes.

"You don't need to stick around for me."

"It's okay," I said, putting on a smile. "I've got nothing better to do.

He lowered his head under the spray. "To be honest, I could use some alone time," he said after a bit.

"You sure?"

"Yeah. I'll see you above deck."

I waited for a moment before taking a step back.

"Okay, but I'll be here if you need me for anything. Anything at all."

"Thanks. I'll be fine," he said all too quickly with that deadpan tone.

I wasn't surprised that he was closing himself off, but I was still disappointed. I sighed. "I'll leave your clothes on the chair."

With that, I set his clothes down and headed back through the crew quarters. I heard shouting and I ran up the stairs, through the galley, and onto the deck.

One of the scouts was pointing to the river. "The *Lady Amore* is a couple clicks to the south, heading our way!"

Tyler was running down from the bridge, followed closely by several others. Clutch, being so much slower, brought up the rear. I caught up to him quickly. "Sorenson's here," I said, though I knew he'd already figured that out.

"We need to be ready for a fight," he said as he settled into his chair. "Do you have all your gear?"

I winced. "Shit. I left my rifle below decks with Jase's stuff."

"You might need your rifle for this one."

Griz's voice came over the loudspeaker from bridge. "All scouts report to the deck. Everyone else, please go to barge Number One immediately. This is not a drill."

"I'll be right back," I told Clutch and headed back to the galley, only to have Jase nearly run into me.

"You left this." He handed me my rifle.

"Thanks." I checked my rifle and slung it over my

shoulder.

"Is it the riverboat already?"

My body shook with anger. "Yeah," I replied, and I narrowed my eyes. "Let's go."

We ran to meet up with Clutch and Tyler. Griz was just coming down from the bridge. He held an extra rifle and looked around. "I guess none of you need one."

Clutch, who already had his Blaser on his lap, grabbed it. "I'll take a spare."

"Do you see Tack yet?"

I jerked around at the voice to see Deb right behind me.

"You should be in the barge right now," I said.

Deb's lips tightened.

"Or you can stay," I quickly added.

I turned my attention to the incoming riverboat. We were in a shallow part of the river, which meant a few zeds washed up on the island every day that we'd have to dispatch. It also meant that the *Lady Amore* couldn't get very close without hitting the river bottom, which was the first perk I'd seen about being on a boat that didn't go anywhere.

Deb's hand flung over her mouth. "Oh, God."

"What is it?" I asked.

Deb pointed to the riverboat. "*No.*"

Every pair of eyes followed.

There, on the bow of the riverboat, Tack was strung up like its figurehead. He hung limply, a dark clump of bloodied hair hinting that he couldn't be alive.

"No, no, no," Deb cried out and then collapsed.

I fell to a knee and wrapped my arms around her. Clutch, his brow furrowed, looked from Deb to Tack.

"Aw, shit. No," Jase said. The sound of his heart breaking couldn't be missed in those few short words.

"We've got incoming!" someone yelled.

I looked up to see flares being fired from the riverboat. Sorenson and his crew had dozens of flare guns, and they were shooting constantly into the air and directly at the towboat. All but one from the first round of flares missed the *Aurora*. The flare that didn't miss landed on the deck and lit up a tarp covering a raft. Kurt lunged for a fire extinguisher hanging near the stairs.

"To your posts!" Tyler yelled, waving his arm. "They're trying to burn us down! Teams Alpha and Bravo, prepare to launch a counterattack from the boats. Charlie, get those barge bay doors closed now! All other teams, get the civvies to barge Two *now!*"

Over a dozen scouts, including Griz and Tyler, ran toward the ladder to head to the boats. Jase and I were on Clutch's Charlie team, which meant we stayed behind to protect the towboat and its barges.

"You heard the captain," Clutch yelled as he grabbed his crutches. "We need to get the big generators running and those doors closed now."

A young man came up and stood there, looking in shock. He'd arrived with Manny and had just joined Delta team a day ago. His eyes were wide and looked like they were about to burst with tears. "I don't know

218

what to do."

"Grab as many fire extinguishers as you can handle and distribute them," Clutch ordered. A commotion of cattle bellowing and pigs squealing came from barge Four. He turned to Jase. "Jase, take lead of Delta and Echo teams. Cash and I will get the bays closed. Save the barges."

Jase didn't say anything. Stress was instantly replaced by a smooth, hardened sense of purpose on his face. "Come with me!" He took off at a sprint, and the other scout followed.

Ever since Tyler had divided scouts into teams, we'd practiced, but we'd never needed more than three teams on a mission before. Delta and Echo teams were made up of only corporals and civvies. "You sure Jase can handle teams right now?"

"He's a natural," Clutch said. "Besides, he needs this. Let's go." He grabbed his crutches again, and we headed into the galley.

Starting the generators was an easy task...except that black smoke was bleeding through the doorframe leading below decks and exactly where the engines were.

CHAPTER XVI

Even with crutches, Clutch kept a good pace. After touching the steel door for heat, I opened it. Smoke dirtied the air and I coughed. Propping the door open with my foot, I tugged off the red bandana I kept tied around my wrist.

"Hold up," Clutch said and grabbed my bandana. He dumped water on it and handed the soaked fabric back to me. "Here. This will help."

"Thanks." I tied the wet bandana around my face while he did the same with a tactical scarf he'd retrieved from a backpack he always carried.

As soon as he had his face covered and his water bottle stashed in his pack again, I entered the short deck. The air wasn't pleasant, but there was no fire here. I looked up to see the heaviest of the smoke hovering around the vents. "The smoke must be coming in through the ventilation system," I said.

"We need to hurry," he said as he hustled around me. Each step of his was staggered as the rest of his body had to overcompensate for legs that didn't play along. He stopped at the door leading to the equipment room that would in turn bring us to the engine room. He touched the door. "It's cool. That's a good sign." He sifted through his backpack and pulled out a flashlight and a flat roll of duct tape. He clicked on the flashlight and taped it onto a crutch. He turned to me. He ran a hand through my hair, and his look softened. "Stay here. I don't know how bad it's going to be in there."

I guffawed and then smacked his hand away. "I should go, and you should stay. I can move faster."

He frowned. "You don't know how to work the generators."

I pulled out my handgun and pressed the flashlight. "Then we go together. If one of us falls, the other will get us out of there."

He turned back to the door. "I knew you were going to say that," he muttered as he opened the door. I shoved my bag against the door to prop it open. Before us was a filthy gray haze, hiding anything and anyone in the large room. Clutch took the lead, moving as quickly as he could, clearly pushing his body beyond what it was ready for.

My eyes burned. Every breath was bitter air. Clutch coughed. I tried to smother my coughs, but it was impossible. I supposed all these doors help protect the well-sealed towboat in case it flooded, but they were a pain in the ass because they retained bad air inside.

For all I knew, the barges were already on fire, in which case we'd be screwed. Even if it was too late to close the bay doors, we still needed water pressure to put out any small fires. We *had* to get the engines running.

When we reached the next door, I could barely see Clutch in front of me. My flashlight couldn't cut more than a foot through the haze. His coughs were about the only way I could stay with him. I grabbed onto his backpack so that we weren't separated. We didn't talk. When I tried, I only coughed more. Tears streamed down my cheeks. A coughing fit nearly had me bent over. Clutch wasn't doing any better, but his crutches seem to bolster our stability.

When he stopped, I bumped into him. Metal clanked, and I found myself yanked forward.

Clutch slammed the door shut behind us. The air was much better — though still not great. The beam from my flashlight cut through the haze to fall on the large engines and the short red generators covering much of the floor.

"Thank God," I said, which brought on a coughing fit.

Clutch headed straight for the engines. He tripped over a cable and fell down, so he pulled himself over to the control box. With my help, he got back to his feet. Using my weight to support him, he flipped a switch.

Nothing happened. He frowned and then struggled to the next motor. Again, nothing happened. He stood there while I watched, feeling incredibly helpless. He was right. I knew nothing about engines and generators and mechanical things. After a long moment, he spoke. "Wes must've turned off the fuel line."

"I looked around the room. Where is it?"

"It's got to be in here somewhere. It should have a gas marking or warning on it."

I propped Clutch against an engine while I retrieved his crutches. Then I began my search. With only a flashlight, it was a tedious search. I tripped a couple times over the cables Wes has strewn across the floors.

"I see it," Clutch said.

I hurried over.

Clutch pointed. "It's too tight with my crutches."

I looked down the narrow walkway between two engines and saw a triangular "Warning: Extremely Flammable" sticker. "I'll get it." I had to walk sideways. It must've been a tight fit for Wes, but it was pretty easy for me. I knelt at the sticker. Below it was a round metal crank that looked like it rotated rather than a switch that flipped on and off. I tried to twist it counterclockwise, but it didn't budge. "Jesus, Wes," I muttered, and put all my strength into it.

Slowly, the crank moved an inch before it picked up speed and twisted a full rotation. I leaned back. "Try it now."

I heard an engine start up. "We're good!" Clutch

yelled out.

Clutch had the engines running by the time I reached him, and had moved to a box of switches that Wes had built to run all the generators. While each of the generators had its own gas tank, Wes has talked about how he had everything set up to run directly off the towboat's gas tank to save someone having to constantly refill the generators.

As the generators started, the noise in the metal room became deafening, and I winced. Clutch rewet his scarf. He held the bottle to me, and I took a long drink before soaking my thin bandana.

"Ready?" He yelled. "We have to close the bay doors now!"

I could barely hear him but nodded. "Okay!"

He grabbed my hand and put it on his belt. "Don't let go!"

After taking a couple deep breaths, he opened the door, and we headed back into the smoky mechanical bowels of the towboat.

The smoke had faded some—probably due to my propping the door open rather than any fires being put out—making the return trip not quite as terrifying as our first time through. My throat was raw, worse than any sore throat I'd ever had before. The smoke was acid to my already stinging eyes. I closed them and held onto Clutch's belt loops as he clumsily took the steps as quickly as he could.

I had to steady him several times when he lost his

footing or didn't get the crutches leveled right on a step. I grabbed my bag, and we burst through the crew quarters and shower room. Finally, when we climbed the stairs and reached the last door, Clutch threw it open, and we tumbled inside the galley. I kicked the door shut, and we both lay there, gasping slightly better air. Who knew how badly the boat or its barges had already burned. Worse, who knew how many zeds the smoke would draw to our location.

"Are you okay?"

I looked up to see Benji standing over us, Frost's Great Dane at his side. Diesel was as tall as the short boy and just as lovable.

"Benji." I propped myself up on an elbow. "What are you doing here? You should be in the barge." The words came out rough, like I was a lifelong smoker.

"Grampa told me to stay in here. He heard the engines start and said he was going to close the big doors." He pointed up, referring to the bridge.

"Good," Clutch said and then coughed.

Outside I could hear shouting. I rubbed my eyes with my bandana and climbed to my feet. Through the windows I could see people running across the deck. Several were pulling a large water hose. "I guess I'd better get out there and help."

As I kneeled to help Clutch, the door leading to the deck opened. Three men entered, with their pistols raised. In the middle stood Sorenson.

I froze. Neither Clutch nor I could draw our weapon

in time, and with Benji and Diesel in the way, I'd never get a clean shot, anyway. Benji didn't move. Instead, he just stood there between us and them. He was likely frozen with fear, but it didn't matter. He was going to get himself killed.

I reached out to pull the boy behind me.

"Don't move," Sorenson ordered. "And get down on the floor now."

I stopped mid-reach. I could hear Clutch's breaths next to me but was afraid to make eye contact with him. *Don't be a hero,* I mentally said to Clutch. I sat back on my heels, waiting for, hell, I had no idea what I was waiting for.

Benji cocked his head. "Are you here to help us?"

Sorenson frowned while he scrutinized Benji. He waved with his pistol. "Move to the side, kid. We need to get upstairs."

Benji didn't move. Diesel's shoulders bunched aggressively and his hackles rose as he stood next to his small master. A deep growl came from his throat and his teeth were bared.

Sorenson was trying to get upstairs? Why? To get to the bullhorn? To open the bay doors again? I glanced at Clutch, but he had on his poker face. I stayed silent, not willing to take the risk of pissing off Sorenson even more.

Benji patted the dog before looking up at Sorenson. "Are you going to use that gun? Because I don't like guns. They're loud. My mom shot a gun by my ear once.

It hurt for a long time."

"Only if I have to, kid," Sorenson replied. "Now, get out of my way. I'm in a bit of a hurry and don't want to hurt you. I need to unhook those barges from this boat."

"Why?" Benji asked.

"Because some of those barges belong to me," he said.

"Why?" the boy asked again.

"Listen, kid. They just do. I need what's on them. Enough."

Benji crossed his arms over his chest. "No." he said sharply. "You look angry. People do bad things when they're angry."

Sorenson could've shoved the boy out of his way. Instead, he took a deep breath and his expression softened. "They hurt my daughter."

"My mom got hurt once."

"It's tough out there, kid. So you see, I have no choice. I need what's on those barges."

Benji shook his head. "Grampa says that people always have choices."

"Well, your gramps is wrong."

"Nuh uh." Benji shook his head even harder. "He's never wrong. He's really smart. He's been around a really long time. He's old. Like you."

Sorenson smirked and one eye narrowed. "Yes, I've been around and seen plenty. I've got to say, I liked the way things used to be a whole lot better than they are now."

"I did, too," Benji said. "I liked school. I had a lot of friends."

Sorenson's lips tightened. After a moment, he held up the hand not holding a pistol. "We're leaving."

"What?" the man at his side asked. "But the barges —"

"We've done enough for one day." Sorenson cut him off with a hard glare. "Everyone's had enough hurt for a lifetime. We're heading back to the *Lady*."

The man who had spoken seemed pissed, while the other looked relieved.

As they backed up to the door, Benji waved. "Bye. Be careful out there."

Sorenson gave Clutch and me one final glance before he turned to leave, like he'd just remembered we were still there.

"Game over, asshole," Jase said from the doorway, his rifle leveled dead-to-rights on Sorenson.

His men jerked around. "You move, I shoot," Frost said as he squeezed inside.

Clutch yanked up his rifle, and I went for my sidearm.

"We were just leaving," Sorenson said slowly.

"Not now, you aren't," Jase replied much more quickly. "Drop your guns."

Sorenson eyed Benji and then spun his pistol and handed it over to Jase. The other two men dropped theirs.

"Benji, are you okay?" Frost asked, cranking his head

just enough to see his grandson while keeping his rifle aimed at Sorenson's pals.

"Grampa!" Benji said. He tapped his leg. "C'mon, Diesel!"

The Great Dane's growling dissipated and he trotted alongside happy-go-lucky boy to the older man, both oblivious to the showdown of firepower under way. Sorenson watched as the pair bounded past him.

"Did they hurt you, son?" Frost asked, tugging Benji against him.

"I'm fine, Grampa," he giggled. "No one hurt me." He pointed to Sorenson. "He's just sad because his daughter was hurt, that's all. He wasn't going to hurt me."

I took a big breath and leaned into Clutch, who was breathing just as heavily. He knew as well as I did that the only reason we were still alive was because of a boy. A boy with Down Syndrome just proved that a little bit of kindness was sometimes more powerful than all the brute force and guns in the world.

RACHEL AUKES

SLOTH

THE FOURTH DEADLY SIN

CHAPTER XVII

We held Tack's funeral the following morning. Griz had used his Ranger skills and somehow managed to climb onto the riverboat and cut down Tack's body sometime during the attack without getting caught. Tack had been executed — shot in the head. That he hadn't been beaten was little consolation to any of us.

Deb refused to leave Tack after he was brought on board. When I stopped by to offer my condolences while she was preparing his body, she seemed oblivious, completely lost in her own world. By morning, she'd regained her composure and now stood strong, her blotchy cheeks and swollen red eyes the only outward signs of her mourning.

Even Manny and his people joined all of Camp Fox on the towboat's deck, just off the back, where the water was deepest. Frost and Wes had spent the night building a heavy casket out of wood leftover from pallets and various metal parts found on the barges so that Tack would find permanent peace at the bottom of the river.

Griz led the service. He and Tack had been best friends, and Griz had to stop several times during his speech to take a deep breath before continuing. After he recited a prayer, he asked everyone to share a story.

No one spoke. Then, after a long minute, Tyler stepped up and told everyone about Tack, the skinny new recruit on his team who wasn't expected to make it a week. He ended by finally sharing Tack's real name. Corporal Theodore Nugent. Yeah, the poor guy was seriously named after a rock star. No wonder he'd always gone by his nickname. We all laughed. Even Deb cracked a smile, though it was still a sad expression.

After Tyler, the stories came easily. Some were short like Frost's straightforward proclamation, "I'd have been proud to call him my son." Others, like Benji's, took fifteen minutes or more. For his story, the young boy went into detail about how Tack had shown up with a foam football for his birthday. Benji went so far as to run back to the barge, with Diesel at his heels, to reclaim the purple ball so we could all see the special present.

Jase talked of the time Tack had gotten him drunk for the first time in his life, and they'd tried to catch a possum with their bare hands. Jase showed us the scar on his hand that I'd always thought bore a striking resemblance to sharp teeth marks.

Clutch and I talked about the time the three of us ran through Chow Town and, by some miracle, managed not to become dinner for five thousand or so zeds.

The service lasted for hours, and we took snack breaks. Everyone was there except for the scouts on duty, but Tyler had instituted one-hour rotations to ensure everyone had a chance to say good-bye while remaining on full alert for herds and the *Lady Amore*.

We cried and we laughed as we celebrated Tack's life. When everyone had finished, Griz turned to Deb. She was the only one who had known Tack well and hadn't spoken yet. "Would you like to say anything?" he asked softly.

She looked across the faces and then touched Tack's casket. "I'm carrying his baby."

A lengthy pause followed. There was nothing that could be said after that. Finally, eight volunteers slid the weighted casket onto a makeshift ramp of two-by-fours. "Lord, grant Tack peace," Griz said before shoving the casket off.

We all watched from the edge of the deck as the casket splashed into the water. It floated for only a second before it descended into the darkness. Bubbles came to the surface, the final glimpse we had of Tack, aka Ted Nugent, a Corporal in the United States National Guard.

I looked up at the zeds surrounding the *Aurora*. There were only a few dozen, having been drawn in by the dark smoke. A few tried to walk through the water and were carried away by the current. Most had a basic sense of preservation and simply stood on the bridge over the river, swaying from side to side as they watched. The herds weren't here yet. Kurt's last scouting run put them out several days. The closest herd had stopped at a large river town, buying us time. If we didn't clear the zeds now watching the camp, they'd surely draw the attention of a herd.

But that wasn't our biggest problem.

The *Lady Amore* sat in the water about a mile south of us, an ominous reminder that we had her beloved captain locked up below decks. The riverboat hadn't shown any aggression since the attack. It simply waited, likely for its missing captain.

"All right," Tyler said. "We've got a lot of cleanup to do. Unless you've volunteered for a cleanup job, everyone stays in barge Number One until the zeds move on. Got it?"

People complained and dragged their feet as they headed back toward the barges.

"We're not doing this for fun," Tyler yelled out. "We're doing this to save lives."

His words cooled down the grumbling a bit, but people still weren't thrilled about being cooped up in a dusty, steel barge.

The *Aurora* was in rough shape. The deck of the boat, with its heavily shellacked wood, was charred in several places. Only one flare had burned through the deck and into the equipment room, which accounted for most of the smoke we'd come across yesterday.

The deck had been repaired, but barge Four, which had taken the brunt of the damage, was a different story. A flare had landed on hay bales, which had lit a fire. Our livestock had been decimated. No animals survived. Most of the animals had died from smoke inhalation, and the cooks were working non-stop to save what meat they could.

Still, we'd been counting on eggs for our breakfasts. Several cattle and hogs had been pregnant, and all of them died in the fire. Finding livestock after the outbreak was tough. It had taken us over six months to pull together the thirty head and several dozen chickens. To replenish our stock would take a miracle. It would take a bigger miracle to hunt and fish enough meat until we could rebuild our livestock.

At least no one had died from the black fumes, although Clutch and I had both suffered from killer headaches all night. We'd gone through a pot of coffee this morning, and it had only taken the edge off our throbbing headaches.

I pulled myself to my feet. "Want to go bug Jase with me before we join the cleanup crews?" I asked Clutch.

He gave a crooked grin. "Hell, yes."

I wheeled him toward the galley, giving him a twirl when we reached the door. He pulled himself up on his crutches, and we headed inside and went below decks. When we reached the equipment room, Clutch called out before he walked through the door. "Hey, Jase, coming in."

Jase waved at us, without taking his rifle off his prisoners. "Hey guys!" He was currently on guard watch over the three prisoners from the *Lady Amore*. The temporary brig was in the towboat's equipment room and was in no way set up to hold prisoners. It wasn't the ideal location, but we figured it would be more difficult to escape than from any barge near civvies. Rather than bars, the prisoners were all handcuffed to chains that had been wrapped around thick pipes. It had a medieval feel to it, but we had to make do with what we had.

Clutch stepped unsteadily down the few steps, using his crutches and upper body strength for support. Since his back injury, his upper body was stronger than it'd ever been to make up for the lack of strength in his legs. He'd also lost weight, making the contrast in muscles all the more obvious. I liked the look of his biceps. His tattoos wrapped around his arms in a sensual way. But his legs were too thin from lack of use, and I worried about how long it would take for him to rebuild muscle.

Jase stood and offered the box he'd been sitting on to Clutch. "How'd the rest of the funeral go?" he asked.

"It was nice," Clutch said as he took a seat.

"Griz did a really good job. The stories were great," I added. We'd worked alongside Tack for several months. When I'd heard the stories from the other residents, I'd realized just how many lives the man who'd rarely spoken had touched. He had truly been an example of actions speaking louder than words. I hated that one more good person had been unfairly stolen from the world.

I turned to Sorenson, who sat on the floor, his wrists cuffed in front of him. His two men sat next to him, one on each side. Their chains were long enough to allow some mobility so that they could reach the single bucket that served as their toilet.

They all watched us. Sorenson with a blank look, the man to his right glowered with disdain, and the man to his left simply looked exhausted. My jaw tightened, and I crossed my arms over my chest. "You killed a good man. A man who would never hurt an innocent."

Sorenson blinked a couple times, but his gaze didn't connect with mine. It was distant, dull. "I lost my daughter yesterday."

"There's no one left alive who hasn't lost someone they love," I said.

Sorenson's gaze sharpened as his brows furrowed. "When I left Nikki with the *Aurora,* she was alive and vibrant. When I watched those two men bring her back," he eyed Jase, "She-she was gone."

"It was an accident," Jase said. "I'm sure Tack would've told you that."

"I am sorry about your man. When I saw what had happened to Nikki, I couldn't bear it."

"And so you killed an innocent man," Clutch said, anger dripping from each word.

Sorenson gulped, frowned, lowered his head, and then shook his head. "It doesn't matter now. I can't bring him back any more than I can bring my little Nikki back."

"It does matter," I said. "Nikki slipped and fell. It was an accident."

"She's telling the truth," Clutch added.

"What happened to your daughter sucks, but it was an accident. What *you* did was murder," Jase said.

Sorenson scowled. "Is there even such a thing as murder anymore? We kill those who used to be family and friends every day, just because they get sick. Who are we to judge what constitutes murder and what doesn't?"

I shook my head. "Tack wasn't a zed. He was a young man who'd done nothing except help return your daughter's body to you."

Sorenson climbed to his feet and backed up several steps. "She was everything to me. Everything I'd done, taking passengers onto the riverboat, all of that was for her. She was the only reason I helped anyone." He picked up the now-lax chain and held it in his hands. He looked up. As long seconds passed, his distant gaze narrowed with intent. "I have nothing without her. Nothing!"

In a sudden rush, he wrapped the chain around his neck and sprinted forward.

I lunged to stop him, but wasn't fast enough. When the chain was pulled tight, Sorenson was yanked back, and he collapsed onto the floor.

"Captain! No!" His men each moved to kneel by him. One pulled the chain from around Sorenson's neck while the other watched as the man on the floor convulsed. I took a single step closer but didn't get within reaching distance of the prisoners. Sorenson's eyes were wide as he fought for breath that wouldn't come. His body shuddered on the floor. After a minute or two, his body became still and his hands fell.

"Is he—?" I asked, afraid to voice the word aloud.

"He's dead," one of his men said without looking up.

"His windpipe was crushed," Clutch said quietly at my side. "There was nothing anyone could do."

I stared at the now-slack chain and then at Jase and Clutch. By their wide eyes, they were as shocked as I was. I swallowed. "Shit."

We were going to have a war on our hands.

"Cash? You around here somewhere?" Clutch's voice cut through the fog.

"Over here," I answered.

"Where's here?"

"At the stern," I said.

I could hear footsteps, then a dark shape morphed into Clutch. He took a seat on the deck and set his weapon down next to him. He'd swapped his wheelchair and crutches for a cane yesterday. The swelling on his spine had finally subsided enough that he had decent control over his legs again. He couldn't jog, but at least he could put one foot in front of another. I'd been terrified that he'd never reach this point, which would've killed his spirit.

"There's not much I can do in this fog," I said. "I can't see five feet in front of me. I feel like I'm just sitting on my ass instead of being on duty."

"At least if we can't see them, then the zeds can't see us. Besides, we can hear better than they can." He handed me a thermos.

"Thanks." I took a sip of the steaming tea and burned my tongue. I winced and screwed the cap back on.

Since Clutch had dropped off his wheelchair with Doc, his mood had improved a hundred-fold. While I still believed he suffered from depression—and he clearly suffered from PTSD—it was nice to see him not staring off blankly into the unknown quite as often.

"This fog could save us," he said. "The zeds may move on since they can't see us."

Until the zeds left, there wasn't much we could do besides quietly get the Aurora back into shape. It was too foggy to go ashore or even down the river on any scouting runs. We'd used up a ton of fuel putting out fires and making repairs. The herds would be passing through any day now, so we couldn't go in search of any livestock. Thank God we still had the grain, though the lack of complete protein this winter would be hard.

"Hopefully we don't have to worry about the Lady Amore any time soon," I said. Immediately after Sorenson's death, Tyler had organized a truce with Sorenson's men. He'd offered them full pardons in exchange for no more attacks. He'd even offered another chance at the trade agreement, which they'd quickly accepted. However, many of us weren't nearly as confident as Tyler was that they wouldn't seek revenge or try to steal from us again. The riverboat had left minutes after we'd returned Sorenson's body back along with his two men, and the boat hadn't returned.

"I still think we should've gone in and hit them hard. They know they're outgunned and they wouldn't try something stupid again," Clutch said. "It all depends on Sorenson's replacement. They could be smart and know the value of working together, or they could be idiots. We'll have to stay on our toes until we know. It's too bad Sorenson killed himself. He was easy to figure out. He was a straight shooter, except that he let his heart get in the way. Whoever replaces him could be more of a challenge."

I nodded and then smiled. "At least we have his speedboat now. I'm looking forward to going for a ride." Tyler had given Sorenson's men one of our deck boats in a "trade" for their speedboat. He wasn't about to let them leave with our .30 cal again.

A light breeze blew through, and I shivered. My clothes were damp from the fog and offered little warmth. I held the thermos against me. "I need to start wearing a jacket."

"Here," Clutch said as he wrapped an arm around me.

I leaned into him, savoring his warmth and the closeness. We sat and watched as the sun burned through the fog. A low haze sat just above the water, but I could see the land over it.

"Look." I pointed to the riverbank. "The zeds have cleared out on the east side. You're right. They're leaving."

Clutch twisted his neck to take in the landscape. "Yeah, but they're still on the bridge and on the west side."

"Hopefully just one more day of us laying low and they'll leave like the others."

"Hey guys," Wes said through a yawn as he approached.

"Mornin'," I said, climbing to my feet.

Wes took a seat on the deck behind the rail where I'd been sitting. The boat was angled in the water in a way that allowed us to watch the bridge and see land from every direction without being seen by the zeds. "Man, I'd rather still be asleep."

"That's all everyone does anymore," Clutch grumbled. He used his cane to push himself to his feet and looked at me. "Feel up to some sparring?"

"You bet." I turned to Wes. "Don't have too much fun."

He scowled, and I headed off with Clutch.

Clutch had a point. Once the critical repairs had been made to the Aurora, there was little left that could be done quietly. It didn't take more than a couple days of relative safety for laziness to set in. Hell, if I didn't have Clutch's persistence at having me spar with him and Jase's contagious energy, I'd be heading back to bed right now out of boredom.

As we walked across the deck, I watched Clutch's legs as his stride nearly matched mine. "You're healing really fast now. I can already tell a huge difference from yesterday."

"Doc said that healing would happen in bursts. All I can tell you is that it can't happen soon enough. I'm sick and tired of being a cripple."

I rolled my eyes, because Clutch may be a lot of things, but he was no cripple. He proved it during our sparring session in the towboat's engine room. Even though his legs were weak, his upper body strength more than made up for it. I almost got in a high kick once, but he'd taken me down with him. I imagined it would always be that way: Clutch the master, me the student. He had too many more years of experience.

After a day of doing little, as the sun began to set, we headed to the commons area in Barge Two to meet Jase for dinner. The area was already filled with people. I stepped into the line while Clutch spoke with Tyler. I looked for Jase, but he wasn't at our usual spot on the floor yet.

I grabbed a tray, and Vicki, Fox's best cook, slid

chunks of white meat onto my tray.

My eyes narrowed. "Fish?"

Vicki nodded. "They finished the nets this morning and fished off the south end of the island so the zeds wouldn't see. Fish for everyone tonight!"

I grinned. "Awesome."

Normally, the fishermen caught no more than a dozen fish using fishing poles. They figured the zeds rotting in the shallow waters scared them off. The livestock from the fire was being dehydrated for the winter, so we'd been living on canned meat, beans, and grain. As I worked my way through line, I noticed everyone was in a better mood. The fresh fish, the zeds starting to disappear, and the repairs to the Aurora relatively complete gave everyone hope.

I sat down on the floor and dug into the fish.

Jase sat down a minute later with his food. "What kind of fish is this?" he asked.

I shrugged.

"It's catfish," Frost said as he and Benji ate a few feet away from us. Diesel had his head buried in a bowl of dog kibble.

The fish suddenly went down like a rock. "Catfish?"

"Wait," Jase said. "Isn't catfish a bottom feeder?"

"Yes, why?" Frost said.

Jase's eyes widened as he looked at me. "Didn't anyone tell the cooks?"

"Tell them what?" Frost asked.

I dropped my fork. "Bottom feeders are tainted from

feeding on zeds. Sorenson said they'd lost a crew member to bad catfish."

Frost grabbed Benji's hand that held a fork full of white meat, but the boy had already cleaned much of his plate.

"Maybe these fish are okay," Jase said to the pair before giving me an oh-shit look.

We jumped to our feet at the same time.

"Where are you going?" Clutch asked as Jase and I ran past.

"To warn Vicki," Jase said.

I took the stairs two at a time to reach the kitchen faster. Halfway up the second flight, a stomach cramp doubled me over.

I felt Jase's hand on my cheek. "Cash, are you okay?"

I clenched my teeth as I grabbed my stomach. "Bad fish."

CHAPTER XVIII

The day was a horrifying blur of dry heaves, chills, high fever, and bizarre dreams. All around me, people moaned and cried. They lay in bed, the slightest move causing them to retch.

Jase and Clutch took turns at my bedside. They helped me and the others without rest. Since neither had eaten the catfish, they hadn't gotten sick. They were in the minority. Thirty-three residents had eaten the tainted meat. They kept all of us in barge Number One and had opened the bay door to let in fresh air.

By night, I finally regained some semblance of myself. I felt like I had one foot solidly in the grave, but I'd lived to see another day. Others weren't so fortunate. I'd seen Mrs. Corrington covered with a sheet and carried out. What a miserable way to die.

Clutch squeezed water from a rag into my mouth.

The other healthy people, like Jase and him, constantly moved about, checking on the sick. Meanwhile, others filled in as scouts above deck to keep watch for the herds or any signs of trouble from the riverboat. Deb was the only person who hadn't eaten the fish that Tyler wouldn't allow to help. Her pregnancy had come to represent the hope of Camp Fox. Tyler didn't want her around anything that could pose a risk to her pregnancy. After Tyler's adamant orders, she'd reluctantly stayed in the crew quarters on the towboat.

I rolled my head to see Jase still with Benji, who was up to eating crackers already. That kid had a cast iron stomach. If only I'd remembered to tell the cooks what Sorenson had said about the fish, then none of this would've happened. I felt so stupid, but was too weak to stay angry at myself. No one had remembered to tell the cooks. Jase blamed himself, and I'd seen Tyler's face when he walked through. He blamed himself the hardest of all.

Twenty-four hours later, I could finally hold down small amounts of water, and Clutch was relentless at sponging drops into my mouth every couple minutes.

The poor man looked utterly exhausted, with dark circles and bags under his bloodshot eyes. I licked my chapped lips. Sometimes, a pessimistic devil sitting in my soul would make me wonder if all of this running and work was in vain, that all we were doing was delaying our inevitable doom.

I lifted my fingers, though they weighed a ton, and

touched his hand that was holding the rag. "You should get some rest."

"I'm fine," he said rather tersely, making it clear he wasn't going anywhere.

"Can't believe I ate catfish," I said on an exhale.

He shook his head and dribbled more water into my mouth. "You couldn't have known."

I closed my eyes.

"You're going to get better," he said. "You don't give up. That's why I brought you with me to my farm at the outbreak. I knew you were a fighter."

When I reopened my eyes, I saw Clutch watching me, taking his eyes off me only to soak the rag again. Sitting there, his broad shoulders cast a shadow over me. His quiet strength showed through his gaze. When he looked at me, I always knew I'd be safe.

I grinned, weakly. "You're an oak."

His confused expression tightened into a look of consternation. He pressed a hand against my forehead, and I treasured his touch.

I needed him to know the truth. "I love you," I said, but my words slurred. My eyes grew heavy.

"What's wrong?" Jase asked, sounding distant.

"Get Doc. She's got a fever."

"Mary Corrington had a fever right before—"

"I know. Get Doc *now*."

GREED

THE FIFTH DEADLY SIN

CHAPTER XIX

Lucky for me, I was both younger and healthier than Mrs. Corrington. My fever of one-hundred-four broke the following morning, but it took me an entire day before I could stand without getting a nosebleed, and another day after that before I could handle a flight of stairs without getting light-headed.

I woke up early in the morning, quietly climbed out of my bunk, and crept past Clutch. He'd been able to move down to the crew quarters once he had no longer needed his wheelchair. Being careful not to wake him, I grabbed my boots, clothes, and gear and headed up to the deck. I stopped in the shower room to finish dressing. Since the catfish incident, I'd lost a few pounds and had to buckle my belt a full notch tighter. Not that I'd had any fat on me before, which meant my body had burned through muscle, and, Christ, I was feeling it.

That was just one of the little things that had changed after the outbreak: there simply weren't overweight people anymore. Without proper food and medical care, things like food poisoning or dysentery were even more dangerous than ever. Everyone who'd gotten sick from the catfish had a gaunt look. At least everyone who'd survived. We'd lost four to bad catfish.

I took a seat on a bench and inhaled deeply the smell of fresh coffee as it finished brewing. Moments later, I poured myself a small cup and headed outside. I walked slowly so I wouldn't slip on the deck still slick with frost. The coffee steamed, and my breath made small puffs in the morning air.

I slurped the coffee, holding the warm cup in both hands, and tried not to shiver. The warm sun was rising, and its light glistened on the wet deck. I headed to my usual spot that overlooked the open river. A light morning fog blanketed the water. An eagle soared above the tree line. It was beautiful, serene. And the best part? No zeds. They'd finally moved off while I'd been sick.

I really thought I wasn't going to make it. I'd never felt so miserable in my life. Thankfully, I didn't remember much of the past couple days. Only Clutch's gentle touch and him never leaving my side.

I set down my coffee and started my yoga routine. Sometime during Downward Facing Dog, Clutch bent over and looked at me.

"Mornin'," I said with a smile.

He stood back up. "I called your name three times."

"You did? Oh. I guess I was in my zone."

"It's good to see you getting back into a routine," he said.

As I changed position, I saw him looking out over the river.

"I feel fine, other than the fact that my body thinks it was in bed for a month instead of days. I can promise you that I'd rather starve than eat catfish ever again."

"You had me worried there for a while," Clutch said.

I stopped and turned to find him watching me with a strange intensity, his eyes full of emotion. Then he quickly turned away. Disappointment panged in my heart. "Well, moving around in the fresh air and stretching has helped as much as anything. It's nice that the zeds left so I can do yoga outside rather than in the dark, stuffy boat."

"We still have to be careful. Yesterday, Jase saw a couple small groups still in the area. There." He pointed. "And there."

I squinted and couldn't find them, but my vision had never been as good as Jase's. "As long as they're not fixated on the *Aurora*, they shouldn't draw any interest of the herds." I stood up and grabbed my coffee.

He took in a deep breath. "Kurt returned from another Jet Ski trip to the north. He thinks the first herd will pass through this area by tomorrow. Tyler wants all boats and a couple Humvees out today to search the area for anything we can possibly grab before the herds arrive. Fuel, food, chickens, anything. We don't know how long we'll have to lay low once they arrive."

I clapped my hands. "I'm ready."

He smirked. "Feeling cooped up?"

"Feeling *very* cooped up."

"Sounds like exactly how I felt being stuck in that wheelchair."

"You were a bit grumpy," I teased.

"Speaking of grumpy, how about you go wake up Jase so we can head out."

I lowered my arms from my stretch. "Want to play rock-paper-scissors for the honor?" By honor, I meant who had to deal with getting a pillow—or worse—thrown at them by a teenager whose one last pleasure he'd held onto from pre-outbreak days was sleeping in late whenever he could. Today was supposed to be one of those days.

Clutch shook his head. "Hell, no. I had to wake him last time. It's your turn."

I scrunched my nose at him and then tossed him my empty cup. "Fine. Wish me luck."

As I trudged toward to the galley, I could hear Clutch chuckling.

When I reached Jase's bed, I grabbed the spear lying next to his cot and took a step back. With four feet of space between us, I gently poked at the pile of blankets with the flat end of the spear. A grumble emerged, and the blankets wiggled. "Go away."

"Wakey, wakey, eggs and bakey," I said softly in a sing-song voice.

I grinned when he grumbled louder and rolled over, taking the blankets with him and leaving his back exposed. "Lemme sleep."

Too easy, I thought to myself. I ran the dull wood bottom of the spear up his spine, and the insanely ticklish teenager jerked up.

He whipped around and went to throw his pillow but held onto it, which was a good thing. It wouldn't have taken much to land me flat on my ass.

I laughed.

He scowled and hugged his pillow. "Not cool."

I laughed. "Rise and shine. We've got a run this morning."

I think he might have actually growled at me, but he did kick his blankets away and sat up. I handed him his spear and he plucked it back.

"I'll see you in the galley," I said, still chuckling, and left him rubbing his eyes.

An hour later, after Jase had time to ingest caffeine and some breakfast, he was back to his usual self. The boats had already left on their scouting runs. We were one of the two teams assigned to make a land run. Jase, Clutch, and I took one Humvee, while Griz and two other scouts took another.

Our Humvee was the easiest to spot out of all Camp Fox's Humvees. It had a coyote head painted on the hood and front doors, thanks to Jase. He'd dubbed our team the Charlie Coyotes and the name had stuck. Luckily, only one zed still lingered around our vehicles this morning. Jase easily dispatched it, and we headed out for a day of adventure.

The plan was that we'd drive east and Griz's team would drive west, since it was far too risky to drive north. We'd check out rural gas stations and farms and meet at the boat ramp in four hours. If any of us succeeded in finding fuel, the six of us would bring a fuel truck with a Humvee lead vehicle back to the places to fill up. Getting the diesel to the ramp was the easy part. Getting the diesel onto the *Aurora* would be a bit more complicated since we had to move it in fifty-five-gallon drums on pontoons.

Jase took his favorite position manning the .30 cal on the back of Charlie team's Humvee. He had a warm leather coat on to fight the late fall chill in the air. I drove. Clutch was by far a better driver, but since his legs were still healing, he rode shotgun.

I drove slowly, even though we had a lot of ground to cover. We had to be careful to avoid the river towns that dotted the river. The good thing with towns every ten miles or so was that zeds tended to group together and hover around populated areas rather than in the fields and around farms. The bad thing was that we couldn't find a single rural gas station clear of zeds. "I guess the fuel will have to wait until after the migration," I said.

"Let's see what else we can find," Clutch said. "Try

that gravel road."

We searched farms for the next three hours, finding only a few dozen cans of food, which we tossed into duffle bags. As I turned off a gravel road and onto the winding river highway, I hit the brakes. "Shit. You see that?"

"They're not biters," Jase called out from above. "What's the plan?"

A group of ragged survivors were standing near a vehicle in the intersection. The van hadn't been there when we'd passed through the area a few hours earlier. Steam pouring out of the open hood gave hint at why it was there now.

It was a group of mostly women, and they looked in rough shape. A man stood by the hood. A hunched-back elderly woman stood in the middle of the road, staring off into the distance. A teenaged girl stood near a little girl playing hopscotch. A pale woman lay against the van. They had crowbars and spears, but no one seemed to be carrying rifles or pistols. Still, it could have been a setup.

Another man walked around from the other side of the van, saw us, and started waving wildly.

Jase kneeled to our eye level. "They've seen us."

"Hold on," Clutch said before he picked up the radio. "Charlie calling Alpha."

A couple seconds later, Griz's voice came on the radio. *"Alpha here. Report."*

"We have a sit rep. Charlie has come across at least

six survivors ten clicks straight east of the RP."

"Are they raiders?"

"Negative. Just civvies. Looks like their vehicle broke down."

"Alpha is heading your way. Do you want to wait for backup?"

Clutch looked at me, Jase, and then back at the group. "Negative. We're going to check it out."

"Roger. We're on our way."

He hung up the radio. "Here's the plan. We'll pull up close. If anything throws off a red flag, we're out of there. We all stay with the Humvee. Only if we're absolutely sure they're safe, Cash and I will get out. Jase, you stay behind the .30 no matter what happens. You never, ever leave the .30, got it?"

"Yes," we both replied at the same time. We'd been together for enough months that we understood one another.

Clutch checked his rifle one more time. "Okay, Cash, take us in nice and slow."

As we approached, the man quit waving and stood between us and the woman propped against the van. The little girl stopped playing her game and jogged over to stand by the man. The other man, the one who'd been standing behind the hood, grabbed the teenaged girl and pulled her to him.

Clutch rolled his window down.

I pulled up alongside the van and stopped, but left the engine running.

The craggy old woman limped over to us first. Her hands were gnarled with arthritis that looked like it'd taken over much of her body. How she'd survived this long was beyond me.

"I need you all to stay at least four feet back," Clutch ordered.

Her gray eyebrows rose, but then she stopped and smiled warmly. "Oh, I'm not any danger to you, I promise. I knew God would answer my prayers. He's never let me down yet. He's really outdone himself this time, sending one of those big Army trucks and strapping, able-bodied young men," she said, her voice crackly. She noticed me and touched her chest. "Oh my. Young men and woman. Well, God bless you for coming. Your timing couldn't have been better. You see, we've gotten ourselves into a pickle." She motioned her people. "We've been on the road for days, only stopping for gas and rest breaks, and I'm afraid we overworked our poor van. Praise the lord for sending you to our rescue."

"Save your prayers, lady. God didn't send us," Clutch said with a grumble. "It was just luck we happened to be passing through."

She chuckled. "Well, you can call it what you like. It's all the same. You're here now. I can't tell you how relieved we are to see you. I'm Margaret Fielding, but you can call me Maggie."

Clutch nodded at her group. "Nice to meet you, Maggie. I'm Sergeant Seibert from Camp Fox. Where are you from and where are you headed?"

"Well, you get straight to business, don't you, young man? I can understand, with all those infected folks out there. We were staying at the Wisconsin Dells, but things went downhill. We were planning to keep driving until we found another group of God-fearing folks like yourselves. In fact, you're the first people we've seen since we've left. I must admit, when our van broke down, my faith was tested. But as soon as I saw your truck, I knew everything would turn out fine."

Clutch didn't speak for a long moment while he scowled at Maggie while she continued chattering away. When he finally spoke, he pointed to the pale woman sitting against the van, and interrupted. "What's wrong with her? Is she bit?"

Maggie turned. "Thank goodness, no. When we ran, Brenda cut herself on some old tin, and I'm afraid it's become infected and she's caught herself a bit of a fever. We've cleaned it as much as we could, but we don't have any bandages or medicine. I don't suppose you happen to have anything that can help her?"

After a moment, he took in a deep breath and grabbed our first aid kit. "I'll take a look."

"Oh, thank you," Maggie said, clasping her hands together.

I narrowed my eyes suspiciously at him, but he didn't make eye contact. He propped his rifle on his seat, unsnapped his holster, swung open the door, and stepped out with his cane in one hand and the kit in the other.

I put the Humvee in Park, grabbed my rifle and stepped out. I only took a few steps and propped my rifle on the hood so that I could get behind the wheel quickly while also keeping a clear view of Clutch and the refugees. I threw a quick glance at Jase to see he had the .30 cal leveled on the refugees.

As Maggie hobbled next to Clutch, she commented, "You don't get around much better than I do."

I smirked when Clutch grunted in response. He didn't like his faults being pointed out. I could only imagine how much it annoyed him to be compared to a little old lady.

As Clutch approached the injured woman on the ground, he nodded toward the man near her who had the young girl pressed tight against his leg. "I need you to take a step back."

The man didn't move. "She's my wife."

"It's all right, Don," Maggie said. "He's here to help Brenda. Let him help."

Keeping a watchful eye on Clutch, Don took a tentative step back, holding who I assumed to be his daughter against him. Clutch went down on his knees before the woman. "I need to take a look. I'm going to have to lift your shirt."

The woman—Brenda—was pale and sweaty. She was clearly in pain, every movement stiff. With a small nod, she let her hand fall to the side, giving Clutch access. Her husband stood tensely to the side, his eyes darting from Clutch to Maggie and back to Clutch.

Clutch gingerly lifted her stained shirt and then quickly dropped it, covering his nose. He winced at me before turning back to the woman.

He pulled out a small syringe from the first aid kit. "This will help with the pain," he said just before injecting it into her thigh. After a moment, her features relaxed and she lay there limply. She looked almost peaceful.

He closed up the kit and pushed himself to his feet, using his cane for support, and faced Don. "I gave her some morphine for the pain."

"Thank you," Don replied.

As Clutch stepped away from the woman, Don's eyes widened. He shoved his girl behind him and he grabbed Clutch's arm. "What are you doing? You have to help her! She needs antibiotics!"

Clutch looked down at the hand on his arm and then pulled away. "There's nothing I can do for your wife. And back the fuck off."

The man glared for a moment before lowering his head. "But Brenda...she needs help."

"I can't help her," Clutch said more softly this time. "It's too late. She has gangrene, and it's too far advanced for anything to help. The morphine will ease her pain for a bit, but there's nothing else I can do. Any supplies we use would be wasted."

"Wha-what?" Don asked, seemingly unable to process Clutch's words.

Clutch said it more bluntly than I would've, but he'd never been one for beating around the bush. He gave me a hooded, tight look as he set the first aid kit back in the Humvee.

The man's bottom lip quivered. The girl hugging him looked up and whimpered. "What's he saying, Daddy?"

"There must be something that you can do," Maggie said, wringing her hands. "It was only a cut."

"Wait!" The man called out. "Maggie's right. There's got to be something you can do. You can't leave her like this!"

His daughter started to cry. Big tears rolled down her cheeks as she clung to his leg.

Clutch grabbed his rifle and shook his head. "There isn't." He turned away. "I'm sorry."

The second Humvee pulled up from the other side, and Griz jumped out.

"They're with us," I told Maggie, though it should've been obvious.

"You can't leave us like this. You've got to help my wife, damn it!" Don cried out.

Clutch ignored Don's pleas and curses, instead focusing on Maggie. "Tell me about what happened at the Dells."

She frowned at the change in subject, watched Don and Brenda for another moment, and finally nodded and inhaled deeply. "I don't understand where they're coming from, but there's so many of them, and they seem to be coming from everywhere. We were so well hidden, we were so far from any town, but they still found us. We lost so many." Her gaze fell and she shook her head slowly from side to side. "Too many."

Griz came walking over, holding his rifle.

Maggie lifted her head, looked at Griz funny, and then broke out into a wide smile. "My, I haven't seen a black man in months, and such a fine-looking young man you are."

Griz raised a brow in amusement.

Clutch spoke first. "How far behind you are the herds, Maggie?"

"Oh," she stammered and fidgeted. "They're not far. Not far at all."

"Exactly how far is that?"

Maggie didn't answer.

Griz motioned to Clutch. They walked around to my side of the Humvee.

"We don't have time for this," Griz said. "Did you find any diesel?"

Clutch shook his head. "Nothing we could get to. You?"

Griz scowled. "It's going to get hard fast without any power on the boat."

"You heard the lady," Clutch said. "We can't keep looking. The herds are nearly here."

"I know," Griz said. "We need to be below decks and silent by the time they show up. It's getting risky staying out here."

Clutch frowned. "What do we do about these folks?

We have the room, but we don't have the food. Not since the livestock was destroyed. We can't leave them here. They'd get slaughtered."

Griz pointed to the west. "There's a farm a few miles straight west of here. We found a black SUV in the driveway that runs. You can't miss it. I can take one of them to go get it. That'll help them get some distance between them and the herds."

"Until they run out of gas," Clutch said. "If we don't take them in, they're zed bait."

Griz gave him a knowing look. "They could distract the herds from us."

My heart pounded. Even though my brain was telling me the same thing, my gut was screaming at me at how wrong this felt.

Clutch gave me a look and his features softened. "We take them with us. It's only six—well, five—extra mouths to feed."

Griz looked relieved but then frowned as he looked at the injured woman. "She bit?"

Clutch gave a slow shake of his head. "Gangrene."

Griz grimaced. "We came across a vet clinic this morning. We have the supplies on board to give her peace. It's the only thing we can offer her."

"I'm not sure her husband and daughter would agree to that," I chimed in. Without modern medicine, people often died horrible, painful deaths from infections. Euthanasia was one of the few things we could offer the doomed, and vet clinics offered plenty of the drug guaranteed to bring painless death.

"Then we give them the choice. They can either stay here with her or come with us," Griz said. "Gangrene isn't contagious, but we can't risk bringing any new sources of infection onto the *Aurora* in case she's got more than a case of gangrene. Not with how many are just recovering now."

Clutch stiffened and snapped around as Don hurried toward the Humvee.

"Stand back," he ordered Don.

Don kept walking toward us. "I heard what you said. You can't leave Brenda behind. You don't know her. She's strong. She'll recover."

"She has gangrene," Clutch said simply, as though that answered everything.

"She may also have contracted a secondary infection that could potentially spread. We can't risk it," Griz added. "Now, please step back."

The man's features morphed from desperation to anger. "So you're going to leave her here to die all alone in the middle of the road? What kind of sick monsters are you?" His fists clenched and he rushed Griz and Clutch.

Griz hit him in the stomach with the butt of his rifle just as Don reached them. "Get on the ground! Face down and arms stretched out!"

His daughter screamed, and the teenager rushed over and grabbed her to keep her from running to Don.

"Keep her quiet," Clutch snapped.

"Don't hurt my little girl!" Don cried out.

"Please," Maggie limped forward. "Let's all take a moment and talk. Don's just worried about Brenda. He doesn't mean anything by it. We've all been through a lot lately."

"She's going to be dead soon," Clutch said. "It sucks, but wishing for something different isn't going to keep her alive."

"She's not coming along," Griz said. "If you want to stay with her, you can."

Maggie wagged a finger. "We're good people. We work hard and wouldn't wish harm on anything. Please don't leave us here."

"The choice is yours," Griz replied.

Don guffawed. "That's no choice. I won't abandon my wife."

"Uh, guys?" I said, motioning to the tree line. "We need to make a decision and fast."

Several deer ran out from the trees and across the road. Deer were skittish creatures, tending to hide unless spooked by a predator, and, there was one predator in abundance around here.

Zeds.

CHAPTER XX

stepped around the Humvee. Don climbed to his feet. No one spoke while we waited to see how big a herd we had to deal with.

Finally, a single shape emerged. We all let out a collective sigh.

Maggie's hand fluttered over her heart. "Oh, thank God."

The huge, mangy wolf — or large dog; it was too hard to tell from this distance — stepped out from the shadows, eyed us as though deciding which would be easier prey, and then slowly turned to follow the deer. The deer had made a large U-turn around us and stopped only a couple hundred meters from where we stood. Wolves had multiplied since the outbreak. Large dogs were now joining their ranks, and these new packs feared neither humans nor zeds. Both became their dinner.

Once the wolf was a safe distance away and no others appeared, I let out the breath I'd been holding.

"Anyone in the mood for some venison for dinner?" Jase said from atop the Humvee.

I glanced at Clutch, and his lips curved upward.

We each raised our rifles. "I'll take the big one on the left."

"I've got mine," Clutch said.

"Three," Jase said quietly. "Two."

We fired at the exact same instant.

Two deer fell, and I grinned, thinking of the first real meal I'd have since the catfish ordeal.

"Let's hurry up and grab them in case the noise draws attention," Griz said.

"They're all yours," I said, still smiling. While I enjoyed eating fresh meat, I hated seeing it when it was still literally doe-eyed and bushy-tailed.

Griz smirked. "I'll haul them back, but I think I've got the better end of the deal. You guys will have to haul this group if they're coming." He gestured toward the small band of stranded newcomers. Then, his features hardened. "I'm sorry, but we can't take in a casualty. It's against protocol. You know that, right?"

I swallowed, glancing back at the woman who was starting to groan again, holding her stomach. The morphine was wearing off too quickly. Don was already growing tense again as he watched us.

"Get us a kit," Clutch said tightly. "I'll handle it from

here."

Griz gave the slightest nod before heading around the back of his Humvee.

"What kit are you talking about?" Don asked. "What are you doing?"

Clutch didn't say anything, and Don turned to me. "What are you talking about doing to my wife?"

My lips tightened and I gulped before forcing the words out. "We can't heal her, but we can take away her pain." I liked to think I could bring peace for someone I loved if they were doomed, but I wasn't so sure I had the strength for it. Seeing the agony on Don's face, I was thankful it wasn't my decision to make.

Griz walked back with a vial and syringe and held it out for Clutch. "We'll meet you at the RP in twenty."

Clutch took it. "See you there."

Griz gave the group a troubled look before heading toward the van.

"What is that?" Don asked, backing up step by step.

"It's an anesthetic," Clutch said and held up the vial. "It's called pentobarbital. Just one shot, and your wife will fall asleep. She won't hurt anymore."

"But she'll wake up, right?" Don asked, his voice rising in octaves. "Right?"

"She won't wake," Maggie said. "That's the same stuff they use to put down dogs for good. They want to kill Brenda." She hobbled over to stand between Brenda and Clutch. She crossed her arms over her chest. "I won't stand for it. I will not allow you to commit murder."

I stood near Clutch, my rifle ready, in case they tried to attack. A quick glance at Jase showed that he had us covered.

Clutch held the vial out to Don. "It's the humane way. Your wife won't feel any pain. She has no chance of recovery and can't come with us. I'm offering her a peaceful way out."

Maggie scowled. "Who are you to decide who lives and who dies? Only God can do that."

"Zeds do a pretty good job at it, too," I snapped.

"Don," Brenda said, her voice barely above a whisper.

He moved like she'd shouted. He dropped down and clasped her hand. His young daughter, being held by the teen, took a couple steps closer.

"You-you must keep Alana safe," Brenda said.

He brushed hair from her face. "I won't leave you. Not like this."

She winced and fisted her shirt. "You have to go."

His body shook as he held back sobs. "No." He turned back to us. "You have to let me take her. We've been married eight years. We've never been apart."

"You're only prolonging her suffering," Clutch said. "She has a day left at most. If you want to stay with her today, we can take one of you to get a vehicle. It's your call."

"You can't give us ultimatums," Maggie countered. "We've done nothing wrong. You're taking all of us with us."

"No," I said, exasperated.

"Take us!" the other man stepped forward, pulling the teenaged girl alongside.

"Hugh," Maggie chided. "We don't leave anyone behind. We stay together. Always."

"If that's how you feel," Clutch said with far more calm than I could manage. "There's a vehicle not far from here. We'll take one of you to go get it."

"You can't leave us!" Maggie cried out.

Clutch pointed to the man named Hugh. "You. I'll take you to get the vehicle." He turned and started walking back to the Humvee, and I stayed at his side. I glanced up to see Jase still standing at the .30, alert and ready.

Hugh ran forward, dragging his daughter with him.

"She stays. Just one of you can come along for the SUV," Clutch said.

The man looked none too pleased, not that I could blame him. He didn't know that Clutch was only protecting us by minimizing risk inside the Humvee.

The man glanced back at his group and then pulled his daughter with him. "I don't need the SUV. Just take us with you," he pleaded.

"Hugh!" Maggie shouted. "You can't be serious!"

"They don't get it," Hugh continued. "We can't stay out here. The herds are coming. I don't plan on staying out here." Then he thrust his daughter at Clutch. "She's all yours to do with as you please. Just take us with you!"

The girl's eyes grew wide and she shoved against her father. "Dad!"

Uncaring, he pushed her again at Clutch. "She's pure! Hali will do anything you want. That should cover our room and board. Don't leave us behind."

Clutch grimaced at the daughter and then glared at the father. "Christ. Do I look like a pedophile to you? You'd sell your own fucking daughter for safety?"

The man winced but then stood firm. "I just want us to be safe. Take us with you. If you leave us behind, the zeds will get us for sure. You don't understand. We barely made it this far."

"Stop it!" Brenda cried out, her pale face twisted in pain. "All of you stop it!"

Everyone turned toward the dying woman. She turned to Don. "You must save Alana."

Don shook his head. "I won't leave you. I can't."

"Save Alana," she said with more strength than I thought she'd be able to muster for how close to death she looked.

He sobbed and then buried his head in her neck. "I love you so much."

"I love you." She looked up to their daughter. "Come here, my little garden sprite."

The young girl ran over to her mother with tears in her eyes. "Mommy!" Though she couldn't have been older than five, she still clearly understood the severity of the situation.

Brenda released her husband and hugged her daughter. Don held both of them in his arms. They cried and kept repeating their love for one another. After several long minutes, Don held out his hand and motioned for the syringe.

Clutch handed it to him.

"Don't do this, Don," Maggie said. "It's murder. Don't let these devils lead you astray."

"Maggie, I need you to look after Alana right now," he said.

When she didn't move, Don yelled, "Do it, Maggie!"

The old woman glowered, but she pulled the crying girl against her.

"You should go through the vein," Clutch said. "It will go faster."

Don's hand shook like crazy. His wife watched him and tried to smile but it was all too quickly drowned by pain.

He'd nearly pierced the skin and then tore away. "I-I can't." He grasped his hair with one hand while the other hand holding the syringe fell limply at his side.

"Okay." Clutch stepped forward.

"No. I'll do it," I said, stepping around him. Clutch had enough nightmares already. He didn't need another one. To make it easier, I'd already figured I'd imagine her as a zed and that I wasn't taking a life. At least, I figured if I did it quickly enough I wouldn't think myself out of it.

He grabbed my wrist, gave me a sharp look, and then

tugged me back. He cupped my cheek and shook his head. "I won't let you do this."

He turned, bent down, and took the syringe from Don. Clutch didn't waste any time. He grabbed the woman's arm and rubbed his thumb over the vein at her elbow.

As the needle pierced the skin, her eyes widened, and she tried to yank away. "No! I—"

Her eyes fell closed, and she never finished whatever it was she'd had to say.

"Brenda!" Don cried out and pulled her to him.

Clutch fell back on his heels, and I pulled him up and away from the pair. He stared at the syringe, gave it a look of disgust, and then threw it across the road.

We stood around, silently waiting as Don held his wife's body. I held onto Clutch, knowing it had nearly killed him to do what he'd just done.

Maggie glared at us. "You committed murder. You are a sinner and will burn in hell."

I glared right back. "We're *all* sinners, lady. And if you don't back off, we're leaving your ass on this road."

Did euthanasia feel wrong? Hell yeah, but the alternative was so much worse. That woman was going to die anyway. We simply took away a few hours of suffering. At least that's what I told myself. I didn't try to think of the few hours of life we also took.

A strange sound in the distance yanked my attention back. "What was that?"

Clutch, shook his head and looked around for the

source. "Sounded almost like a jet."

I looked to the sky but saw no trails. The ground...I bent down and put my hand on the pavement. The slightest sensation of a vibration. The noise, while distant, was becoming audible. There was no breeze today, yet the leaves began to tremble on the trees.

"No! They're here!" Hali yelled.

Hugh twisted around and reached out to me. "We have to go!"

"I've got a bad feeling about this, guys. I think we'd better boogie," Jase called out.

"It's too late," Maggie said, standing stoic, looking toward the north. "They're already here."

My brain finally deciphered the sound of a gigantic swarm of mosquitoes into a hundred thousand moaning zeds. Cold filtered through my blood, and my breath came short. My legs nearly gave out.

The first herd had arrived.

CHAPTER XXI

Clutch yanked open the back gate of the Humvee and motioned everyone in. "Move it!"

"But our things," Noah said.

"We're going to be packed like sardines the way it is," I said.

"No time!" Jase yelled. "Move it, people!"

Hali didn't even hesitate as she shook free from her father and bolted for the Humvee. Jase grabbed her arm and pulled her on board. No one else had yet moved.

I rolled my eyes. "We'll come back and get it later," I said. "Now, get inside or else you're getting left behind."

My words finally got through to Hugh, who then caught up with his daughter.

Maggie was still praying over Brenda's body, and Don stayed by his wife's side. "I can't leave her here like this."

I ran over and squeezed Don's shoulder. "We have to go."

He wiped his eyes and picked up his wife's body. He laid her inside the minivan and closed the door.

"Come on, Cash," Clutch said, climbing into the front seat of the Humvee.

I ran around the front of the vehicle and climbed behind the wheel. Don pushed Maggie in and then climbed in, holding his daughter in his arms.

"Daddy! Mommy's still back there!" the little girl cried.

Jase pounded on the roof. "Everyone's on board. Go!"

I stepped on the gas, and we lurched forward. Don's kid was crying for her mother, and everyone was talking over one another. Clutch pointed to a lone zed on the roadside, and I swerved around it. Shots from Jase's .30 cal echoed non-stop through the Humvee. Alana cried out and covered her ears.

I glanced in the side mirror and saw zeds pour out from the woods. I would've said, "Holy shit," except my jaw was clenched too tightly to speak. I sucked in air.

Clutch said something, but I couldn't hear.

"Would you guys please shut the hell up!" I yelled, rubbing a hand down my legs one at a time before gripping the wheel just as tightly again. "I'm trying to get us out of here."

They quit trying to talk above the .30 cal.

"Drive," Clutch said. "I'll keep an eye out for the herds."

I had the gas pedal floored and didn't let up until we reached the bridge. Every muscle was tight. I slowed down only to pull off the road, and then drove down the steep slope of the east bank and stopped hard just before the ramp. Griz and his team already had their payload loaded on the pontoon and were waiting for us.

Griz's smile faded when he saw us. "What happened?"

"The herds are here," Jase said as he jumped down.

"Shit."

Everyone tumbled out of the Humvee and toward the pontoon in a chaotic mess.

"Where are we going?" Maggie asked.

"Get us out of here," Clutch ordered Griz.

"You don't have to tell me twice." Griz jumped behind the wheel and started up the boat's engine, and we scrambled for seats on the pontoon. Little Alana clung to her father. Jase had managed to grab one of the duffels filled with canned food on his way out off the back of the truck. Maggie limped on last, nearly tripping over one of the deer carcasses as she found a seat.

I helped shove the pontoon away from the boat ramp, and Griz throttled the engine full forward to get us into the river. But we weren't safe yet. We still had to get to the *Aurora* without attracting the attention of any zeds. It only took one zed to home in on us, and others would notice. Griz ran the engine full-out to close the short distance to the barge.

"Is *that* where you're going?" Hugh asked.

"Yes," I said, and then turned to Jase, who was busy searching the surrounding area. "Any sign of them yet?"

"Not yet," he said without looking at me.

"Hopefully we were able to get in enough distance between us and them that they won't find us," I said as we pulled up to the dock.

Fortunately, the small dock for the *Aurora* was on the south side of the towboat to better hide us from predators. "We should be safe now, as long as they don't smell or hear anything," Griz said.

"Not if they see anyone on the deck," Clutch countered and squeezed Jase's shoulder. "Hustle up and warn Tyler."

"You got it." Jase leapt off the boat and climbed up the rope ladder.

Wes waved from the deck above and lowered the platform.

Tyler's voice came over the loudspeaker. "Code Red. Code Red."

He didn't say anything else, and he didn't need to. Everyone had been prepped for this moment since we'd arrived at the *Aurora*.

Maggie, Don, and Alana were sent up on the platform since none of them were in any condition to climb the ladder. We slid the deer onto the platform with them, not wanting to let the meat go to waste. I scrambled up the ladder as quickly as possible, with Clutch coming up right behind me.

Griz was already moving the newcomers toward the barge.

Jase waited for us. "Everyone's headed below decks. I think we're set."

We crossed the deck as quickly as Clutch could walk and entered the galley. The room was packed, but no one said a word. Not even prayers were voiced aloud. People huddled together, many holding hands. I squeezed my way through to look out a window.

Time dragged by more slowly than my Corporate Finance class my junior year at college. I focused at not making eye contact with anyone except Clutch or Jase. We played cards, but even that grew dull. I eventually settled on daydreaming about flying the Cub over fields free of monsters.

As the sun set, dark shapes filled in the landscape, making the land look like an eerie ocean of ripples. By morning we'd know if they'd zeroed in on the *Aurora*. Until then, all we could do was wait.

And so we waited.

We were able to move above deck freely after the sun had set, though silence was critical. With over fifty people crammed on board the Aurora, whispers and the sounds of shuffling feet were the only breaks in silence. We'd all prepared for this moment, we'd practiced it over and over. But the five newcomers were foreign to us and our plans, adding a huge element of risk to our plans. Maggie and Don avoided us, glaring at me whenever our paths crossed. I wanted to glare right back. Instead, I tried to take the higher road and simply ignore their unthankful asses. Hali, still pissed at her father for offering her up, had isolated herself in a corner of barge One.

Even though Clutch thought it too risky, Tyler allowed Vicki to cook the deer for dinner since the wind was out of the north and the bay door was closed over the barge. Everyone ate in silence. The tension was higher than it had ever been.

Through the hull, the sound of the moaning herd made nails on a chalkboard almost melodic. As I lay in my bunk and stared at the springs and mattress of Jase's bunk above, I prayed that they would have moved on before morning. I tried to sleep but settled for staring at the ceiling.

I headed up to the galley sometime before dawn. I didn't bother checking my watch. Upstairs, Jase was kneeling on a bench, his hands clasped and his head down. Clutch sat at a table nearby, cleaning his rifle. I took a seat next to him and watched Jase. I hadn't seen him pray since we'd buried his dog, and it worried me to see his façade gone.

Clutch glanced up before turning back to his work.

"He's been at it all night," he said softly, also looking worried.

Seeing Jase's ragged appearance, it was clear the stress was getting to him. His hair was mussed and dark circles underlined his eyes. I headed over to the countertop and poured a cup of coffee, and then set it down next to him.

He looked up, startled. "Oh. Thanks."

I sat and wrapped an arm around him. After a moment, his tension gave way and he leaned into my embrace. "It'll be okay," I murmured. "We're safe here."

He nodded slightly before reaching for the cup and taking a drink. Holding the cup, he watched me for a moment, and then placed his forehead against mine. "I hope we're safe." When he pulled away, he put the cup down and traced the fresh scar on my face and he winced. "That's still a doozy."

"Do you think it'll hurt my chances at getting a date?" I asked.

He gave me the smallest hint of a smile before he looked back out the window and wrapped his hand around the cross he wore.

I sat there, with my arm around Jase, while he prayed. Clutch eventually joined my side. We watched the night sky turn from black to dark gray with hints of gold in the east. As light gave definition to the shapes and trees, any hope I had plummeted.

I could make out the zeds filling the bridge and road to either side. Not a blade of grass remained. They'd filled in the entire area to the west, disappearing into the trees, and were still spreading out. Our Humvee at the boat ramp was being rocked as zeds fought to get whatever they smelled inside.

A leaf in the wind caught my eye, and I noticed it was blowing north, which meant the wind had switched direction sometime during the night. My eyes widened, and I grabbed Clutch's arm. "The wind."

He looked. After a moment, he nodded tightly and then pointed at the zeds. "I think we just entered hell."

"No," Jase said.

Clutch wrapped an arm around him, then another around me. I clung to him but could find no comfort in the embrace. My stomach clenched with terror. A tear rolled down my scarred cheek as I held onto Jase and Clutch and stared outside. One hundred thousand pairs of eyes were focused on Camp Fox, and they looked ravenous.

GLUTTONY

THE SIXTH DEADLY SIN

CHAPTER XXII

Two very long weeks later

"It seems like the ones in back and on the edges are moving on," Tyler said as he walked down the steps and into the crew quarters. "Only problem is that there's still at least fifty thousand or more out there sticking around."

"Figured that was the case," Clutch said while he did another lunge. "I have to hand it to them. Once they zero in on something, the bastards are persistent."

"It really sucks being at the bottom of the food chain," I said, matching Clutch's lunge.

Eight of us were going through daily exercises. We'd just finished several sets of push-ups and sit-ups. We tried to keep it interesting by having each scout come up with an exercise, but after a while, even that got old. There were only so many variations to a push-up.

But the herds outside just kept coming. Even though it seemed like tens, if not hundreds, of thousands continued on their journey, enough stayed behind, seemingly too hungry to continue for the slight chance for prey. Two herds currently surrounded the *Aurora* from the bridge and both sides of the river. They couldn't reach us, not through the water, but at least a hundred tried — or were pushed — each day, and at a couple dozen of those made it onto the island. I'd quit looking out the window on the fourth day. It made it easier to pretend that we weren't caught in the middle of the world's worst shit storm.

"C'mon. Just one."

I turned to see Griz with his open hand stretched out.

Jase shook his head. "No way. Go find your own."

"Why? You have a whole case of them."

"I risked my life for them." He held up a half-eaten candy bar. "These Snickers are my one and only joy in life so you'll have to pry it from my cold, dead hands."

"Don't tempt me."

When I turned back to Tyler, he had moved closer to Clutch.

"We need to ration harder. Vicki says we need to move to a diet of at least ninety percent grain," Tyler said in a low voice. "Without fresh meat and vegetables, we're going through our food stores four times as fast as we calculated."

Clutch's lips thinned. "People aren't going to like to hear it."

I winced. They weren't going to like to hear that news at all, but we had no other option. Heading to the mainland was out of the question. Worse, enough zeds had fallen in the water and scared the fish away, not that I could yet take a bite of fish without gagging. More and more zeds were washing ashore and now lingered on our island.

As long as the zeds were out there, we were stuck in what could easily become our tomb. "We need to get the zeds away from the *Aurora*," I said my thoughts aloud.

Tyler chuckled. "Want me to get on the bullhorn and order the zeds to leave?"

Clutch was watching me all too closely.

"I'll do it," I said after a moment. "I'll lead the herds away from the river barge."

"Cash..." Clutch warned.

I gave him a pleading look. I knew the odds. I'd been an actuary before the outbreak, but I figured the odds out on the river couldn't be any worse than staying on the boat. Staying on the boat was only delaying the odds. "If we don't do something, who knows how long the herds will stay. If we wait until we are out of food, it'll be too late. You know how long it took to build up the reserves we're burning through. The winter may kill the zeds, but without our livestock, it's going to kill us, too. I'll take a boat and run the Pied Piper plan."

"We've only tried that with tiny herds, a few dozen zeds at most," Tyler said.

"The plan hasn't failed yet," I countered.

Clutch watched me for a moment—it was a calculating gaze—and then turned to Tyler. "I'll lead the mission. I want Cash and Jase to stay on the *Aurora.*"

"Like hell," I said. "Camp Fox needs you more than it needs me."

Clutch grabbed my arms. "What happens when you come up against a lock or a dam?"

"I'll figure out something. What would you do?"

He shook his head. "Leading them away is one thing. How are you going to turn around and get past them and back to the boat?"

"I'll bring plenty of supplies and hide out until the coast is clear."

His brows rose and his lips tightened.

"The idea could work," Tyler mused. "But it's dangerous. It's awfully dangerous."

"What other option do we have?" I asked. "If I fail, you still have time to figure out other options."

"If *we* fail," Clutch added. "We're a team."

I tried not to look relieved, but the idea of not having Clutch along terrified me. I smiled and gave a single nod.

"I'm in," Jase said, and I looked around, realizing we'd drawn the attention of everyone in the room.

Clutch glared at Jase. "Now, hold on a minute."

"This is a Charlie team mission, right?" Jase asked. "I'm a Coyote. You're not going to make me sit this one out. We're in this together."

Part of me wanted to scream at Jase to stay behind

where it was safer, and I suspected it was exactly how Clutch felt about both Jase and me. But Jase was right. We were in it together.

Clutch sighed. "We don't even know if the plan could work on this scale."

"What could work?" Manny asked as he entered the quarters.

"We're forming a small team to lead the zeds away," Tyler said.

"I'm in if the kid ponies up a candy bar from his stash," Griz said.

"Heck, no," Jase said, and the two poked jabs at each other.

"This is not something to take lightly," Tyler said harshly. "I won't order anyone on this mission. It will be volunteers only."

"Well, son of a bitch. You guys can't go without me," Wes said. "I'm the best mechanic around here. With a herd that big, you can't afford to break down."

Tyler held up his hands. "Whoa. That's enough. Five of you will fill a boat and have eyes in every direction. Clutch, you're senior officer so you have lead. Now, we all need to take time to think through this. If anyone backs out, I won't hold it against you. Everyone, take sixty. We'll meet in the galley in an hour to work out the mission details."

Clutch nodded. His features were still set hard, so I rubbed his back. He sighed and looked from Jase to me. "I know trying to talk you two out of this is a waste of breath, so either of you want to spar instead?"

I grinned. Whenever he was stressed, he needed action. Of course, I was the same way. "You bet."

"Yeah, why not," Jase said after stretching his neck from side to side.

I grabbed my thermos from my bunk. By the time I returned, Jase and Clutch were already chatting about setting up the boat.

"Mind if I join you guys?" Griz asked as he caught up.

I motioned him along. "Only if you're ready for an ass whooping."

Griz chuckled. "Oh, it's not me who's —"

Shouting erupted from above deck and I snapped around. "What's going on?"

We ran up the stairs and to the galley. Outside, Maggie was screaming at the herds. "Go back to hell, you devils! You'll never get to us! Never!"

"Shit," Griz muttered. "Our first cuckoo has flown."

No!

I reached for my pistol, but the others bolted outside, and I followed.

Griz reached her first. He yanked her back and covered her mouth. "I should've figured out you'd be the first to go nuts."

She mumbled something but he kept her mouth covered.

I scowled at Maggie, keeping my hand on my holster. "Fucking nut. You trying to get us all killed?"

Lucky for her, Griz still had his hand over her mouth because if I heard what she seemed to be saying, I might have changed my mind and shot her right then and there.

Clutch and Jase helped drag Maggie back inside.

Before I reentered the galley, I looked out at the herds to see every pair of eyes watching us. The wind whipped at my face.

"Well, that does it," Clutch muttered. "This mission just became critical."

"Yeah," Jase said. "The tough part is that it sounds more like Mission: Impossible."

I swallowed and turned away from the ocean of zeds.

No, it wasn't just an impossible mission.

It was a suicide mission.

CHAPTER XXIII

All Camp Fox squeezed into the galley the morning we left. It was standing room only in a room made to seat twenty comfortably. Weighted down with food and gear, I followed Jase as he weaved through the crowd. I noticed Hali squeezed his hand briefly as he walked by, and I smiled.

Maggie, who now had a scout assigned to her twenty-four/seven, eyed us with her usual glare of disdain and suspicion. Thanks to her, zeds had proof that we were still here, and their numbers were growing. Her little tirade guaranteed Camp Fox would remain under siege until we starved. I craved to put a bullet between her eyes.

Even so, she wasn't the hardest to deal with in the room this morning. Everyone else watched with hope. They put all of their faith in us to save them. If our gamble failed, everyone would starve to death because of us. Those were the ones I really avoided eye contact with, as their gazes followed us silently through the room.

On the island, we chose a deck boat instead of the speedboat since we could load a lot more extra fuel on it. The .30 cal was useless, and we only had to be faster than the herds. The speedboat also couldn't hold nearly the amount of supplies a larger boat could. And boy, did we fill that boat. After all, we had to be ready to live on the river for up to a couple weeks.

Tyler and several scouts had speared the zeds on the land by the *Aurora* so we could load and get out. Even then, hands reached up from below the surface at us. A vision that would no doubt haunt my dreams for the rest of my life.

While I strapped down our food and gear, Clutch and Jase tied the leftover deer organs to the sides of the boat. Vicki had saved the deer organs "for a rainy day." The sweet, iron smell of deer innards was strong and unpleasant but not as bad as I would have expected. Vicki had devised a cellar system on barge Four that helped preserve food, and surprisingly the deer had only the slightest smell of decay.

I pulled out one more item from my backpack, unfolded it, and strung it up on the flagpole at the back of the boat. The wind was just strong enough today that the American flag flapped proudly in the breeze. I sat back and admired it. "I think we're all set."

Griz tossed me a life vest.

I looked at it and scowled. "It's going to be harder to shoot with one on."

He shrugged his vest on like it was body armor. "We play it safe. No unnecessary risks."

"As soon as you know the herds are moving on, get back here as soon as you are safely able," Tyler said.

I gave him a salute. "Aye, aye, captain."

His eyes narrowed with the hint of a smile before he turned and climbed up to the deck.

Kurt had spent much of his childhood boating and water skiing, so he was our pilot. He was also the only one who hadn't volunteered. Tyler had assigned him to the Pied Piper team since we needed Kurt's experience with boats.

We had a perfect team for the mission. Jase had eagle eyes, so he sat at the bow along with Griz, who was a master at strategy. Clutch and I, both crack shots, sat across from each other behind Kurt to have our sides covered. Wes, our mechanic, sat near the motor to keep an eye on our six. I also suspected the engine vibration comforted him as he couldn't swim and really disliked water.

"Everyone ready?" Kurt asked.

A chorus of yeses replied.

He backed the boat from the shoddy dock that had been hastily constructed our first days on the towboat. Wes had a long stick to push away any zeds close to the motor. Kurt piloted the boat slowly and smoothly, and I appreciated that his nerves didn't relay through the controls.

Things started to feel *real* when we pulled around the side of the *Aurora* and the herd came into sight. I felt like we were the stars of a sold-out concert. Kurt pulled the boat around, and we moved away from the river barge and toward the zeds.

The boat rocked gently in the river current as Kurt piloted it forward, into the U-shape of zeds on the surrounding land and bridge. The zeds looked like extras in an old-time horror film. Filthy, they were all the same shade of brown-gray. Most were emaciated. Many sported fresh boils and old injuries.

"Don't get too close," Clutch warned. "We don't want zeds to start dropping in on us."

It was like someone had wound up the zeds. What had been slow shuffling before became a frenzied dance as we approached. When we approached the center of the U-shape, their moans reached a crescendo.

"That's close enough," Griz said, sounding nervous.

I didn't blame him. I was practically frozen, and it wasn't just because of the cold air. My hands trembled, and I gripped my rifle to me like it was my lifeline.

Kurt cranked on the CD player, and the previous owner's choice in music — Motor Boat City's "Pontoon" — blasted through the speakers. If the smells of deer organs and visuals of uninfected humans weren't enough to snag their attention, they couldn't ignore the noise. We hadn't had time to rig up louder speakers, but the stock speakers seemed to be doing the trick. Dozens of zeds tumbled into the water, pushed in by zeds behind them.

"Think we got their attention?" Kurt asked.

"Yeah," Clutch said. "We don't want them to keep falling in the water."

Kurt brought the boat closer to the western bank and turned the boat toward the south and cut the engine, letting the current do the work. As we drifted past the *Aurora*, the deck was empty and I could see no signs of inhabitants, though I knew everyone was watching from the galley.

Back on the towboat, we had debated for less than two minutes whether to lead the herd south or north. Leading them north seemed counterproductive. Leading them south meant that we had to lead them past the *Aurora*, but it was the direction they seemed naturally inclined to head.

The plan was to lead the herds far enough away—at least twenty miles—from Camp Fox and then hide in a cove until they had all continued in their migration. We had no map of the river, so it would be all guesswork, and we were counting on Kurt's experience to help navigate the river. We'd loaded up enough fuel to run for at least three days straight, but the plan was that we wouldn't need much.

We used paddles to keep the boat close—but not too close—to the western bank, so that the zeds from the east would work their way across the bridge to the west.

Without the engine, the music blared even louder. Wes had rigged up a second battery so we wouldn't drain the primary one.

Jase stood up and shaded his eyes. "It looks like they're all following. Even the ones way in back are moving. Cash, you were right. They're just like lemmings."

I leaned back on the white vinyl seat. *Thank God.* We'd been counting on the zeds sticking with their herd mentality. That once a critical mass moved, the rest would tag happily along. Zeds weren't very bright, to say the least, and it wasn't too hard to outthink them. Except what they lacked in brains, they made up for in numbers and ferocity.

Unfortunately, no matter how simple and fool-proof the plan was, when you're surrounded by a hundred thousand zeds, it just might not matter. Predictability can fly out the window. Griz and Jase relied on prayer to make the difference. The rest of us were relying on luck.

The current carried us faster than the herd walked so Kurt started the engine every thirty minutes or so to bring us back to the herd. It was a slow process. Two hours later, we were barely a mile south of the *Aurora*. At this rate, it would take us an entire day to get the herd out of the sight of the towboat and its barges, and a few days to get the herd back on their migratory path.

When the sun reached high in the sky, Kurt lifted the boat's sunshade. The music dampened the constant moaning. Wes had long since fallen asleep, his snores filtering through the wide-brimmed straw hat covering his face. If I closed my eyes and ignored the smells, the boat ride was almost tranquil, and I could pretend it was just another day on the water, in a world where the outbreak had never happened. There was a sense of safety in the boat, knowing that the zeds couldn't swim out to us. When I opened my eyes to a landscape filled with zeds, with zeds reaching out to us as they stumbled along the riverbank, reality soured my daydream.

For lunch, we each had a can of tuna and some flatbread. We didn't carry water. Instead, we carried carbon-filter straws made for camping, and drank directly from the river. Every time I leaned over the side of the boat to drink, I had a near panic attack from imagining hands reaching up and grabbing me. Fortunately, the only thing out of the ordinary was a faded beer can floating by.

We chatted, but small talk was hard ever since the outbreak. Without sports, politics, and celebrities, there were only so many things a person could talk about that didn't dredge up the topic of death or zeds.

I stared off at the treetops that lined the Mississippi. "This river has a lot of levees and little islands," I mused.

"It shouldn't be too hard to find a good hiding place once they get back on their migration," Griz said.

"The landscape can change within just a few miles.

Let's hope there will be cover available when we need it," Kurt cautioned.

"Hey guys. There's a lock and dam coming up. We'll be there in a few hours at this rate," Jase said as he pulled out his binoculars.

"How's the lock look?" Clutch said from behind Kurt.

"Nuh-uh," Jase said. "It looks like it's blocked by a big boat."

"Damn. I was hoping we'd get lucky and the lock would be clear," Kurt said.

"Can we get through another way?" Clutch asked.

"Doubt it," Kurt said.

Clutch muttered a string of profanity, his words echoed by complaints and curses by every single one of us. When she wasn't being a bitch, Nikki had told us how various crews had opened all the locks after the outbreak to travel the river easier. We'd been counting on having a wide open path. With a lock blocked, we quite literally had nowhere to go except back.

I looked at my watch and tried to mentally calculate our location. We'd been on the river for nine hours. I bit my lip to keep it from trembling. "We can't be more than four or five miles from the *Aurora*."

"That's not far enough," Griz said and turned to Clutch. "What's the plan, Sarge?"

Goosebumps flitted across my skin. Once we reached the lock, we'd be fucked. The zeds would close us in. We couldn't turn back without bringing the herds with us to the *Aurora*. There were no islands or outcroppings of trees to lose the zeds in.

Clutch's lips thinned as he looked at the herd and then ahead toward the lock. After a moment, he spoke. "We keep going."

Tension throbbed between my temples as I wracked my brain for ideas, but there were few options in a wide open river. We passed a couple outcroppings of dead trees, which would offer some cover, but we were still dangerously close to the river barge. An hour later, the game changed when we could see which boat was blocking the dock.

The *Lady Amore* was sitting sideways in the lock. It looked like it had tried to shove past the smaller boats and logs jamming up the lock but had gotten itself stuck. Without Sorenson to captain the riverboat, it looked like Sorenson's remaining crew lacked the skill to navigate through the open locks and around dams.

"Oh, hell," Jase said.

Clutch made his way toward the front of the boat where Jase was. "What is it?"

There are zeds all over the lock. It looks like they're dropping down onto the boat."

"What do we do?" Kurt asked.

"Our primary objective is to deter the herd," Clutch said bluntly. "Everything else has to come second." He turned to Kurt. "Will that small grouping of islands and trees over there work to hide us?"

Kurt bit his lip as he thought for a moment. "It

should. It's nice and close to the lock, so as long as we get there without them seeing us, it may work. Why?"

"Because the riverboat is going to draw their attention from us," Clutch replied.

Kurt frowned. "There might be people still on board."

Clutch narrowed his eyes. "The *Aurora* is counting on us."

"He's right," Griz said quietly. "We're not far enough away. If we turn around, we could lead them right back to the *Aurora*. The *Lady Amore* will distract them enough that they'll forget about us and then keep going. It's the only way."

Clutch unsheathed his knife. "Turn off the music, Kurt. Griz, help me cut the meat loose."

As the pair started to cut the cords holding the deer organs onto the sides, Kurt shook his head as he started the engine and turned the boat around. "I don't like this. It's not right."

"And exactly how do you expect us to rescue anyone in that lock?" Clutch asked as a chunk of deer meat plopped into the water.

"It's not right, but tell me what in this godforsaken world is right," I added, frustration bleeding over my compassion.

"They wouldn't have saved us," Wes said from my right. "Besides, we'd all die if we tried to help them."

Kurt remained silent. He piloted the boat against the current, bringing it in between a small island and a group of tall dead trees with their trunks underwater. I peered into the trees on the tiny island. A zed's hollow gaze leveled on me, and I shivered. It walked to the edge of the bank and stopped at the water's edge. It didn't growl or try to come closer. It only watched me inquisitively.

Kurt dropped the anchor before spinning around to face Clutch. "What now?"

"We wait."

And that's exactly what we did.

We had nowhere to go. As long as the herd was still here, we couldn't go north without drawing their attention. The south was blocked by the lock and dam. We had to ride out the herd. An occasional scream blasted through the groans of the herd, and I winced each time. I focused on breathing in the smell of the river water and tried to imagine I was in a different world, one without zeds, but the relentless sounds were an iron maiden to any daydream. I curled up into a ball and covered myself up with a blanket as I watched the zed watching me while everyone on board the *Lady Amore* was eaten alive.

CHAPTER XXIV

'd hid and waited zeds out plenty of times, but this time was the hardest. Kurt was right about one thing. It felt wrong to sit by while people were slaughtered. I racked my brain for solutions, but it came down to the fact that Clutch was also right. There was nothing we could do for the riverboat. We were too late by the time we'd first seen it. Anything we did now would put both our lives and potentially every Camp Fox life at risk. The mission had to come first. The *Lady Amore's* demise was our wild card. It was the only thing available to distract the herds from both us and the *Aurora*.

We waited while the zeds that fell onto the riverboat gorged themselves on its occupants. No one spoke, not even when I could hear someone screaming for help. To better hide our scents, we covered ourselves with blankets, which also helped to ward off the cold. Only our heads peeked out so we could watch for any approaching zeds, but the blankets did little to muffle the sounds.

The zed on the riverbank just stood there and stared, strangely not in a frenzy to reach fresh food. Its gaze seemed more curious than vicious. Still, I would've preferred to kill it, but it would have been a waste of a good arrow since the zed couldn't reach us. Instead, I kept a close watch on it while the sun set.

When sunlight morphed into moonlight, the lone zed remained easy enough to spot. Its jaundiced eyes reflected light in the dark akin to a cat's. Fortunately, unlike cats, zeds' vision sucked at night, making their eyes a giveaway to us, as long as the moon was bright.

Clutch assigned shifts using hand signals, but I don't think anyone slept. The constant moans of the herd cut through any imagined sense of safety. It sounded like a madhouse orchestra, with every instrument out of tune, and every note a screech. For the first time, I could *almost* commiserate with Maggie. I wanted to scream at the zeds to stop. They were driving me mad, but I was sane enough to know it would do no good. Instead, I focused my hate on Maggie, blaming her for our situation—even though I knew she wasn't to blame. If she hadn't gone nuts, someone else would have broken eventually. Still, hating her helped ground me.

Sometime during the night, we huddled together for warmth, rotating as we went on and off night watch. Each of our breaths made a tiny white puff in the night.

It had to be below freezing because frost built on the wispy edges of my hair.

By morning, we were all snuggled together in the center of the boat, except for Clutch who'd taken the final night watch. Kurt copped a quick feel under the blanket, but I pretended I didn't notice. Even though I wanted to kick him in the nuts, there were just some things a woman learned to deal with when outnumbered ten to one by men in the field.

I opened my eyes and found Clutch watching me. I smiled, and he returned one of his all-too-rare smiles before turning back to watch the river. Suddenly warmer, I closed my eyes, making sure his smile stayed imprinted in my memory. There were too many bad memories in my head already. I had to work hard to keep the good ones. I spent the next several minutes dreaming of our cabin and snuggling with Clutch. He gave me that smile before kissing me and pulling me to him.

Unfortunately, Kurt's groping ruined the fantasy. When his fingers crept to my inner thigh, I decided I'd rather be out in the cold than under a blanket with him, and I shimmied out with a grumble. His finger looped around my belt, but I gave a sharp heel to his stomach, and he let go with a grunt. Clutch cut Kurt a hard look before giving me a questioning look.

I replied by focusing my smile completely on him and sitting next to him on the frost-covered seat. Cold wetness seeped through my cargos and into my bones. I shivered, and Clutch wrapped his blanket and a cold arm around me. He was shivering too, and I snuggled into his embrace. I found my breathing found a pace with his, and I placed my hand over his steady heartbeat. He leaned toward me and pulled me possessively closer. Feeling a rare peacefulness, we watched the sun rise over the trees.

Behind us, the zed on the water's edge had disappeared at some point before morning. We'd gotten lucky that the herd had followed us along the western bank of the river. If they'd taken both sides, we were just close enough to the eastern bank that we could've been seen or sniffed out.

I figured we deserved the luck. All too many times, we'd been unlucky, and it had become expected. Statistically, things were bound to go our way once in a while. But when they did, like now, it felt unnatural and worrisome. Not that I was worried enough to not savor our temporary fortune.

Jase and Griz joined us next. Jase grabbed my arm. He had a huge grin on his face as he pointed toward the lock. I looked and my mouth opened. I grabbed Clutch's hand but he was already looking, too.

The herds were moving on!

My heart nearly leapt from my chest and I squeezed Clutch's hand. A line of zeds had begun to head south, and the ones left around the lock were following. It would take them a long time, but their trajectory was clearly the opposite direction of the *Aurora*. I hadn't looked earlier because I was afraid of what I'd see. I grinned like a little girl as I snuggled in between Jase and Clutch and we spent the next several hours watching the exodus in silence.

By lunchtime, I was starving. Clutch had finally given the okay to eat. Last night and this morning, we couldn't risk the smell of food getting out. While we waited out the herds, we crunched as quietly as possible on nuts and some kind of flatbread cracker that Vicki invented. Even after letting each cracker sit in my mouth to get soggy, they still crunched. With every bite, I grimaced, wishing Vicki sent something mushy along, but I was too hungry to go without food, and so I kept crunching away.

It wasn't until nearly six hours later that Griz and Clutch broke the silence.

"Don't hate me for saying this, guys, but I think we ought to check out the riverboat," Griz said with an almost pained expression, like the words hurt to say them.

"Too dangerous," Clutch replied. "I can still see the back of the herd. Too much noise could draw their attention back this way."

"There might be survivors," Kurt said.

"There will definitely be zeds," Clutch countered.

"Just think of how much food and supplies are on that boat," Wes chimed in.

"And how many zeds do you think are on that boat between us and any supplies?" Clutch asked.

RACHEL AUKES

"You're lead on this mission, but what's the harm in just going in near enough to scout it out?" Griz said. "As long as it's stuck in the lock, it could be an emergency food run if it's not too heavily damaged. Besides, we can't head back to the *Aurora* yet, not until the herds are further away."

We all watched Clutch hopefully. While I trusted his judgment—his gut was never wrong—a part of me imagined the *Lady Amore* as the *Titanic* and that we could rescue any survivors who remained. Since the outbreak, nearly everything we did revolved around simply surviving. The chance to save even one person from the zeds brought hope that we could eventually win this war. Even though the realistic part of my brain pointed out the hopeless odds of surviving a zed herd.

Clutch sighed. "All right, but we wait until we are sure the herd can't see, smell, or hear us. So, dig in. We have at least a couple more hours to wait."

And the waiting continued.

Three hours and forty-seven minutes later, Clutch broke the silence. "Okay. We'll go in slow and keep to the east bank. We can't do a thing to draw the herd's attention, got it?"

We all came to full attention. No one smiled because we all knew that going near anything where zeds had been a day earlier was dangerous.

"It's the right thing," Kurt said as he climbed into the pilot's seat.

"Before we go, take five," Clutch said. "We're not

heading into that clusterfuck half-cocked."

After we checked and double-checked our weapons, Kurt started the motor, and then reached back and pulled up the anchor. He kept the motor at idle as he weaved through the trees that had camouflaged us all night. The wind was out of the northwest, so any noise from the boat was carried harmlessly to the southeast.

Once clear of the trees, Kurt cut the engine, and we rode the current toward the lock. We all searched for survivors as well as for zeds. No zeds remained on the ledges, but I could already make out at least a hundred on the top deck of the riverboat. Kurt kept the boat on the eastern edge, so the tall, concrete lock served as a wall between us and the migrating herds. Even though they were now several miles away, we'd all long since learned that one of the secrets to survival was to be overly, obsessively careful. The other secret? Having a shitload of luck.

"Careful not to get caught in the lock," Griz said.

"Trust me, Sarge. I know what I'm doing," Kurt replied.

I'd almost echoed Griz's words. The riverboat blocked the entire opening to the lock, with smaller boats and debris lodged around it. Kurt pulled the boat closer and slowed to a stop.

Any hope I had of finding survivors, or at least access to food and supplies, was quickly drowned. The riverboat was *filled* with zeds. Through the windows, we could see zeds standing shoulder-to-shoulder.

"We're not going in there," I said quietly. "Any food or supplies is a lost cause."

Clutch grimaced. "The riverboat is a no-go. Let's head back to the levee."

Kurt started to turn the boat around. Something thumped against the hull.

Griz leaned over the edge and then staggered back. "The water is full of zeds! They're floating just below the surface. Get out of here!"

Kurt throttled forward, but the motor ground and then died.

"They're getting tangled in the props!" Wes cried out.

"Grab the oars," Clutch ordered. "No gunfire."

We all lunged for oars. I dipped mine in the water to paddle and hit something solid. I pulled back and tried again. This time, something heavy nearly pulled the oar right out of my hands. I gasped and put all my weight into yanking the oar out of the water, and a zed still holding the oar reached for the boat. Every nerve was on edge as I twirled the oar free. I swung and cracked the zed's skull, and it fell back below the surface.

My brow furrowed with confusion. Zeds couldn't swim, but these hadn't sunk yet. Then it hit me, and my heart thumped harder. These zeds were climbing on one another to get to us. "Jesus, how many fell off the lock?" Goosebumps covered my skin even as adrenaline sent a surge of heat through me.

Everyone was too busy dealing with zeds clawing at

the boat to say anything except curse the zeds. We were making no headway, and more hands were grabbing onto the sides. We wouldn't live much longer if we didn't get out of there soon.

Frantic, I swapped the oar for a machete and hacked away any arms that managed to grab onto the boat as the guys continued to paddle. Every foot we made north was a battle against both the current and the relentless zeds. Even in the cold temperature, sweat ran down my face. My arms ached and I struggled to keep a firm grip on my machete.

After fifty feet or so, fewer zeds reached up the sides, and the boat moved more smoothly through the water. I swapped my machete for the oar and paddled upriver. With all of us rowing, it took only a few minutes to close the rest of the distance to the trees where we'd hidden last night. Once there, Kurt threw out the anchor and then collapsed on his seat.

"Jase," Clutch said. "Do you see any zeds heading this way?"

Jase pulled out his binoculars and looked to the south, and then to the other directions. "No. It looks like the coast is clear."

"Good," Griz said on a sigh. "Wes, get that engine fixed so we can get the hell out of here."

"You don't need to tell me twice," the older man said. He stepped out onto the deck and opened up the engine cover. Water splashed. "Agh! Help!"

I jumped over the seat and grabbed Wes by his belt.

His arms were thrashing around while he reached out. A zed was trying to pull him into the water and had his head underwater already. Wes lost his balance, and it became a tug-o'-war as I tried to pull him back. His yells were garbled by the water. Others joined in, and we all tumbled onto our backs on the deck, yanking Wes back with us.

I jumped up to make sure we hadn't brought the zed with us. "Holy shit, that was close."

"Ah, hell," Clutch muttered.

I turned around and saw the blood. "No."

Wes lay on his back, looking up with utter terror in his eyes. He was holding his neck, where crimson covered much of his shirt. He coughed and blood leaked from his mouth. I fell on my knees. His lips moved, but no sound came out. With blood loss came lethargy. His features relaxed. He looked around to each of us, though his eyes couldn't seem to focus. He reached up and touched my face.

He went to say something, but coughed and wheezed as he bled out on the deck. I knelt by him, my hand on his chest, offering what little comfort I could. There was nothing we could do. We waited until he lost consciousness, and tears caused my vision to blur, and I could do nothing but watch. I didn't wipe the tears away. Griz and Jase recited a prayer. Even Clutch joined in, the first I'd ever heard him pray. I couldn't find my voice.

His breathing became shallow until I could no longer

feel it under my palm. His heartbeat disappeared seconds later. "He's gone," I said bluntly and without emotion, even though inside I seethed at the unfairness of it all. Jase tugged me back toward the main area of the boat, and Clutch stepped in. He swung his machete and then rolled Wes off the back of the deck. In the water, the zed tore into him like a piranha. My tears stopped, blocked by numbness, and I sat there, watching my friend be eaten by something that used to be human.

LUST

THE SEVENTH DEADLY SIN

CHAPTER XXV

We made it back to the *Aurora* just before sunset. Once we'd killed and disentangled the zed in the prop blades, the motor had started. It had run rough — some things were probably bent up inside — but it'd gotten us back to Camp Fox.

We'd returned to receive five minutes of fanfare, but then it was right back to work. Our problems were nowhere over yet. We found ourselves in an endless debate about what to do next. The herds had moved on, but a couple hundred zeds had stayed behind, watching us from the bridge that crossed the river. That number wasn't even counting the hundred dead or nearly dead scattered on the ground that had been trampled by the herd. Those would be easier to clean up but still posed some risk to walking to the vehicles.

The next morning, Griz led another Pied Piper boat,

but the zeds we'd dubbed the "bridge bastards" remained undeterred. Over the next few days, we tried scouting runs to the north using the river since we couldn't get to our vehicles. Traveling under the bridge was dangerous, and we had to speed under each time. With no land vehicles parked to the north, we were limited in our search radius, and the riverfront had been picked clean by other boats on the river like the *Lady Amore*.

We'd brought a pontoon full of scouts to the nearest river town to empty the grocery store, but bandits had beaten us to it. They must've been right behind the herds because every place we went showed signs of being recently picked clean. Every vehicle we came to that looked like it could run was missing its keys. Likely, the only reason bandits hadn't come across our vehicles yet was the bridge bastards.

Without access to vehicles, we were running on borrowed time. We couldn't get the fuel or food we needed without making land runs. Relocating from the *Aurora* was deemed not an option. Tyler had queried the residents, and no one had wanted to leave. They felt safe there and were tired of looking over their shoulders.

So another option presented itself, one the residents embraced and the scouts balked at. Of course, none of the residents planned to get their hands dirty. They planned on watching us from the safety of the barge.

"We'll have to burn them at sunset, so the smoke

won't be seen," Griz said before leaning back in his chair.

"It's risky," Clutch added. "We could set the whole countryside on fire."

Tyler shook his head. "Not if we control it. We'll set up boundaries."

Clutch's eyes narrowed. "Tell me. Exactly how are we going to dig up ground and not get torn to shreds?"

"Fine," Tyler replied. "We'll skip the boundaries. So what if the fire spreads? It won't reach the *Aurora*."

My eyes widened. "It could spread over miles and miles. We could destroy everything around here. Any food, animals, everything."

"Why does it matter?" Kurt asked. "There's no one left out there but bandits, anyway. A fire would destroy a lot of the rotting corpses and clean up the countryside."

Clutch clenched his fist but stopped himself before he hit the table. "Sure, the fire will take out all the zeds in this area, but it could also destroy any plants and wildlife. We'd be dealing with the same issue we have now, and that's no food."

"We still have the grain," Tyler said. "Deer are faster than zeds and can run. We'll hunt them later."

"It sounds too dangerous," I said.

"It's safer than using up our ammo on them," Kurt said.

"I disagree. We can't waste our gasoline," I said. "I think it's safer to shoot them, but I'd prefer to find a third option."

"Gas will start going bad before we use it all up," Kurt replied.

Griz stood and poured himself a cup of tea. "The people need to be free from zeds. Being watched by zeds day in and day out wears on morale. They need the break. Even if it's only for a few months."

"And when spring comes?" Clutch countered.

"We have no idea if they'll even come back," Kurt said, rolling his eyes and sighing in exasperation. "Every month, they rot away more and more. They can't last much longer before their bodies completely fall apart."

"We've been saying that for months now," Clutch said.

Jase finally spoke up. "You're not thinking straight. You're all too desperate to live without zeds. Going after a couple hundred zeds is really dangerous. We've never done anything like this before. We'd have to burn them to the point that they can't physically move, or else they could still survive."

"Then we need to make sure they are thoroughly burned because not going after them is even more dangerous," Tyler said. "Every day we can't get to our vehicles and start land searches, the bandits clear out more of the surrounding area."

"Well, if this boat is the new permanent location for Camp Fox, we need to make sure it's not going to float away in the spring floods. The residents need to kick up their efforts at turning this from a temporary base to a home," Griz said. "We'll have to focus completely on building up our food reserves. Vicki thought we should build a greenhouse so we can grow vegetables this winter."

The banter was giving me a headache, and I rubbed my eyes. We could argue these points until the zeds died off, even if it was twenty years from now. None of these discussions would keep us from starving. "Even if we find enough food to last the winter, we'll need acres and acres of land in the spring to feed everyone. How can we do that if everyone stays on the *Aurora*? Who's going to farm it?"

"Staying on the *Aurora* long term is too risky," Clutch said. "Griz makes a good point about the spring floods. How the hell are we going to anchor the towboat and barges here so we don't get washed away or broken apart in the spring?"

Tyler came to his feet and leaned forward on the table. "We've been rehashing this for too long. This isn't a democracy, and the matter is no longer up for discussion. As commanding officer of Camp Fox, the *Aurora* is hereby renamed Camp Fox, so deal with it. Since it's no longer our temporary location, we need to strengthen the infrastructure to support us long term." He pointed at the window. "We're burning those bridge bastards outside tomorrow and converting this camp into a sustainable fortress. Anyone who isn't one hundred percent on board with me as CO—

commanding officer—is free to leave right now."

There were no retorts, and I assumed everyone had been stunned into silence like I had been. I stared at Clutch, who was looking right back at me. I was sure I looked as frustrated as he did. In the corner, Jase sat with his head in his hands. I didn't know the answer, but this plan had too much complexity and too many risks to feel right.

"You heard the captain," Clutch said, the sergeant tone coming through his voice. "We've got a bonfire to plan and a base to protect."

At fifteen hundred hours, twelve scouts in full gear loaded onto two pontoons and headed around the southern edge of the island to stay hidden from the bridge bastards. Zeds lingered on the small island, and we skirted around them rather than kill them, to not draw the bridge bastards' attention. As we broke away from the island, I thought about the plan. It was a simple plan that seemed like a wasteful use of precious fuel and ammo while putting eight people at risk. The plan? Pen the zeds in on the bridge, and burn them. Shoot any outliers.

My pontoon, led by Clutch, was tasked with sneaking onto the eastern shore, where there were more trees to hide our approach. Trees could also hide zeds, but they tended to shuffle their feet, while we could move nearly silently. We were counting on the zeds' tendency to herd together and hoping that one of those herds weren't lingering in the woods. Our pontoon's job was to lay gasoline on the east end of the bridge while the west team distracted the zeds.

The other pontoon, led by Griz, was to distract the zeds' attention from our movements until we were in position. Then, they'd land on the western shore, so we could burn the bridge bastards from both sides.

Clutch, the eternal pessimist, wasn't so confident things would go that easily. He'd voiced concern about the fire weakening the bridge, which could mean we'd have to find another bridge to cross the river. He'd talked about how few explosives were needed in Afghanistan to bring down a bridge if they were placed right. He'd said that a hot enough fire at the wrong points of the bridge might do the same. Only problem was that we didn't have a single bridge expert or engineer among us. So, the general consensus was that a gasoline-fed fire wouldn't burn long enough to weaken the steel and concrete structure.

Tyler had made it clear that he was the boss, and if we didn't like it, we could leave. Honestly, we were tempted. Clutch, Jase, and I had even talked about it last night. But Jase was adamant that Camp Fox needed us far more than we needed them. It was our duty to help.

Everyone craved to be free from zeds. Hell, I wanted it, too, but they were letting hope overshadow their logic. If we took out these zeds, there'd be more. There were *always* more.

When Clutch and Griz each gave their *ready* signal, our pontoon went east while the other went west. The island sat on the eastern half of the river, so our trip to the shore was brief. The pontoon hit the riverbank, and we all lurched forward. After regaining my balance, I looked over the side to make sure no zeds had washed ashore with us. Jase was the first to jump out, and I followed. Landing at the dock would've been far easier, but the bridge bastards would've seen us. Instead, Clutch picked out a heavily wooded area on the eastern bank a quarter-mile south of the dock.

"Let's move out," Clutch said in a hoarse whisper as he joined my side. "We need to be ready to go the moment the West team engages."

Four men on my pontoon each carried a five-gallon gas jug. Both Jase and I had our hands free since we were on point to take out zeds in the woods. One on point was probably good enough, but Clutch always believed in being doubly prepared.

I had my rifle slung over my shoulder, and my machete held at the ready. Silence was crucial until we were in position. Jase and I led the four others through the woods, each of us with two men following behind.

The leaves had turned colors, and many had already fallen, allowing sunlight to reveal a zed lying next to a log. The zed couldn't walk and was in pretty rough shape. Jase finished it off with two swings so that it couldn't make noise and alert others to our presence.

We moved slowly, being extra careful to not slosh the gasoline. We came across a second zed, but it had been torn apart, likely by wolves or wild dogs. When the trees opened onto the road, we saw the devastation Camp Fox's vehicles had taken while parked on the eastern bank. All had smears of zed sludge. A couple had been rolled over. A HEMTT sat askew in the road. Trampled zeds dotted the road.

For our pontoon, Kurt was going to drive the fuel truck while Joe, another one of Tyler's trusted guardsmen, shot gasoline onto the zeds to make sure they'd burn to death. The five-gallon jugs were to set up a wall of fire at the end of each bridge to help hold the zeds in. As the fastest runner, Jase's job was to light the fire. I had my usual job as sweeper to shoot any zeds that got too close to the scouts managing the fire.

The bridge was big. It spanned the width of the Mississippi, which made penning the zeds easier. Except that herding zeds was a lot like herding cats—a whole lot easier said than done.

Careful to avoid the zeds on the ground with some life still left in them, we looked under the vehicles to make sure no other zeds were waiting to jump out at us. We squeezed between the Humvees and HEMTTs and made our way toward the bridge. We paused at the last fuel truck we came to. Kurt set down his gas can, and opened the door. A second later, he stood back and gave a thumbs-up.

We stood behind the vehicle closest to the bridge, a big HEMTT, which would be our RP (rendezvous point). Clutch signaled to me, and I climbed up the back of the HEMTT. Jase came up right behind me. Until Jase started the fire, Clutch wanted him with me to provide suppression fire, but I knew it was also to keep us both safe.

Once I had my rifle set up, I noticed the pontoon in the middle of the river. The West team was in play. I motioned to Clutch, and he nodded. He signaled to our team and the four men with gas cans—Clutch, Kurt, Bryce, and Joe—jogged toward the bridge, though Clutch's jog was more of a walk. The bridge bastards were completely entranced by the West team, who was slowly making its way to the western riverfront. The zeds followed, mimicking the direction of the pontoon and moving onto the western half of the bridge.

The East team poured gasoline in a thick line across the eastern opening of the bridge.

So far, so good.

Clutch signaled to Kurt and Joe, and they took off at a sprint for the gas tanker truck. Clutch stood there, in plain sight, at the end of the bridge in the middle of the road. Bryce stood off to the side, more skittish.

Once Kurt and Joe both gave a thumbs-up that they were in position, Clutch waved his arms toward Griz's team's pontoon. They waved back, and went under the bridge to where they'd go ashore on the western bank.

"Hey!" Clutch shouted.

Several zeds toward the back of the group turned.

"Yeah, you! Come and get me, you dumb fucks!"

It was irresistible bait, and I wanted to run to Clutch and yank him away from danger. The zeds moaned as they changed direction to head back down the bridge toward Clutch. The West team crept up around the edges of the bridges and started pouring gasoline across the bridge, just like the East team had.

Clutch waved at the zeds and gave them the bird. "Come on, you slow shits!"

I had to remind myself to scan the entire area, not just the bridge, with the noise Clutch was making.

Behind me, the gas truck's big engine started, and I turned to see Kurt pull the truck out and back it toward the bridge. Joe was on top of the tank holding the hose. When Kurt approached the bridge, Clutch stepped to the side with Bryce and held up his hand. Looking in the side mirror, Kurt stopped the truck.

Clutch and Bryce climbed up on the back of the HEMTT, and I could hear them take position around us.

"You're up, Speedy," Clutch said.

Jase held up a lighter. "I'm way ahead of you." He got to his feet, climbed down from the HEMTT, and sprinted toward the bridge.

Movement in the tree line caused me to adjust my aim. I fired.

"Nice shot," Bryce said after the lone zed fell.

While I continually scanned the landscape, out of the corner of my eye I saw Joe stand on top of the truck and started spraying gasoline over the incoming herd as the truck pulled slowly away from them. They continued until they reach the end of the bridge.

Joe waved frantically. "I can't get the hose to turn off!"

The zeds were nearly to the truck.

"Leave it! Get out of there!" Clutch yelled, motioning them to us.

Joe continued to work with the hose and then finally tossed it away. Gas continued to spray out. With the engine still running, Kurt jumped just as Joe was climbing down the back. A zed grabbed Joe's leg, but Kurt shot it several times until its gripped relaxed enough for Joe to tumble onto the ground. He regained his footing and took off at a sprint along with Kurt toward us.

As soon as Kurt and Joe passed Jase, he lit a small, weighted rag and tossed it onto the gasoline-soaked bridge. Fire erupted down the line, forming a wall of flames across the western end of the bridge. Jase ran back toward us and was back up on the HEMTT in a couple seconds flat.

Even though they weren't smart, zeds tended to step back from fire. That was, if they weren't preoccupied with trying to get to us. These zeds stepped right into the flame, like we were counting on. As each gas-soaked zed touched fire, it went up in a whoosh.

Garbled hisses came from deep within the flames. Human-like shapes writhed and moved in a macabre dance in the fire. The zeds that passed through the flames made it several feet, sometimes even more, before they finally collapsed into abstract, angled shapes as their bodies cooked and brains melted. Zeds smelled horrible, but barbequed zeds smelled even worse. Burning rot and flesh made my eyes water, and I swallowed back bile to keep from throwing up.

Clutch put a hand on my back. "Don't look."

I hadn't realized I'd been staring.

Clutch and the others climbed down to dig up the ground to prevent the fire from spreading. As they frantically worked, I forced myself to scan for zeds coming at us from other directions. But my gaze kept going back to the charred zeds burning at the edges of the flames. Another memory to haunt my sleep.

We couldn't see the flames spread from behind the wall of fire, but it didn't take them long to reach the gas truck. A massive explosion blasted us and rocked the HEMTT. I clenched my eyes closed, but the heat nearly cooked us. My eyes watered and my cheeks felt seared, and I leaned my face against the cooler metal of the HEMTT. Once my tears slowed, I looked back up to the fire. Heat still tingled against my skin though we were a couple hundred feet away. Even when we were confident the zeds were all dead, we still had to wait until the flames died down before we could return to the *Aurora*. Not that we had any way of putting out the fire. We could grab buckets of water from the river, but it wouldn't make a dent on the searing flames that hadn't yet died down.

An hour passed, and the flames still didn't die down, even though the bridge was made of steel and concrete. Dread filled my gut, and looking at each of the men up there with me, they were thinking the same thing. I didn't understand all the science behind fire, but my lack of knowledge didn't change the fact that the bridge was burning.

A screeching sound of bending metal made me jump to my feet. My mouth opened. I pointed, and yelled out, "Did you see that?"

Clutch's jaw clenched. "I see it. The bridge is going to collapse."

CHAPTER XXVI

There was nothing we could do as fire-tortured steel made horrendous cries. The northern edge of the bridge gave way first. When the arch's cables snapped, the pavement curved before setting off a chain reaction of concrete and rebar porpoising down the bridge. An avalanche of fire, steel, and dusty concrete plummeted into the Mississippi with a sonic sizzle. Much of the bridge sunk, sending up waves down the river. Many huge chunks of debris still littered the surface and burned while the current grabbed at it.

"Oh, shit." I could no longer watch for zeds. I stood and helplessly stared as the burning debris floated directly toward the *Aurora*. My hand flew to my heart and I clutched my shirt. My stomach churned as people ran out on the deck, screaming and shouting. When the first debris slammed into the towboat, I gasped.

Someone fell off the edge and screamed the ten short feet down to the water, where the sound was abruptly cut off. As debris piled up against the boat, both it and its barges rocked.

The two barges that had been barely hanging onto the rest of the group broke away with a drawn-out metallic screech. Small flickers of fire erupted the grain in barge Number Eight into dark clouds of smoke.

I jumped off the back of the HEMTT before remembering to take a cursory scan for zeds. I stopped, found none, and ran up to Clutch, whom everyone had been gathering around. "What do we do?"

"They need our pontoons to speed up evacuation. Bryce, Kurt, and Joe, you're with me on the pontoon to help with rescue at the *Aurora*."

"How about me?" Jase asked.

He pointed to where I'd spent the last couple hours. "You and Cash need to keep this area clear of zeds, so Camp Fox can safely land. Make sure none of these grounded zeds can endanger people as they get to the dock."

"Okay," I said.

Clutch and the three other men took off running toward the woods and back to the pontoon. "Be safe," I called out, but I had no idea if he'd heard me.

Griz's pontoon was already in the water and halfway back to the *Aurora*, but they were having trouble zigzagging through the debris and kept having to back up and go for a different route.

I swapped my rifle for my machete and made a winding path through zeds on the ground. I stopped at each one that still had life in it and swung. Jase and I carved a path to the boat ramp in ten minutes. We spread out to make a wider path.

"Hey," Jase called out. "Three tangoes at my eleven o'clock."

I jogged back up the eastern bank and followed his finger. I saw the shapes exit the trees across the road. "I'll start on the right."

I had my rifle out and had taken two shots by the time Jase took the last one. After making sure no more emerged, I turned around and headed back toward the ramp. I lifted my rifle and looked through my scope at the *Aurora*. Clutch and his team had made it onto the towboat. People were running at him like a flock of sparrows. Against the rail, Clutch was shoving people back who couldn't take the ladder. Many were weighted down with bags, and I could see Clutch was yelling and motioning at them to drop their things. No one seemed to be listening.

When the smoke blocked my view of Clutch, my heart clenched. "Be safe," I whispered, suddenly knowing in my heart that I didn't care if anyone made it to shore as long as Clutch made it back safely.

"What?" Jase asked.

Anger at the stupid fire hardened my features. "Nothing."

The flames had engulfed the outer four barges and

were already spreading to the four closest to the towboat. All of our grain...gone. My heart pounded, and I found it hard to hold my rifle. At least the fire hadn't overtaken the closest barges or towboat yet, but smoke was shooting out from everywhere. I could still make out barges Four and Three through the haze, where Kurt was taking a crate of ammo from another scout who'd just emerged from our armory. Smoke bled through where the bay doors met in the middle. "Hurry," I whispered as they carried out our irreplaceable supplies.

A fire shot up, and Kurt disappeared. I squinted to see smoke and flames pour out from a hole where Kurt had been standing a second earlier. *Oh, God.*

"The fire—" Jase didn't finish.

The sound of automatic gunfire drowned out the sound of everything else, and we both ducked. I quickly realized it wasn't automatic gunfire but the sounds of ammo going off in the fire. My legs were suddenly wobbly and I leaned against our Humvee that still sat next to the boat ramp.

We were about to lose everything. Our food, ammo, everything. And there wasn't a single fucking thing we could do except watch Camp Fox quite literally go up in flames.

CHAPTER XXVII

Embers showered down like glitter around the *Aurora* while ammo continued to go off in barge Three by the box-load. Clutch's team was already on board the towboat and helping with the evacuation. Joe brought over the first pontoon packed shoulder-to-shoulder with coughing, crying people. Joe's face was covered with black ash as he pulled the pontoon up to the dock on the eastern bank by what was left of the bridge.

Jase and I looked at one another, and then we both ran toward the pontoon. Other than smoke inhalation and shock, no one looked seriously injured. Jase and I helped anyone who seemed to be struggling off the boat and onto the bank. Once it was clear, I jumped on the pontoon to where Joe was curled over the steering wheel. "What do you need help with?"

Joe's reply was smothered by a cough, although he

eventually looked up with tearing, bloodshot eyes and gave me a thumb up.

I held my rifle out to him. "I can take the next trip. Can you cover the people here?"

He nodded, still holding his chest.

"I'll drive," Jase said as a matter-of-fact and set his rifle down next to him.

I sat down just as he throttled full-forward, and the pontoon cut through the water. Midway, we met Griz's boat, also filled with people. All of the barges were covered in flames, and the towboat was covered in smoke. Someone plummeted into the water to our right as we headed around the boat to the boat dock. I couldn't make out who he was because as soon as he surfaced, something yanked him right back under. I searched but could find no one under the murky water.

I swallowed and sat back. As we approached the dock, a zed was chewing on Hugh, while his daughter Hali was trying to pull him free. He looked unconscious, which was small consolation. I grabbed Jase's rifle and fired two shots: one into the zed and one into the doomed victim. Hali stood back, stunned, her big blue eyes and mouth opened wide. Jase cut the engine and jumped out. `

He wrapped his arm around Hali and led her back to the pontoon. "I've got you. It's going to be okay now." She went with him like she was a robot, seemingly oblivious to his presence.

On the other side of the dock, the deck boats were

being filled, with Deb leading the effort. I searched for Clutch but didn't see him anywhere. I handed Jase his rifle back. "I'm going to find Clutch. Can you keep it clear down here until we get back?"

He looked at me directly and gave a single firm nod, still holding Hali with his other arm. "Hurry."

I ran for the ladder and waited for two scouts to climb down. Both were laden down with olive drag duffles. As soon as they were on the ground, I grabbed onto the ladder. "Just about everyone is down, and this is the last of the supplies we could get to," one of them said with a hoarse voice. "The final team is wrapping up on deck now."

I didn't wait. The metal was warm under my palms, and I climbed as quickly as I could. As soon as I reached the rail, I pulled myself over and stood. There was fire shooting up through the deck everywhere. Smoke burned my lungs, and I coughed on the black air. The bow was engulfed in flames. Two charred bodies lay hunched over in the fire, and I prayed neither was Clutch.

Frantic, I searched for anyone alive on the chaotic deck. Then I saw them. My heart leapt and air shot from my lungs. Clutch was helping a man down the edge of the deck onto the lift. Right behind him, Tyler was carrying Maggie who was quacking on about something. Even in this hell, I couldn't help but smile in relief at seeing Clutch and Tyler. Keeping a hand on the rail, I hustled to meet them, careful to avoid burning or smoking deck boards. I reached out and grabbed his arm, just to feel him and know he was real. "Is that everyone?"

Clutch, his face blackened, frowned in shock. "What are—"

"Is this everyone?" I asked again. "Can we leave now?"

"I think so," Tyler said.

I noticed the unconscious man Clutch was dragging was Don. But his daughter wasn't with him.

My stomach dropped. "Where's Alana?"

Clutch and Tyler looked at each other.

"Shit," Clutch said. "I didn't see her."

"Where'd you find Don?" I asked.

"The bridge," Tyler said.

I patted Clutch's chest. "Get to the ground. I'll see you guys below!"

His eyes widened. "No! It's too dangerous!" Clutch yelled.

I pursed my lips. Every nerve in my body was shouting to stay with Clutch, but I couldn't leave a child behind to burn. My bottom lip trembled. "Get those two to safety," I said and then burst away before I changed my mind. Clutch yelled after me, but I kept going.

"Alana!" I shouted and coughed. To my right, flames licked at the varnished wood and I flew up the outside stairs, taking the steps two at a time. When I saw no one outside the bridge, I jumped inside. "Alana!"

I could barely hear her whimpering above the noise

of the fire, but I heard her. Jesus. Why did kids always have to hide? I bent over and found her hugging herself under the navigator's station. "Come here. I'm bringing you to your daddy."

She didn't move, and I didn't plan on taking the time to encourage her to come out on her own accord. I grabbed her arm and yanked her out. She cried, but I didn't take time to console her. A crying kid was a hell of a lot better than a dead kid. I lifted her into my arms, and ran outside and down the steps. The heat was excruciating. Alana kicked and squirmed, and I nearly dropped her. Suddenly, Clutch was there, and he took the girl from me.

"You're supposed to be on the boat!" I yelled, angry that he was still in danger.

He ignored me, and I followed him down the steps. It was hard to move fast when trying not to breathe. Alana continued to wiggle in Clutch's arms, but he was able to keep a hold on her. By the time we'd reached the deck, fire lapped at the deck boards all around us.

"Catch!" Clutch called out to Tyler, and then tossed the girl.

She flew several feet through the air. Her scream stopped abruptly when Tyler caught her. She sobbed in between coughing fits. He put her down next to her father on the already full platform and she clung to him. Tyler looked up. "We'll see you on the ground."

Tyler worked the pulley system that Wes had built, and the platform lowered. I glanced over the edge to see the hull around the aluminum ladder smoking. I bent over and touched the ladder with a gloved hand. It hissed like a hot iron, and I yanked back. "It's too hot."

Clutch frowned and then squeezed the pulley's ropes used for the platform. "We'll rappel down the ropes once Tyler's down."

Heat seeped through the rubber soles of my boots. I nodded quickly. "Got it."

The wood cracked beneath my feet. I grabbed for the rail, but was too late. The floor gave away, and I found myself falling into a furnace. My hands scrambled to grab onto anything. Clutch gripped my wrists, and pulled me up. The heat sizzled straight through my clothes, and I clenched my teeth against the oven temperatures.

When he pulled me to my feet against him on the deck, my breath came out and I leaned my forehead against his hot neck. I looked up at his burned red face. "You caught me."

His frown was overcome by his intense gaze, and he squeezed me hard against him. "I'd never let you go."

A tear escaped my eyes and I squeezed him right back. "Good" was all I managed to get out.

Flames licked up from the hole. Clutch twisted us around and before I knew it we were sliding down the outside of the hull. I made myself as small as I could and clung to him like a koala bear. I fought to keep from coughing, trying to keep completely still so that he could more easily handle both of our weight. I didn't know how he managed to support both of us, but he did. As soon as I felt his legs hit the wood dock, I stood but refused to let go.

"Come on, guys!" Jase yelled out.

Clutch and I looked around at the same time to see Jase standing alone on the dock. When I didn't see the pontoon, I frowned. "Where's the pontoon?"

"Tyler's driving it back," he replied. "Come on."

Clutch grabbed my hand and we hurried behind him across the island. Zeds reached out to us, but we ran past them. The speedboat came into view behind a thick bush. The motor was already running. We tumbled onto the floor while Jase backed us away from the bank.

As Jase navigated through the debris- and zed-infested water, I looked down at Clutch. He brushed his thumb across my cheekbone as he looked into my eyes. I mean, he *really* looked into my eyes, as though I was the only thing in the world, and it was perfect. His warm breath tingled my lips. After a while, he smirked. "There's not a single thing I could say right now that wouldn't sound completely idiotic."

I smiled, closed my eyes, and rested my head on his chest. His heart, still pounding from our narrow escape, beat strong. My head rose and fell with each breath he took. "Try it."

He didn't.

"Hang in there, guys," Jase said. "We're coming up on the dock."

I grudgingly rolled off Clutch and sat up. Clutch

pulled himself onto a seat. It took several long minutes while we waited for boats to be moved before we could get to the ramp. When we stepped onto the rocky soil, Tyler was waiting for us with a hard look. "Take ten to regroup and load into your Humvee. We're heading out to the first house we find and staying there tonight."

None of us replied or acknowledged. We simply trudged up the rocky bank. At the top, I turned around to see the *Aurora* lit up like its namesake.

After I reclaimed my rifle from Joe, I headed back to our Humvee with the Charlie Coyote on the hood. Jase already had the engine running.

Two hours later, after the sun had long since set, we lay on the living room floor of an old two-story farmhouse with nineteen seventies decor. My eyes burned from smoke, and my skin still felt hot, even in the cold house. Exhaustion forced me into a sleep that I don't think my mind would have otherwise allowed. Not with all the fresh images of flames, lost friends, and burnt corpses filling my head.

When I awoke some time later, I found Clutch and Jase awake, one sitting on either side of me and leaning against the wall. I pulled myself up, squeezed in between them, and wrapped an arm around each of them. With my "family," I felt safe. But the devil was in the details. Sure, I felt safe right now, but we had no home, no food, and no weapons. Nothing except for what we had on our backs, and outside it was snowing.

NEW EDEN

CHAPTER XXVIII

Thirty-two Fox survivors remained after the fire, but more should have survived. Most of those who died were lost below decks when they went in to grab their possessions. It was a funny thing how, even at the end of the world, people were so attached to their possessions that they risked their lives for them.

The final casualty, Don, was found dead this morning when he didn't wake. Doc figured the man had succumbed to an internal injury since his lower back was bruised and distended. His daughter, Alana, refused to let go of him and had to be dragged away. She screamed until she fainted.

The snow covered everything in a light blanket of white, making the world look deceptively clean. The house smelled like pungent smoke since no one had washed up last night, and we only had the smoky, filthy clothes on our backs. It took nearly an hour to hook up the only surviving portable generator to the well pump, and another four hours for everyone to wash up with ice cold water.

We didn't get on the road until noon, and we had no breakfast or lunch served. Vicki, with some help from Joe, had collected wild leaves and made tea to curb everyone's hunger. About a dozen of us, who always wore "every day carry" packs, had protein bars and water filters. I'd given one of my bars to Benji but none to anyone else. It wasn't because I was selfish. It was because we needed to maintain our strength so we could find food for the others. It didn't stop people from eying me with disdain as I zipped up my backpack and slid it over my shoulders, though.

Clutch and Tyler had constantly told people to always carry emergency bags, but few actually did. I wanted to tell each and every one of them to fuck off, that I'd gladly give any one of them a bar if they were willing to go find food. Except they didn't want to earn the bar. They just wanted the handout.

"Let's load up," Tyler announced to the room full of people, without making eye contact with anyone.

I frowned. Always before, Tyler had an underlying warm tone to his words. Since yesterday, everything he said was hard and to the point. He kept his arms crossed over his chest, and he didn't even respond when Vicki hugged him. It was like he'd completely closed himself off from everyone.

"I'll take the lead vehicle," Tyler said. "Griz and Jase will take the scout vehicle. They will advance ahead of the convoy and recon any houses for food. Clutch and Cash will cover our flank. We'll head north until we can safely cross the river. We'll stop outside the first town we reach today to split up and search for food. Any questions?"

"Why don't we stay here?" someone asked. "Have the scouts go for food like they've always done."

"Since we know the area around the river has already been picked clean, we need to move on. There's nothing here for us."

"What's our destination?" Frost asked. Diesel sprawled around Benji, both napping next to the older man. Frost had never given the dog any food meant for people, but when the *Aurora* burned so had all of Diesel's kibble. The dog, just like everyone else, no longer had anything to eat. Already, the griping had started. Complaints that the dog would take precious food.

Complaining about a dog wasn't a serious issue, but it revealed the mood of Camp Fox. If relationships were collapsing the first day on the road, we wouldn't last three days before everyone was at one another's throats.

"We're heading back toward Fox Hills since we're familiar with the area and the herds should've passed through there at least a week ago. We'll stop along the way at any place that's safe and has food, including every military base and armory so we can replenish our gear."

"What if we don't find food," someone else asked, and several others chimed in agreement.

Tyler didn't even pause. "Then we go hungry."

After Tyler's uncharacteristically harsh response, no one else voiced any more questions.

Fifteen minutes later, everyone had split into four Humvees, one HEMTT, and the two gas trucks. With fewer people and no gear, all other vehicles were left behind simply because we didn't need them anymore.

Less than an inch of snow covered the ground, so we didn't have to deal with shitty road conditions on top of everything else. Griz and Jase pulled out first in Bravo team's Humvee—the one with a pinup girl painted on the hood—and disappeared out of sight. Clutch and I had time to wait since we would be the last vehicle to head out. I was glad I was with Clutch rather than Tyler since Tyler's mood had been so sour since the fire.

Not that anyone was in a cheerful mood.

I drove, and Clutch stood behind the .30 cal. We'd decided we would switch positions every hour so neither of us would get too cold. This morning, we'd counted our rounds that we kept in the Humvee. Just over two hundred for our rifles and fourteen hundred for the machine gun. Not bad, but I would've liked to have had ten times that for a cross-country trip.

Tyler led the convoy and he kept us slow, below thirty miles per hour. That speed allowed plenty of time to prepare for any zeds that discovered us, and made it easy for Clutch and me to alternate positions. The slow progress also allowed for a chance to admire the beautiful day outside. Snow dusted the trees lining both sides of the winding river road. A gentle breeze pressed against the branches, sending maple seeds spinning to the ground like tiny helicopters. The sense of peace was surreal, given all the chaos in our lives over the past several days.

Jase reported in on the radio every thirty minutes. He and Griz had found a dented can of creamed corn under a kitchen counter at one farm. Two other farms offered nothing, and all three farms had clearly been looted. Whether the looters were still alive or not, we couldn't know, so Tyler warned Griz and Jase to proceed with caution.

The road map showed that the closest bridge over the Mississippi was near Parkerstown. If the zeds had cleared out of town, Tyler announced we'd camp there for the night after searching every store and house. With a large sporting goods store, it offered the possibility to restock gear. That was, if it hadn't been looted yet.

The convoy came to a stop before us, and I craned my head out the window to see why. "Do you see anything?" I asked Clutch.

"Everything looks clear up ahead," he replied.

Tyler's voice came over the radio. *"Contact across the river in the trees. Looks like a single troop with eyes on us."*

I scanned the tree line across the river, but didn't see anyone. "Do you see him yet?"

A moment passed. "I have him," Clutch said. "Looks Army issue."

"Scout vehicle to proceed with extreme caution. Make contact only if you're confident he's Army. Report back in ten."

Griz's response came. *"Roger. Scout vehicle closing in now."* Then he tacked on, *"If he's military, he's a damn beautiful sight."*

I scowled at the idea of Jase and Griz heading blindly into a possible ambush. Tyler and Griz had far more faith in an altruistic military structure than I did. I'd figured that the world collapsing didn't exclude the military. Still, we needed food, shelter, and protection. If this guy was the real deal, then we couldn't *not* make contact.

After a few more minutes, the convoy moved forward again. The next hour was tense as I kept waiting to hear from Griz, but there still was no response by the time we reached Parkerstown. Rather than leading us into town, Tyler brought the convoy to the huge store not far from the river.

We parked in the open parking lot. Several snow-covered cars sat, but there were no fresh tire tracks or footprints in the snow. The glass entrance doors were shattered, leaving the building wide open. Joe and Bryce pulled their Humvee close to the entrance. They stepped out and after a minute of looking inside, they walked through the doors.

They emerged about fifteen minutes later. One pulled

out his handheld radio, and Bryce's voice came through. *"All clear. Not a single zed on initial pass. The place looks to be cleared out of ammo and guns."* With the exception of Clutch's handheld radio he'd had with him when we'd burned the bridge bastards, all the other handhelds were all still on board the *Aurora*, making Clutch's a valuable commodity.

"Roger that," Tyler responded. *"All right everyone, we're camping in here for the night. All scouts report to the front to make a full clearing pass. Everyone else, stay in your vehicles until I give the all-clear."*

The two gas trucks couldn't get the same frequencies as the military vehicles, so Tyler stopped by each to relay his orders.

"That means we're up," Clutch said as he climbed down. We still had our rifles, but the scouts off duty when the fire broke out on the *Aurora* couldn't get to their rifles in time. Many still had their machetes and swords, but were at a definite disadvantage if shit hit the fan now.

I grabbed my rifle and stepped outside. My boots left sooty prints in the snow. When Clutch joined my side, we headed slowly toward Tyler.

Scouts now made up about half of Camp Fox. Before the fire, three out of every four Fox survivors were scouts, and nearly all were Guardsman. Manpower had been Fox's greatest strength. But when civilians ran out during the fire, many scouts ran in to save who and what they could. So many had been lost. Camp Fox wouldn't intimidate any enemy now.

As we approached the huge store, I noticed the pile of burnt bodies near the building. Still covered with snow, I could only assume — and hope — they were zeds. I stepped through the doors. Glass crunched under my boots.

Inside, we walked under a ceiling of antlers that led to a wide-open space of clothes and merchandise. Much of it had been knocked over and shoved into piles. "Spread out," Tyler said. "Stay in pairs and yell if you come across a tango." He pointed to each team and then in a direction for them to head. After he motioned for us to head toward the boat section, Clutch and I started walking.

As we searched our section, I couldn't help but admire the rows of new boats and jet skis. "This place is a goldmine."

"I agree. There's plenty of gear still here that we can use," he said. "But I'd bet any food is as far gone as the ammo. We'd better find something for everyone by tomorrow or else their moods are going to turn shitty."

"Shittier, you mean," I said with a smirk, and we continued our search.

After making sure the store was absolutely, positively clear of zeds, Camp Fox was reestablished for the night in the hunting area toward the back of the store. The entrance was blocked off with a Humvee.

As people settled in new clothes and sleeping bags, Tyler tried to reach Griz and Jase on the handheld, but the signal was weak in the building. He decided it wasn't worth the risk of going outside after dark, and set up his sleeping pad and bag next to the wall.

"Do you want Clutch and me to go check on them?" I asked hopefully. The idea of being safe and comfortable while Jase and Griz was who-knew-where and caught up in who-knew-what seemed like a betrayal, and the guilt was eating at me.

Tyler didn't look up. "No. Get some rest."

"They might be looking for us."

"We need to keep everyone as centrally located as possible. I can't risk sending out scouts at night. I'll try to reach them again in the morning."

I never moved and watched him for a moment. He had his hands in his pocket and he seemed to be staring off into nowhere, though his jaw was clenched tight. "You want to talk about it?"

"No."

I stood there for another long moment and finally sighed. "Okay. Sleep tight."

I started to walk away, but then Tyler said something I couldn't hear.

"What's that?" I asked.

He nearly collapsed as he sat down. He rubbed his temples before looking up. "I screwed up."

I frowned and took a seat next to him. I placed a hand on his shoulder. "How so?"

"The fire." He leaned back against the wall. "It's my fault."

Confused, I cocked my head. "How is it your fault? The plan was solid. No one knew the bridge wouldn't hold."

"I ordered the mission. It's my fault."

Clutch, who'd just walked up, handed Tyler and me each a plastic bottle with a price tag still on it. "Water," he said. "It may still have a bit of charcoal taste, but it's okay to drink."

"Thanks," I said and waited for Tyler to continue. When he didn't, I did. "Someone had to take charge on the *Aurora* or else we would've kept debating until it was too late. You may have ordered the mission, but I volunteered for it. If you're looking for blame, it falls on every single person in this room. We're all in this together. Wins, losses, they belong to all of us."

Tyler's lips pursed and he looked off to the side.

"You know something?" Clutch asked after taking a drink from his own bottle. "If you didn't feel the weight of making tough decisions, then I couldn't ever respect you. I've got to admit, I didn't like you at first. I wanted to kick your ass, to tell the truth, but you earned my respect. You're the right leader for Camp Fox. You're not afraid to lead but you've also held onto your compassion. That's rare nowadays. You're exactly what we need."

Tyler's brow rose and the tension seemed to bleed from his features. "You mean that?"

Clutch held up a hand. "Jesus. Don't expect a hug or anything."

Tyler chuckled, and it was the first time I'd seen his smile for some time. "You two had better get some rest. Who knows how long a trip we've got ahead of us."

Reluctantly, I set up a sleeping bag next to Clutch, and we waited for Jase and Griz to show up. Vicki warmed up the camping area by lighting fires in small charcoal grills.

Near dawn, shouting snapped me awake. Blinding light from flashlights shone on us from every direction, and I shaded my eyes, searching to make out the source. Shots were fired, echoed by cries and more shouting.

"Faces down! Don't move! If you move, we will shoot you!"

Before Clutch and I made startled, terrified eye contact, I saw one of our assailants dressed in full camo hunting gear.

Bandits.

CHAPTER XXIX

"Jesus. Except for their vehicles, these guys don't have shit," one of the bandits said to the man in charge while we all knelt on the freezing ground outside the store.

One of the bandits had moved the Humvee that blocked to the side and was now rummaging through all of our vehicles. "Where's your food?"

"We don't have any," someone said.

Every single one of the bandits had a mean look, like they were all pissed off at the world and thought they deserved special treatment now. The leader, missing three fingers on his left hand, had the cruelest look of all. One of his men had called him Hodge, and we all avoided meeting his gaze. He had a mean look, like he'd been this way even before the outbreak. His eyes—cunning like a fox—seemed devoid of any emotion as he looked over the Camp Fox survivors like we were nothing more than cattle.

Our backpacks sat, opened and empty of contents, in a pile behind him, along with our coats. All of our weapons had been confiscated and carried into the store. The bandits who had disarmed me had been overly thorough. I'd wanted to scream and bite as they'd groped, but I'd stood perfectly still with a clenched jaw, afraid of what they'd do to Clutch if I'd reacted. When one was busy checking under my bra with his cold hands, he commented, "Too bad. This one wouldn't be too bad looking if her face wasn't so messed up."

The other one chuckled. "Easy fix. Just turn her around."

Clutch managed to tackle that one before three others knocked him to the ground. He'd gotten a black eye and swollen cheek, but they moved on from me after that. I felt sorry for the other women, who received the same treatment.

When Mary was grabbed, her husband lunged forward and they kicked him in the stomach. As they dragged her back toward the store, she begged them to stop. Her husband, still holding his stomach, climbed to his feet and ran toward her. A bandit raised his rifle, and my eyes widened. Shots cut through the night air, and I jumped. He collapsed, and she screamed. The bandit holding her punched her and she went limp. Tension hung in the air as she disappeared inside.

"If any of you idiots try something stupid like that," Hodge said, pointing to the body. "You're going to end up the same way. Got it?"

No one moved.

Hodge weaved through us, looking at each person one

at a time. As he stood behind us, he spoke. "Many of you are wearing uniforms. Are you associated with New Eden?"

No one spoke.

Something moved, and somebody cried out. I swallowed back my fear.

"I've never heard of New Eden," Tyler said from several feet to my left.

The leader came walking around and stood in front of Tyler. "If you're not with New Eden, what base are you with?"

Tyler didn't answer.

Hodge bent to stare him down, his smooth brown hair covering some of his face, but Tyler stared straight ahead. "Yeah, you're military, all right." He looked up and narrowed his eyes at Clutch. "I'd bet quite a few of you are." He walked over to Deb and held his pistol to her head. She whimpered and tightened her lips. "Since I'm not, I'll ask one more time. What base are you with."

"We're with the Camp Fox National Guard base," Tyler ground out.

Hodge lifted his pistol. "Never heard of it, but that doesn't matter. You military folks are all in bed together, so you are going to help me."

"Please," Vicki said through shivers. "We're hungry. At least feed the children."

The leader looked up. "Tell me boys. How does a beggar earn food around here?"

"Fuck for it or fight for it," several bandits replied in unison.

A cruel grin curved upward on Hodge's face as he bent

down to get eye-level with Vicki. "So, which is it going to be?"

Her lips tightened, and she didn't answer.

He stood, nodded to his men, and they walked around and yanked the adult men forward and made them kneel in front of us. I bit back my cry when they pulled Clutch away and made him kneel with the others. I wanted to lunge forward, to grab him and run, but I didn't move, feeling like a failure.

Soon, every adult man was kneeling in a row before us in the snow. Clutch and I never broke eye contact. I'd never seen him look as pissed off as he did right now. I prayed he didn't do something stupid and heroic. Hodge walked behind each of them, holding his pistol in his hand. "So tell me, which one of you are in charge of this little group?"

No one spoke.

"I'm not going to ask again." He nodded to one of his men, who went to stand next to Vicki, holding his pistol against her temple. She closed her eyes, and tears fell down her cheeks. "In three seconds, I'm going to have my colleague here kill this woman."

He looked across our faces. "One."

Clutch opened his mouth to speak. My brows furrowed, and I shook my head once. *Don't you dare.*

"Two."

"I'm in charge," Bryce said hurriedly from next to Tyler.

The leader's brows rose as though he was genuinely surprised, and he sauntered over to Bryce. "You? Really?"

"You've got me. Release my people. They've done nothing wrong," Bryce added. Even though his voice cracked, he put on a good act. I almost believed it myself.

"No, I don't believe I will." He raised his sidearm, and clicked off the safety.

"Stop!" Tyler yelled. "I'm Captain Tyler Masden, commanding officer of Camp Fox."

Hodge smirked. He grabbed Bryce's hair and yanked his head back to look him in the face. "That was stupid of you. I already knew that asshole was in charge. Everybody knows that whoever speaks up first is a hero, an idiot, or in charge. Usually all three are the same."

He looked up to his men. "Get them to their feet."

Tyler, Clutch, and the other fifteen men were pulled to their feet by the eight bandits. I could see in Clutch's, Tyler's, and all of the Fox men's eyes that they wanted to turn and attack. We outnumbered them, but they outgunned us. It would be a massacre.

The leader stood in front of Tyler. "Now I know how far I can push you and how loyal your people are to you. Disappointing on both counts."

He walked down the line of Fox men and back to Tyler. "You are going to help us draw that New Eden squadron into an ambush."

"We won't help you," Tyler said harshly.

"I should clarify. I don't need your help. Your *uniforms* are going to help us draw the New Eden squadron into an ambush. Now, strip."

It took rifles shoved into their backs for them to take off their fatigues. As a scout, I wore fatigues, too, but I wasn't ordered to take off mine, probably because I was smaller and mine wouldn't fit any of the bandits. I knelt there and watched as Clutch and the others pulled off their boots and stripped down to their T-shirts, socks, and underwear.

They stood nearly naked in the freezing morning air, their breaths making cloud puffs, while two of the bandits carried their clothing away. Goosebumps covered Clutch's tattoos on his arms.

"Hey, Hodge. We'd better hustle," a bandit called out as he came running up. "The New Eden pricks are just about to cross the bridge."

I think everyone's gaze turned toward the bridge in the distance. Trees with golden and red leaves blocked much of the view, but it was impossible to miss the squadron of heavily armored vehicles approaching in the distance.

"Well, then." Hodge checked his pistol. "Thank you for your service."

He walked over to Tyler, held his pistol to Tyler's temple and fired. A thunderous shot broke the silence. A woman screamed. Tyler fell face-forward, and a pool of dark blood spread out from around his head.

Air flew from my lungs and I couldn't breathe. My heart felt like it'd stopped. Someone clung to me—Vicki, I think—and I embraced her numbly. Ice zapped the strength from my legs, yet I somehow managed to stay on my feet. My vision swirled. Not Tyler. He couldn't die. He was too good to die.

People cried out. Hodge held his pistol against Bryce's temple and looked across our faces. He fired, and Bryce collapsed. He moved to the next man, again looked across the group of survivors, and fired.

My mouth opened as I watched in shock as the bandit stopped next to Clutch. My world spun and my legs gave out. I reached for Clutch. "No!"

CHAPTER XXX

Instead of executing Clutch, Hodge nodded to one of his men who raised his rifle and slammed it down on Clutch's head from behind. He collapsed into a pile. Tears fell down my cheeks, and I realized the leader was watching me with keen interest.

"You're a bastard," I said simply, the ice in my body having given way to boiling hatred.

He smiled broadly. "You see," he said. "I keep the ones with something to lose. It's entertaining the things I can make them to do to try to save each other. I think I'll have fun with both of you."

Never, I thought to myself.

"Boss," one of the men said. "They're coming up fast."

He looked toward the bridge, before turning to his men. "Get the rest inside. We'll finish later. We have to get changed before the squadron arrives."

"On your feet," one of the bandits ordered, waving

his gun at us.

Clutch was just coming to with a groan, and I helped drag him up. The back of his head had a wet spot from an open gash. I slid his arm over my shoulder. His skin was freezing cold. Deb came up and grabbed his other arm. The bandits rushed everyone back into the store and back to our small campsite. The seven small grills still had glowing embers from last night's fires.

Deb and I helped Clutch onto his sleeping bag, and I wrapped my bag around his shoulders. I swallowed and my eyes blurred. The shock of everything was starting to give way, and adrenaline and the cold made me shake nearly uncontrollably. I held tightly onto Clutch, and he wrapped his arms around me, shaking just as much.

"I can't believe they shot Tyler," Deb said in a monotone voice.

All but two bandits disappeared into the back. The pair who remained kept their rifles leveled on us while the others changed. One of the bandits was busy admiring his new rifle: Clutch's Blaser.

Less than a minute later, Hodge came out in Guardsman fatigues, walked over to the pair standing guard over us, and said something I couldn't hear. When he turned to us, his eyes narrowed. "If any of you try to run, you will be shot. Got it?"

He didn't wait for a response. He left with the others dressed in clothes our guys had been wearing minutes earlier, and I wanted to see his blood stain the clothes he stole.

I clung to Clutch, partly to warm him and mostly because I needed to feel him—his breathing, his heartbeat, his *life*. His breathing steadied my own, and I felt my pounding heart return to a level where it didn't feel like I was having a panic attack. After a minute or two, his grogginess wore off and he no longer swayed or shook as badly. He gingerly touched the back of his head and winced. "*Fuck.*"

I looked up at him. I wanted to ask if he was okay, but when I opened my mouth, a sob threatened to get in the way.

He cupped my face with both hands. He didn't kiss me, only pressed our foreheads together as though he needed the physical connection as much as I did. Tears streamed down my cheeks. He brushed away a tear with his thumb. "Sh. Don't cry," he whispered softly.

The soft words were such a contrast to his rough palms, yet both were full of emotion and I leaned into him. "I almost lost you," I whispered back, my voice cracking.

He looked up and glared at the bandits, each on opposite sides of our indoor campground, before looking back at me. "You shouldn't have cried out," he whispered. "They'll use me to hurt you now."

If I hadn't cried out, he'd be dead right now. Rather than saying that, I simply shrugged.

Around us, the remaining Fox survivors all sat in shellshock. Many were crying in despair and loss, some stared blankly into nothingness, and others looked downright pissed, like they were about to go kamikaze on the guards. I don't know how I looked to them because I was feeling all of those emotions at the same time.

Tyler's rumpled blue sleeping bag sat empty, along with a few others, and I turned away, not having the strength to think about the permanence of what had happened. I could only hope that Jase and Griz were safe.

The two bandits didn't stop Benji as he walked around the clothing racks, picking out clothes and bringing piles to each of the men. Diesel barked from one of the back rooms. The dog had gotten lucky. When Diesel had growled when the bandits manhandled Frost, one of the men had raised his rifle to shoot the dog, but the bandit leader took a shine to the dog and claimed him as his. Though, I wasn't yet convinced the leader wanted Diesel as his pet or for dinner.

"How did everything go so wrong?" I finally asked against Clutch's tattooed chest. "What do we do now?"

He watched the guard, and didn't speak for at least a minute. His body tensed and his gaze hardened. "I'm getting my rifle back."

CHAPTER XXXI

"**L**et me know if the guard on the rock looks this way," Clutch whispered.

I frowned, peering into his brown eyes. "Okay."

I could feel his arm move behind me. *Oh.* Careful to reveal nothing, I forced myself to stare blankly in the bandit's direction as Clutch signaled to the other scouts. The bandit was lounging on a manmade rock next to a stuffed bear.

The game continued for several minutes. Clutch signaled while I kept an eye on one guard and he watched the one nearest us. I squeezed Clutch's thigh any time the man I watched looked in our general direction.

"We're set. We just need a diversion now," Clutch whispered finally.

I tried to think of anything I could do to distract the bandits. Outside, I could hear the sounds of big engines, signaling the approach of New Eden. I hoped they saw through the bandits' charade, but I couldn't count on it. As I concentrated on thinking of a diversion, I noticed Vicki watching us intently. Her cheeks were splotchy from crying. With the slowest movement, she gave a nod like she knew Clutch was up to something. I supposed, since she was sitting in between Clutch and the other scouts, chances were she was quite aware of exactly what was about to happen.

Vicki stood abruptly.

The bandit nearest us swung Clutch's rifle around. "Whoa there, lady. What do you think you're doing?"

Vicki pointed to Deb, who was lying on her side. "She's pregnant. If she doesn't eat soon, she'll lose the baby."

"So? Why would I care?"

Vicki took a deep breath and then untucked her shirt. "I'm buying her a meal."

It took a moment for her offer to register, and a then huge grin spanned the bandit's face. He looked up to his partner. "What do you think?"

The other bandit shrugged. "As long as you do it in here, the boss won't care. Just keep your rifle on them."

The bandit turned back to Vicki. "You got yourself a deal. A meal for the broad. Come here."

She stood adamant, and her jaw jutted out. "Give her something to eat first."

He thought for a moment and then shrugged, reached into his vest pocket, and tossed a small bag to Deb. "Okay. Done. Now, get over here," he motioned to Vicki. "Grab onto that clothes rack. Face your friends."

I found myself holding my breath as Vicki took slow, tentative steps to the bandit. I slowly pulled away from Clutch so he could make his move, whatever it may be. My arms wrapped around my abdomen on their own, and I swallowed back fear and hate.

The bandit grabbed Vicki's belt and yanked her to him. He almost put his rifle down to go for her pants, and then seemed to realize he was still guarding us. "Pull your pants down."

She moved stiffly as she undid her belt and unbuttoned her jeans, one slow button at a time. He watched her, but every second, he glanced nervously up at us. As soon as she unbuttoned the last button, he turned her around and yanked her pants down. "Grab that rack. Don't let go or else."

She reached out and grabbed the silver bar. I felt Clutch move away from me, and I'd nearly forgotten why Vicki was up there. I heard the sound of big engines outside. The New Eden squadron had arrived.

Vicki stood there. Her determined gaze leveled above our group while the bandit struggled with unfastening his belt and pants with only one hand. The other bandit had leaned forward, captivated by the scene and oblivious to Joe and three other scouts inching closer to the rock. Clutch still sat next to me, but I noticed he now had his feet poised under him, like he was a sprinter at the gate.

The bandit finally had his pants undone, and he grabbed Vicki's hip. As he moved close to her, she shoved her head back and nailed him directly on the nose.

"Uh! Bitch!" he cried out, taking a step back, momentarily stunned.

She grabbed the barrel of his gun, and he tried to yank it from her. Clutch shoved off and closed the ten feet to them with more strength and agility than I thought he had regained. I jumped and ran after him. A couple shots fired from the direction of the other bandit, but I didn't look.

Clutch reached the bandit as soon as he yanked the rifle from Vicki and knocked her to the floor. Clutch tackled him, and I grabbed the bandit's rifle and kneeled on his wrist. He cried out, and I pulled the rifle free. Clutch chopped the guy in the throat and rolled off him. The guy got to his knees, struggling to breathe.

Vicki reached for the rifle. I handed it to her. She raised it and shot the bandit in the gut. He took a step back, tripped, and lay there, holding his bleeding stomach. She handed the rifle back to me, fastened her jeans, and then headed back to the group. I'm guessing she was aiming lower, but I didn't care as long as he was down.

Several had gathered around the other, clearly dead bandit, and I saw Joe on the floor, a stream of blood trailing from his neck. Deb looked over and sadly shook her head.

Outside, there was yelling, and then the sound of gunfire erupted. Several bandits sprinted into the store. Hodge, whose eyes were already wide, froze when he saw us, and anger tightened his visage.

"Incoming!" I yelled. I tumbled with Clutch behind a toppled display and handed him his rifle.

Clutch shouted, "Everyone, take cover! Head for the back rooms!"

He laid down cover fire while the women and children ran. The scouts took up position behind various forms of cover. The bandits fired wildly as though they were trying to decide which direction they wanted to go. White fuzz exploded from sleeping bags. Someone cried out in sharp pain.

"We need to get to a better position." Clutch looked around. "This way."

We ran and slid across a sales counter. No one seemed to be firing at us, but the entire store was filled with the sound of gunfire, and I suspected the bandits were now shooting at the New Eden soldiers and not us.

"I'm going to give you a push, and we'll take position there behind that big support beam." Clutch pointed.

I looked up at the rock ledge filled with various stuffed animals. Toward the middle, just above the giant aquariums, was what I figured had to be the support beam Clutch was talking about: a tree trunk going from floor to ceiling.

"Ready?"

I nodded. We both climbed onto the glass counter. I jumped up at the same time Clutch heaved me, and I flew onto the ledge above. He tossed me his rifle and then climbed up. I slung the rifle over my shoulder, grabbed his jeans, and helped pull him up the last bit. We ran around the animals and behind the disguised support beam. Clutch crouched, took aim, and fired. I was behind the beam and couldn't see, but knew that since Clutch hadn't fired a second shot, a bandit had just gone down.

A grenade exploded, and I peeked around the other side of the beam. Dust and flames flickered near the front sales counters. Then, a massive explosion shook the building. Something big and black crashed down onto me, and I tumbled off the ledge and into the stagnant fish tank below. The falling object landed on top of me, knocking the air from my lungs and pressing me against the bottom of the tank.

I tried to shove out from under it—a stuffed grizzly bear—but it weighed too much. Stale water filled my nose and crept down my throat. My lungs burned as I struggled harder against the bear. I grabbed at its fur and tried to twist away. Blackness and stars overtook my vision. A pounding sound reverberated through the water, and I felt a wave around me as the water flowed away. I coughed and breathed, but the bear was still crushing me. Arms yanked at me. My limbs were going numb, and I felt like I was falling.

"Cash. Godammit, look at me, girl."

The voice sounded like Clutch but it was so distant. Gradually, it drew closer and louder until I found myself coughing water and sucking air.

"Thank God," Clutch said as he held me in his arms. "Are you okay?"

After a final cough, I held up my thumb.

He gave me a hard kiss and then pulled me to my feet before I'd even realized what he'd done. A blend of shock and thrill brought me back to reality.

"They're bringing this place down with artillery fire. We need to get out of here."

CHAPTER XXXII

Clutch practically dragged me through the store. I recognized a couple of the bodies lying motionless on the floor, but, thankfully, nearly all of the Fox survivors were nowhere in sight. I had to believe they'd made it out okay. No one was shooting at us. The fight seemed to have moved back outside, but rounds were still going off everywhere around us. When we reached the hallway under the Exit sign, Clutch took the lead.

We ran past a room where Mary's body lay crumpled next to a desk, her lifeless eyes staring at us. Not far from her, I saw our weapons in a big pile. The bandits must've dumped them there when they were in a hurry to prepare for the New Eden guys. I stopped and pulled Clutch back. "Wait. We'll need these."

He stopped but didn't let go until he noticed the weapons. We rushed into the room, and I picked through the pile to find my rifle and knife. I couldn't find my pistol, so I just started pulling out anything that looked like something I could use. The entire time I focused completely on the weapons and refused to look anywhere even close in the direction of Mary's broken body.

Clutch did the same. I noticed he kept his eyes focused on the weapons, looking at each one. We each took the best machetes, knives, spears, and sidearms. Clutch even grabbed an extra rifle, but I took only mine to keep the weight down. The last thing he picked up before he came to his feet was Tyler's sword, still in its sheath.

"He would've wanted you to have it," I said between slinging what I could over my shoulder and fastening everything else in my weapons belt.

His brows rose but he quickly regained his composure. "Let's go."

We hurried toward the exit. Clutch threw the steel doors open, and we found three soldiers aiming their rifles at us.

"Whoa!" Clutch yelled, holding his rifle up. "We're not bandits!"

They didn't lower their weapons, but one soldier nodded in my direction. "They don't look like bandits."

"Where are you from?" another soldier asked. "And you'd better answer quick."

"I'm with Camp Fox," Clutch replied. "Sergeant Joe Seibert with the 75th Ranger Regiment."

His answer seemed to suffice because the soldier motioned toward the parking lot. "There's a HEMTT by the road. You can join the rest of your group on it. You'd better hurry."

We ran around the corner of the building and the HEMTT came into view. It was surrounded protectively by Humvees. A soldier I didn't recognize was lifting five-year-old Alana into the back.

Our biggest challenge was getting to the HEMTT. The bandits had taken our keys and now had our vehicles, making the battle closely matched. Every few seconds, a bandit ran out from behind one of our Humvees and lobbed a grenade at the New Eden vehicles as another bandit drove slowly, using the Humvee as a shield.

Rounds went through the Humvee's window, blood splattered, and the Humvee sped forward until it ran straight into one of New Eden's Humvees. Red and violet flames burst from the ensuing explosion.

"Wait. Look!" I pointed to a bandit trying to reload the .30 cal on our Humvee.

"Son of a bitch." Clutch took off as quickly as he could run toward the Humvee. He lifted his rifle and shot the bandit in the back. Clutch handed me his rifle and we both climbed up onto the back of the Humvee. He manned the .30, turning it from the New Eden trucks to the bandits in the Camp Fox vehicles. Three bandits stood on the back of Camp Fox's HEMTT. One had a rocket launcher while the other two had rifles, laying down cover fire. Clutch and a soldier from New Eden zeroed in on the risk at the same moment. Two bandits fell with shots from different directions, but the bandit with the launcher fired before he fell.

I watched as the rocket shot through the air, leaving a smoke trail behind it. When I realized its trajectory, I cried out. "No!"

My shout did nothing to stop the rocket from hitting the HEMTT. The vehicle went up in an explosion. Fire engulfed the large vehicle. Debris flew twenty feet in every direction.

Every single person that was here from Camp Fox was on that HEMTT. Everyone we'd fought to protect over the past several months, everyone we'd saved from the fire, everyone we cared for, was gone in a single blast of heat. I don't know how long I stood there, numbly watching the HEMTT burn. All my senses seemed to shut down until the sounds of battle grew in volume.

The New Eden soldiers fired .30 cal rounds back at the bandits, but the sounds of gunfire were growing less and less frequent. Either they were running out of ammo or they were running out of people. Artillery and grenade blasts rang in my ears.

I looked at Clutch to find him staring at the burning wreckage. Slowly, his jaw clamped shut and his eyes and lips narrowed. He maneuvered the .30 cal and began firing relentlessly at the bandits. The sudden sense of loss was blanketed by adrenaline-infused anger. "Kill them all," I ordered, though my words were drowned out by machine gun fire.

Clutch turned to me. "I'm out."

I looked around. The store behind us had become a massive fire. The soldiers who had been around back came running around the store, and were gunned down as soon as they appeared. I twisted to find the source and then saw the bandit who'd given Clutch a black eye standing behind one of New Eden's .30 cals. The Humvee took off, and I saw Hodge in the driver's seat.

I jumped up onto the roof of the Humvee and took aim. I didn't account for their speed properly, and my first shot missed. My second clipped the bandit's neck, and he fell off the back. It'd been awhile since I'd killed a man, but the fact didn't faze me. In fact, I found pleasure watching the blood spray from his neck.

I aimed at Hodge, but he turned sharply, and I couldn't get a clear shot. He pulled out of the parking lot and sped onto the road. I fired off three shots, but I doubted any found their target. Even if we took off after him in our Humvee, we'd likely never catch up in time. So, Clutch and I watched helplessly as the bastard drove off.

When he disappeared behind the trees, I noticed that there were no more sounds of gunfire. Fires crackled everywhere, and I heard someone calling for help.

Unlike massive climatic scenes in movies where the bad guy got his due, this battle had simply...ended.

My ears were ringing, and my adrenaline numbed

my nerves. I stared off at the burning HEMTT. Across the parking lot, no one was walking. There were bodies everywhere, but no one was standing. There was no one left except us.

"We're all that's left," I said emotionlessly, though I knew my emotions were still in there, too beaten down by hopelessness to dare rise. "There's no one left."

Clutch wrapped an arm around me and I found myself holding onto him like he was my lifeline. "We have each other."

CHAPTER XXXIII

O ur first pass through the aftermath was search and rescue. Out of all the Camp Fox survivors, New Eden soldiers, and bandits, we found only one person who wasn't dead or near-death. Marco, a soldier from New Eden, had taken a shot to his helmet and had been knocked out cold. When he woke, it took him some time to come to grips with the loss of his entire squadron. For the first few minutes, he moved restlessly around, counting vehicles and searching for his squadron. When he finally realized they were all there and he was the only one left standing, he collapsed.

Once Marco came to terms with reality, Clutch asked him several questions while I sat and stared at the fires. The HEMTT continued to smoke, but no more flames licked out from the vehicle. I could only imagine the smell of so many dead inside. I tried not to think about any of the bodies belonging to someone I cared about. There'd be too much time for thinking later.

New Eden was a new super-city in Colorado formed by the military at Cheyenne Mountain. Dozens of squadrons just like Marco's had been sent out with the sole mission to save any survivors they could after the herds passed through. On their mission, they'd run across a feudalistic, ruthless group called the Black Sheep that was quickly spreading across the Midwest. The bandits who'd taken us hostage were from that group, and Marco showed us the mark on one of the bandit's body: a brand of a ram's head with curled horns.

"At least we got all these guys," Marco said. "If any got back to their captain, they'd likely come back at us with a vengeance."

I shook my head. "No. Their leader got away."

Marco's face fell before fear widened his eyes. "He'll bring back reinforcements."

Clutch climbed to his feet. "We'll be out of here long before then. But we should hurry and get wrapped up here, just in case."

I looked up to see Clutch holding a hand out to me. I took it and he pulled me up and into an embrace. Strangely, I never cried, even knowing that I'd never see Jase again, or anyone from Camp Fox, again. It broke my heart, but my brain refused to process anything. It felt like I was on autopilot, and the circuit breaker to my emotions had been turned off, and I was thankful for that small mercy.

Later, as I walked around and inventoried the wreckage, Clutch and Marco collected dog tags and carried the dead of those we knew as close to the burning store as we could in hopes the fire would take care of them before the zeds found them. When we came to Tyler's body, neither Clutch nor I could move. For the longest time, I simply stared at Tyler's limp form. I noticed Clutch did the same. His lips quivered, then he sobered and we carried Tyler away from the burning building and laid him under a tree. Clutch walked back to a Humvee and returned with a shovel. As he started digging a hole, I also grabbed a shovel and helped.

The ground was soft, but it still took a while to dig a shallow grave. Clutch grabbed Tyler's shoulders and I grabbed his legs and we lowered him as gently as possible. We stared down at Tyler's peaceful, though bloodied, features.

"Lord," Clutch said. "Bless this soldier who gave his life in the service of others. Watch over his grave so that he finds peace."

"Amen," I said with him. It was the first time I'd heard Clutch pray.

"Sorry for your loss," Marco said.

Startled, I turned around, not realizing he was standing there. I swallowed, unable to find any words. It wasn't that I was hollow inside. Anger, terror, despair, grief, misery, it was all there but isolated in a safe room. I could feel the emotions boiling like a volcano, but there was a heavy, cold stone covering the top of the volcano, letting nothing escape. It was like my body and spirit had split and were fighting to come back together.

My body went through the motions. We buried Tyler and went back to work pulling together anything salvageable. Every vehicle had taken hits, but some were still in decent shape, so it was just a matter of siphoning gas, and tossing weapons, ammo, and supplies in a pile to sort out what could still be used.

As I carried a gas can from our old HEMTT, a dog barked. The sound was deep, hair-raising, and familiar. I turned to see a Great Dane bound out from the woods, followed by someone I'd never expected to see again. I set the can down and stared. "Jase?"

At the sound of his name, he jerked and then saw me. His eyes widened. He took a step from Hali. He started to jog and then run. "Cash!"

He picked me off the ground and twirled me around.

When the realization hit me that it was really Jase, something snapped inside, and tears poured out. I hugged him so hard. I grabbed his jacket hard enough that I swore I should've been able to tear it. I kissed his cheek over and over. In between sobs, I was able to cry out, "You're alive! How?"

"When we met up with the New Eden guys, they wouldn't allow us to radio you in case we were connected with the bandits they were following. Once they figured out we were all right, we couldn't reach Tyler on the radio. So we joined up with them to find you. It was pretty easy to find the Camp Fox vehicles sitting out in the parking lot. When I saw Tyler…"

He sighed and shook his head. Hali came over and stood by us. Jase gave her a look before continuing. "I thought we were too late. Then, those guys came out wearing our fatigues, the New Eden CO figured out the ambush right away. He sent several of us around the back of the store to look for survivors, and that's when we saw Deb and Vicki run into the woods. Griz and I went after them while a few soldiers stayed behind to get anyone else. It took us a while to round up everyone hiding. I've been searching the woods forever for you."

I stared at him for a moment. Then I punched him in the arm before embracing him again, unwilling to let him go in case he was an illusion. "I thought you were dead."

He guffawed. "I was going to say the same thing. Don't scare me like that ever again."

Over his shoulder, I saw other familiar faces emerge from the woods and I smiled.

Diesel led the way for Benji and Frost. They walked up to us, and Jase patted the boy's shoulder while the dog circled us, seemingly unbothered by the recent violence. "It turns out Benji is pretty dang good at hide-and-seek."

Griz was walking with Deb and Vickie.

"Thank God," I said on a sigh. "I thought we'd lost

all of you."

"We're Camp Fox," Jase said. "We're too tough to die." He looked around. "Where's everyone else?"

I frowned. "They're gone."

"Gone where?"

I tried to swallow the lump in my throat. "They're dead."

It was Jase's turn to frown. "Wh-what?"

The others had also heard me. Vickie and Deb clung to each other. Hali walked into Jase's arms. Griz gave us his back. Benji started asking his grandfather complicated questions.

Clutch came over, and Jase's face lifted.

Clutch stared at Jase, his mouth opened wide, as he looked him over in disbelief. After a pause, he stomped forward and pulled Jase into his arms. Each had their eyes clenched shut as they hugged each other.

"You're all right," Clutch said, his voice unsteady and muffled by Jase's coat.

Marco jogged up to us. "We have to hit the road. There are zeds heading this way from both the east and the west. All that artillery noise and smoke probably drew their attention."

I jogged out to look down the road and saw a few dozen zeds making slow but steady progress toward us. When I looked the other way, I saw several dozen more. "They must've been too decrepit to migrate," I wondered aloud.

"All right, Frost, how about you help Benji and the

others load up." Clutch waved his arm toward the Humvee I'd been loading up. The one with the coyote head painted on the hood. "Scouts, let's double time it and grab any beans and bullets we can."

"Beans?" Benji asked. "Why beans?"

"Food," Clutch corrected. "Find any food you can."

I smiled. "We're going to need a second Humvee."

He slowly returned my smile when he realized the meaning of my words. "Yes, we have too many people for one Humvee."

Several hours later, we were back in Iowa on the first leg of our trip west to New Eden. When the sun crept low in the sky, we set up camp near the Des Moines River for the night.

Charred zeds swayed like totems on the other side of the river, the side closest to Des Moines. They had no eyes or ears or noses, but they remained. They were an ominous reminder of why we kept from crossing the river and nearing the city. I refused to watch them.

I also avoided looking at the skeletal ruins of Des Moines's tallest buildings. I hadn't seen my parents since the outbreak, and I'd accepted the fact that I'd never see them again, that they never got out, along with a million other doomed souls in and around the city. At least I knew they were at peace. The bombing had taken out most of the zeds in the city, with the exceptions of the charred zeds—burnt beyond recognition—standing like shadowy guards at the edges of town, always on the lookout for prey.

The military hadn't bombed a wide enough radius to take out all the zeds, but they had done their job on the central part of the city. Bombs weren't precise and would've taken out uninfected and infected alike. Bombs existed only to destroy and took out anything in their path. They were a bit like zeds in that: they were both destroyers.

After taking a cold-water bath, I sipped some pine needle tea and lay in the back of the Humvee with Clutch and Jase. Our legs tangled around the machine gun, but we'd all slept in more uncomfortable positions before. In fact, having both with me, safe and sound, was the best feeling I'd ever had.

Deb lay awkwardly around the back bench seats, and petite Hali fit comfortably up front. Griz, Marco, Vicki, Frost, and Benji were still working out the sleeping arrangement in the other Humvee, though I suspected Benji would tell them how it'd be. Diesel lay curled in a ball next to the vehicle, outwardly sound asleep, but I knew from experience he'd bolt awake at the smallest threatening sound.

Camp Fox had taken a heavy hit. It would never be the same, but enough of us had survived to continue the effort. Yet, I knew that as long as I had Clutch and Jase with me, things would turn out okay.

"There's one," Jase said, pointing to the sky.

"That makes twelve," Clutch said.

I closed my eyes and savored this moment, knowing that we'd be on the road again tomorrow, running from who knew what and heading toward something I wasn't sure I trusted. When I opened my eyes again, I relished the night's peace where there were no zeds and no bandits and no death.

"Another one," Jase said.

"Eagle eye, I swear," I said with a smile.

Clutch chuckled. "Thirteen."

It was probably a meteor shower, and we all enjoyed the distraction. It was by far the best entertainment we'd had in some time. Before the outbreak, I would've gotten bored. Not now. Tonight, we were together and safe.

"Oh, there's one." I pointed.

"That's a satellite, silly," Jase said.

Clutch chuckled, and we both joined in. Lying in the back of that Humvee, without any manmade lights to block the sky, we laughed as we continued to count the shooting stars.

The saga comes to an end in Late 2014
Deadland Rising

AUTHOR'S NOTE

Loosely based on Dante Alighieri's "Purgatorio" (the second poem of the three-part *Divine Comedy*), *Deadland's Harvest* covers the continuing journey of Cash and her guide, Clutch, through the zombie apocalypse. When this story begins, Cash (representing Dante) has gained experience and confidence from surviving the "Inferno" in *100 Days in Deadland*, and is better prepared to handle the deadly sins, of which she and others are found guilty. Since they are the *deadly* sins, there is plenty of death to be found in each section and chapter (paralleling the poem's cantos).

As with the first book in the *Deadland Saga*, *Deadland's Harvest* is a tale of suffering and spiritual growth and a continuation of the story of the human condition. As with "Purgatorio", each terrace purges a particular sin in an appropriate manner. At its heart, *Deadland's Harvest* is about penance. Cash and the Fox survivors cannot move on until the sin is recognized and acknowledged. There are implications to each deadly sin, portrayed by either survivors or zeds and often resulting in the deaths of innocents.

At the macro level, *Deadland's Harvest* is focused more inwardly than *100 Days in Deadland* and you'll see the main characters evolve in their own way. Cash, like Dante, begins to take accountability for her own life (and sins). Clutch (representing Virgil and later, Beatrice) continues as her guide, but their roles become more balanced through their journey as Clutch morphs from purely her guide to her love. It takes Clutch awhile to transition from the guise of Virgil to Beatrice. He must overcome his PTSD and injuries and open his heart to Cash. Only once he becomes Beatrice can he finally become the leader he needs to be. Similarly, Jase also morphs from a supporting character to a man in his own right by taking on the role of the great Statius.

While there are plenty of "Purgatorio" Easter eggs in this novel, I also intentionally broke from Dante Alighieri's storyline to stay true to the *Deadland Saga*. For example, this story does not start on Easter but instead starts exactly six months after Easter. For ease, I labeled the name of the first section "Purgatory" rather than the various levels of ante-purgatory.

I kept true to the themes and symbols in "Purgatorio" as much as possible. Here are just a few images you'll find similar between the two stories:

- In Purgatory, Clutch, Wes, and Cash hide from a herd of zeds (representing the penitent) traveling slowly, "like a flock of sheep." Later in Purgatory, Cash needs two keys to unlock their path to continue. In this case, one key opens the hangar, and the other starts the airplane.
- In Pride, Cash, like Dante, is guilty of the first deadly sin, which others have suffered for.

- In Wrath, black smoke erupts on the *Aurora* when the *Lady Amore* shoots flares at the barge.
- In Greed, the earth trembles as the herds arrive.
- In Gluttony, the starving zeds (again representing the penitent) surround the *Aurora*, which represents the fruit tree forever out of reach and surrounded by a river.
- In Lust, the Fox survivors are so desperately eager to be free from zeds, they set a fire that burns out of control and leads to their punishment. The survivors, representing the penitent, walk through flames as they struggle to escape the fire, the punishment for lack of self-restraint.

For the full list of Easter eggs, visit my website at www.rachelaukes.com.

I hope you enjoyed this story. Stay tuned for Deadland Rising, where Cash, Clutch, and Jase journey through "Paradiso," the final poem of Dante's Divine Comedy.

ACKNOWLEDGMENTS

With many thanks:

To my editor, Stephanie Riva, for taking a decent story and making it so much better.

To Glenda Moleski for working miracles. I couldn't have done it without you.

To my husband for hanging in there through all the crazy times.

To Sarah Lyons Fleming for your genius and humor.

To Al Rowell for the help and great ideas.

To Nicholas Sansbury Smith, Michael Koogler, Amber Schmidt, and Linda Tooch for the helping out on the ugly first draft.

To the Bards of Badassery — Elle J Rossi, Cynthia Valero, and Beth Ciotta — for keeping me from falling off that cliff.

And especially to all those making sacrifices to keep our world safe.

ABOUT THE AUTHOR

Rachel Aukes is the bestselling author of *100 Days in Deadland*, which was named one of the best books of 2013 by *Suspense Magazine* and one of the best zombie books by the *Huffington Post*. She also writes romance under the pen name Berinn Rae, including Stealing Fate, a *USA Today* recommended read. Rachel lives in Iowa with her husband and an incredibly spoiled sixty-pound lap dog. When not writing, she can be found flying old airplanes and trying (not so successfully) to prepare for the zombie apocalypse.

Connect with Rachel at:
http://www.RachelAukes.com

"I don't read many women who write horror
as well as Stephen King and Clive Barker
and Rachel Aukes does!"
~ *My Seryniti*

ALSO BY RACHEL AUKES

"Go get the book, you'll love this one."
~ *Zombie-Guide Magazine*

THE AMAZON BESTSELLER

In one day, the world succumbed to a pestilence that decimated the living. In its place rose a new species: vicious, gruesome, wandering zombies with an insatiable hunger for the living. Welcome to Deadland.

ISBN 978-0-9899018-0-2

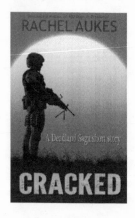

EXCLUSIVE EBOOK

Cracked: A Deadland Saga Short Story is the tale of Captain Tyler Masden and his platoon during the outbreak.

Read it free on the author's website:
http://www.rachelaukes.com

COMING SOON

"…A stunning exploration of the human spirit: survival and greed, good and evil…a microcosm of today's society wrapped up in a dystopian novel. Rachel Aukes has written a modern take on a classic. I for one, cannot wait for her next book."
~ *Suspense Magazine*

The Fox survivors outlasted the herds, but they're not safe yet. In the final installment of *The Deadland Saga,* a new, even deadlier threat faces Cash, Clutch, and their small group of survivors.

ISBN 978-0-9899018-2-6

SURPRISINGLY
ADEQUATE
PUBLISHING

WILL BE AVAILBLE WHEREVER
BOOKS ARE SOLD

Made in the USA
Lexington, KY
09 June 2014